HER EY

"Don't rip me up here," he begged. "Enjoy your first waltz. We can fight tomorrow if you wish. But you can hardly blame me for investigating the woman I was told had evil designs on my ward."

Penelope sighed. "Lady Avery has always hated us."

"That is another situation we can discuss later. Are you sure you have never waltzed? You dance with winged feet." His fingers caressed her back, sending flames racing into every extremity.

She reminded herself that he was using seduction. She couldn't think. He twirled her faster, pulling her closer into his arms. His pupils blurred, his gaze seeming to draw her very soul out for his inspection. Every nerve shivered in delight as his thigh brushed her own under the cover of her billowing skirt.

"What are doing to me?" he murmured so softly she barely heard. "Witch."

Mesmerist, she responded, but only her lips formed the words.

SIGNET REGENCY ROMANCE
Coming in March 1998

Gayle Buck
Tempting Sarah

Dorothy Mack
The Gamester's Daughter

April Kihlstrom
The Reluctant Thief

LORD AVERY'S LEGACY

Allison Lane

A SIGNET BOOK

SIGNET
Published by the Penguin Group
Penguin Putnam Inc., 375 Hudson Street,
New York, New York 10014, U.S.A.
Penguin Books Ltd, 27 Wrights Lane,
London W8 5TZ, England
Penguin Books Australia Ltd, Ringwood,
Victoria, Australia
Penguin Books Canada Ltd, 10 Alcorn Avenue,
Toronto, Ontario, Canada M4V 3B2
Penguin Books (N.Z.) Ltd, 182-190 Wairau Road,
Auckland 10, New Zealand

Penguin Books Ltd, Registered Offices:
Harmondsworth, Middlesex, England

First published by Signet, an imprint of Dutton Signet,
a member of Penguin Putnam Inc.

First Printing, February, 1998
10 9 8 7 6 5 4 3 2 1

Prologue

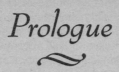

Devon—May 8, 1812

"Of course I'm goin' home!" Hiccups punctuated the slurred words.

The ostler shrugged, swallowing the rest of his unsolicited advice as he held the gelding steady. Lord Avery had never been a man who accepted even implied criticism.

Gareth, Lord Avery, stumbled twice before he managed to mount. His lurching set the stars to swaying overhead. Why had he broached that last bottle? The Golden Stag was known for the quality of its spirits, and the company had been congenial, but that had never led him to overindulge in the past.

At least the evening had started congenially, he corrected himself as he passed the last cottage. When had it changed? Senseless images danced in his head. Something wasn't right. Unnoticed, his hands slackened on the reins, allowing Pegasus to veer off the road.

Business. That was it. Why had he been discussing business at the Golden Stag? Mr. Isaacs had not been there. Nor had he been in his office, so the trip to Exeter had accomplished nothing. He would return, of course, and then the banker would accept his latest offer—must accept it if Gareth was to find peace again. He shivered. One hand patted his jacket pocket, verifying that the papers were still there. Not that his cryptic notes would mean anything to another—they merely jogged a memory not as good as it used to be—but carrying them made her seem closer. *My love, my heart. Damn, but I need yo—*

Pegasus stepped in a hole, nearly unseating him. He should not have downed another bottle after bidding his friends farewell. And he certainly should not have left for home after doing so. It would have been better to stay the night—as the ostler had suggested—but he had already been on his way out when that stranger drew him into a private parlor, and changing his mind never occurred to him. What was the fellow's name again?

He frowned.

Meredith. Stanley Meredith. They had played several hands of piquet before Meredith announced that he was looking for investors in a canal venture that would make them both rich. Or so he claimed. But Gareth did not need—

Without warning, the last bottle of wine spewed onto his horse's neck, where it was rapidly joined by four brethren and the mutton stew served in the Golden Stag's common room. Pegasus took exception to such treatment and bolted, leaving Lord Avery sprawled on the ground, still retching.

The moon had cleared the eastern hills by the time he staggered to his feet. He leaned against a tree, holding his head until the world stopped spinning. A glow to the west defined Exeter, barely a mile away. It might as well be in France. The fall had done something to his ribs, leaving him feeling very odd indeed. He stumbled back to the road, forcing his thoughts past the thick wine fumes as he considered his health.

His coat. That's what was wrong. It was too tight. His fingers fumbled to undo its buttons, but the numb digits could not accomplish even so simple a task. He shook his head. It wasn't the coat. His cravat was too tight. He tugged it loose as he tottered along the verge. Fashionable clothing was not made for exercise.

By the time he heard hoofbeats, he was gasping in painful snorts and wheezes that made his close-out coat pinch even tighter. Only extreme effort raised a leaden arm to signal the approaching curricle.

"My Lord Avery, what happened?" exclaimed the driver.

"Meredith?" He had barely choked out the name when his coat shrank three sizes. Cold sweat broke out on his brow. "Help—"

Meredith disappeared, replaced by a radiant woman beckoning him closer. "Come, my love. All is forgiven. We may share eternity together."

The man Gareth had most wronged nodded in agreement, smiled, then joined a black-haired woman and faded into the distance.

But Gareth could not believe them. "All? Even—?" He patted his breast pocket in horror.

"Some transgressions are. not wholly wicked, my dearest love," she assured him, drifting closer on a wave of peace and hope. "You have erred often, but good can yet come of your sins. The stage is set. Now the other players must choose their own courses."

"I don't understand."

"*He* will explain. Are you ready?"

Lord Avery smiled, the long years of pain and sorrow vanishing in an instant. "Together at last. He is merciful, indeed, my love. Oh, how I've missed you!"

Rejoicing at his unexpected reprieve, he grasped her hand and accompanied her to the light beyond.

The man calling himself Meredith remained in his curricle. Only his eyes moved, calmly watching. Pain exploded across Avery's face; one hand clutched his chest; his eyes rolled into his head as he crumpled to the ground, wearing an oddly beatific smile.

Instinct had urged him to follow the inebriated lord. Instinct never failed him. The moment Avery breathed his last, Meredith snubbed the ribbons. In seconds he had rifled Gareth's pockets and regained his seat, turning his curricle back to town.

Nought but the moon remained to watch over the earthly remains of the third Lord Avery.

Chapter One

~

"This is absurd!"

Richard Avery, sixth Marquess of Carrington, raised his quizzing glass to grimace at his reflected image. Kesterton had trussed him up like the veriest dandy, with a blue satin jacket, embroidered white waistcoat, and silver pantaloons. His cravat was tighter than he preferred, tied in an intricate variation of the oriental that cut into his chin with its unaccustomed height. He snorted.

"Your lordship promised her ladyship," Kesterton reminded his employer, twitching the last wrinkle from the close-cut jacket.

"Who cares what I wear? There is not a chit in the house who sees aught but my title and purse," he grumbled. "I could dress as an American savage, and they would still simper and bat their vacant eyes."

Kesterton merely handed him his gloves.

Richard dropped his quizzing glass and headed for the door. Complaining was beneath his dignity. He knew how the game was played. Duty demanded that he secure the succession, a task he could not accomplish without a wife. His mother was pressing him to wed, and at three-and-thirty he could hardly blame her. Nor could he protest a dearth of candidates. She was giving him ample opportunity to make his choice, entertaining constantly in town and holding frequent house parties at Carrington Castle, each including a good selection of eligible young ladies.

And her taste was not an issue. Unlike some mothers, she did not sponsor weak-willed, brainless chits in an attempt to preserve her own authority. Her protégées included every conceivable sort, from ignorant to bluestocking, inept to accomplished, antidote to beautiful, clinging to independent, impoverished to well dowered, breathless seventeen-year-olds to assured widows. Their only commonality was the breeding necessary for a marchioness. But he had accepted none of them.

The world considered him hard to please, a description he abhorred, for it made him sound like a fussy eccentric. Yet every candidate possessed at least one intolerable fault. The current guest list was no exception: Lady Evaline's fluttering lashes made him dizzy; Lady Edith's giggles rasped his nerves; Ernestine agreed with even ridiculous statements; Martha never spoke above a whisper; Maude laughed immoderately; Melanie contradicted him; Caroline was clumsy; Cora mistreated her maid; Charlotte's mother was a harridan; and on and on. . . .

Were any of them capable of friendship? He wanted more from marriage than a dutiful bed partner, an accomplished hostess, or an ornament to grace his arm. Was that too much to ask?

Unwilling to spend the half hour preceding dinner with fawning misses and calculating parents, he slipped into the library. Were they too stupid to recognize their own insincerity, or did they believe him incapable of doing so? He was tempted to plant a facer on the next girl who called him handsome. He wasn't. Nor was he witty, charming, or entertaining. He had too many responsibilities to waste time on frivolity. And though he considered himself well-read, he knew many who were more intelligent, starting with his friend Mark.

He paced the room, finally stopping in the last alcove. The door opened as he was pulling out a book on Coke's agricultural experiments. But before he could make his presence known, the intruders spoke. He stepped farther into the corner.

"Oh, good, no one is here," exclaimed a girl. "Let's wait until the final bell. Mama will never think to look for me in a library, and I simply cannot face *him* again."

"What happened?" demanded her friend. "Surely he didn't take unwelcome liberties! I never met a colder man."

"Of course not! He is not *that* sort. Sally claims he doesn't even keep a mistress."

"She would know." Both girls giggled. "Her mother would die if she found out how much Sally hears from her brother. But if he didn't steal a kiss under the stairs, why are you afraid of him?"

"I am not afraid, even if he does glower most of the time. He is so old I cannot feel anything for him. But he spoke to me for all of five minutes this morning, and smiled while he did it. You know he disapproves of everything, so his good humor convinced Mama that he means to make me an offer. I will die if he does! Can you imagine living with such an iceberg?"

"It would turn me to stone."

"Oh, Lizzy! If only Sir Harold could cover Papa's debts, we could marry. I love him so! But Mama turns livid at the very suggestion. They will never approve his suit."

Lady Angela Bradburn. Richard identified her as she paused to stifle a sob. And the other was her bosom bow, Miss Elizabeth Sandbourne. His face twisted into a frown. Angela had been flirtatious since her arrival, but she did not even pretend to be sincere about it. That had piqued his curiosity, though he had never considered offering for her; she was barely seventeen. Pity welled up, and he shook his head. Lady Bradburn was a shameless schemer who would use her daughter to better her own social standing. Poor Angela.

"What will you do?" asked Elizabeth.

"I don't know." Lady Angela's voice trembled. "Mama is so determined to attach Carrington that I fear she will try something dishonorable. Papa has already announced that we will not go to London next Season. But you know how Mama loves society. She condemns his efforts to improve our estate, and counts on a wealthy son-in-law to repair his fortune so she can resume her place in town. How can I fight her? It will be four years before Harry and I can wed without their consent. I can never dodge her schemes that long."

"Have you considered eloping?"

"That would destroy Harry's career," Angela admitted with a sigh. "Scandal is not tolerated in government circles. You know that."

"Then you must resign yourself to Carrington. Thank heaven I do not need to consider him. My parents will never force me to wed without affection."

"You do not like him, either?"

"I don't dislike him," objected Elizabeth. "He has been all

that is polite. But he is too old, too harsh, too solemn, and not nearly handsome enough for my taste."

"Nor mine."

The dinner bell rang.

"Come on," urged Elizabeth. "Mama will scold if I am late."

"As will mine. Perhaps if I flirt with Mr. Walper, Carrington will leave me alone tonight. How I wish I was of age!"

Richard stepped from the alcove and frowned at the library door. Matchmaking parents were bad enough, but indebted ones were despicable. He had already sidestepped one compromise plot in recent months and had no intention of succumbing to another. His eyes hardened. He had seen enough of this house party to dismiss every chit from contention. Summoning a footman, he sent his regrets to his mother and requested a tray in his room. But he did not immediately leave the library.

Those two girls were honest and intelligent, rare traits in the *ton*. Elizabeth needed no help, but Lady Angela was another story. She would make an ideal wife for a rising diplomat and did not deserve the misery that Lady Bradburn would force upon her. Lord Bradburn had gamed away considerable sums the previous Season, though not enough to threaten him with debtor's prison. He had apparently faced his folly and was bent on addressing his problems. But if his wife was determined to sell their daughter, there were any number of lecherous rogues who would be willing to buy. Picturing her in the arms of one of society's reprobates did not bear thinking on, especially when she had already found a man she could love. Pulling out a sheet of crested stationery, he sharpened a quill.

> *My Lord Bradburn,*
>
> *It has come to my attention that Lady Angela and Sir Harold Compton wish to wed. Please consider his suit. He has gained much respect in government circles, earning the patronage that will raise him to the heights in time. Already he has acquired the means to support a wife in style.*
>
> *No one deserves a spouse who loves another. If Lady Bradburn compromises a wealthier gentleman into taking Lady Angela, I will be compelled to ruin both of you in the eyes of society.*
>
> *Carrington*

Sealing the missive, he summoned his secretary. "See that this is delivered tomorrow morning."

Cawdry's brows lifted, but Richard refused to explain. At first light, he turned his curricle down the drive.

"You *what?*"

Penelope Wingrave stared in horror at her fifteen-year-old half brother. Michael shuffled his feet for several seconds before meeting her eyes.

"I lost a hundred pounds at piquet."

"How could you!"

"I am so sorry, Penny," he choked out. "I know I shouldn't have done it, and I swear it will never happen again, but I must send Gerald the funds immediately. There is no way to honorably renege. How could I hope to return to school?"

Sighing loudly, she took a turn about the bookroom. Michael's return for long break had filled her with joy, though she had hardly recognized him when he walked through the door. He was six inches taller than on his last visit, boding ill for her budget, for he would need yet another new wardrobe when school resumed. His voice had dropped at least an octave, and his already slim physique had turned positively lanky. But the joy was short-lived. Within minutes he had exploded disaster in her face. A hundred pounds. Where could she possibly find a hundred pounds? Yet ranting would do no good. She took a deep breath, resuming her seat behind the desk.

"What happened, Michael?"

"There was a party for Wiggy." Michael paced the room in turn. "His great-uncle died last month, leaving him the barony. He had barely known the man, so you can understand that it was cause for celebration rather than sadness."

She nodded.

"Gerald arranged the festivities down at the Laughing Pig." He hesitated.

"I suppose everyone was rather foxed," she said helpfully.

"Exactly. There were cards and dice and—" He hesitated again.

She could fill in the rest. Those who had not already discovered women would have done so that night.

"I never understood how heedless one can get while in one's

altitudes," he admitted with a groan. "I paid no attention to either the stakes or the cards. Before I knew it, I was a hundred pounds down. I quit immediately, fearing that staying in the game could only make a bad situation worse, but there is no way out of the debt."

"It is done," she said with a sigh. "At least you had the sense to avoid trying to reverse your luck. That rarely works."

"But what are we to do?"

"Send a draft to Gerald, of course. Your reputation is worth more than a hundred pounds."

"I am so sorry," he repeated. "Where will you find the funds?"

"It will have to come out of the next mortgage payment," she acknowledged, holding his gaze so that he could not mistake her meaning.

He blanched. "But that means we could lose everything."

"We could. You know how close to the River Tick we live. But let us not worry about that yet. We have two months to find replacement funds. Perhaps the pottery orders will expand. Or the price of plumes may rise again. We will contrive."

"Dear Lord, Penny. How could I have been so stupid? Should I throw myself on the banker's mercy?"

She shook her head. "We cannot give Mr. Isaacs cause to call in the loan. Our situation is precarious enough without courting his doubts. Somehow we will find the money."

"I am so sorry," he repeated in a voice choked with tears.

"It is done. We must learn from the experience and move ahead. If nothing else, this demonstrates the difference between you and your school friends. Despite your breeding, you have no title. And with fourteen others between you and Uncle Raymond, there is no chance of acquiring one. Most of your friends are bored heirs who spend their time on drinking, gaming, and debauchery rather than learning. You must remain firm to avoid falling into their habits."

"True." He dug at the carpet with the toe of one boot.

"I am not trying to draw the ridicule of the other boys onto your head," she disclaimed with a sigh. "But we haven't the money to increase your admittedly paltry allowance. Thus you cannot join their extravagant pastimes. If the pottery works out, that may change, but for now paying tuition is all that I can manage."

"I understand." He met her gaze squarely, determination stiffening his chin. "And I am grateful that you can do this much. I won't let you down again."

Footsteps raced along the hallway.

"Michael!" shrieked Alice, tossing her bonnet to the floor as she flung herself into her brother's arms. "When did you get home? How was your trip? Oh, I could kick myself for not being here when you arrived, but we did not expect you until dinnertime. Goodness, how you've grown!"

Laughing partly in jubilation and partly in relief at escaping Penelope's scold, he set her away. "Easy, Allie. It's good to see you, too, but am I permitted to get a word in edgewise?"

Alice giggled. "Of course. It was just the shock of seeing you here. And so tall. I have to look up to you now. Doesn't he look like Papa, Penny?"

"That he does, more so every year. And that is fitting, for you take after your mother."

"I wish I could remember her," said Alice with a sigh. "But this is no time to be maudlin. When did you get back, Michael?"

"Barely half an hour ago. Where were you?"

"In the village." She retrieved her bonnet and a small package. "The pins you needed, Penny. And you'll never guess who I met."

"Who?" Michael smiled indulgently at his sister.

"Terrence Avery. It must be three years since he last spent long break here."

"But how could he not return home with his father so recently gone?" asked Penelope gently.

"Of course." Alice blushed. "How stupid of me. Come along, Michael. Let's leave Penny to finish her work. You won't believe what Ozzie was doing last week . . ."

Penelope watched her half siblings leave. Much as she loved them, she would never be as close to them as they were to each other.

Terrence's return boded ill, but perhaps he was cut from a different cloth than his father. Never had a death been so welcome, though the thought was unchristian, at best. But the late viscount's demise had removed one of her more pressing problems. Too bad fate had replaced it. Michael's debt already weighed down her shoulders. Despite fifteen years of juggling the demands of their small estate, the burden never grew easier. So many things could destroy them—another rise in prices, bad weather, accident, disease, fire . . .

Enough! She rarely felt sorry for herself, but today she could not help it. So much responsibility left her weary.

It had started at age twelve when her stepmother died in childbirth. Though they had never been close, the woman had been kind to her, taking her on outings, overseeing her education, and even supporting her on those occasions when her father's indifference turned to antagonism. Walter Wingrave had dearly loved his second wife, falling into a prolonged melancholy after her death that even his long-awaited heir failed to mitigate. Weeks would pass between visits to his children. She did not mind on her own account, but he had previously doted on Alice, who was too young to understand the change.

So she had been left to look after Alice and the newborn Michael. The servants helped, of course, but even in those days they had a limited staff. Her only rewards were an absent-minded thank you when Walter eventually questioned the nursery arrangements and the trust implied in his will, which appointed her as their guardian.

When Walter's failing health removed his last interest in worldly affairs, she assumed control of the estate, appalled to discover that it was both run-down and heavily mortgaged. She fired their hidebound steward and initiated the changes that would eventually produce a comfortable income. Walter's death had led to her biggest battle—convincing a skeptical banker that she was an acceptable steward. The bank could have called in the loan or insisted that she hire a man to oversee operations. Either action would have cost them the estate. There was no money for additional help. But she had won the day, for the books showed an improving financial picture in the years she had run Winter House.

Now she faced a new challenge. Their resources would not cover a hundred-pound gaming debt. How was she to replace the money before the next payment was due?

* * *

Lord Carrington restlessly paced the terrace at Bridgeport Abbey, his eyes fixed on the flagstones at his feet instead of the spectacular view.

What was he doing here?

Escaping. And not just from his mother's house party, which surely must have died a natural death by now.

He grimaced, rejecting every one of his supposed reasons for this unannounced visit. Running away did not accord with his position in the world, but that was exactly what he had done. Why else was he intruding on his closest friend barely two months after the man's wedding? There were plenty of other places he could have gone—London, Brighton, any of half-a-dozen estates he had not visited in over a year, his ward's estate, the homes of friends who were not in need of privacy. Yet he had come here, needing a holiday from both business and matchmaking.

Not that Mark had questioned his arrival. He had a standing invitation from both the earl and the new countess, but it was gauche to arrive at this time. Despite their professed pleasure in his company, he felt decidedly *de trop*. And more than a little envious. They were so very much in love.

Elaine was already expecting, so excited that she discussed her condition freely, even around Mark's six-year-old daughter. Worse, the Bridgeports matched wits in a continuing quotation game that left him feeling ignorant and stupid, for he could identify less than half of the lines that they threw at each other. Nor could he follow the silent conversations that arose from the uncited surrounding text and brought a blush to Elaine's cheeks or a rakish sparkle to Mark's eyes. Even young Helen could cite facts he did not know. It was all rather lowering, more so when he realized that despite being Mark's closest friend for five-and-twenty years, he was acquainted with only one facet of the total man. Before his marriage, Mark had been a notorious libertine and renowned Corinthian. Who would have believed that he was also intimately familiar with poetry and philosophy? Even Richard had not suspected such interests.

But he was not ready to return home. His mother would never condemn his unannounced departure, but she *would* be disappointed. And how could he explain his objections? His ideas were changing, but even he was not yet sure how. He had always wanted a wife who could look past the marquessate and see the man beneath the title, a wife who cared for more than social position, a wife who was also a friend. But now he wanted more—a wife whose eyes would glow with pleasure, who could share conversation or silence in equal comfort. After a fortnight at Bridgeport Abbey, he yearned for the love that Mark had found. Yet he had no idea how to find it. He could be peg-legged, squint-eyed, and mad without affecting girls' fawning flirtatiousness and simpering smiles.

And time was running out. He must settle the succession. He had worked too hard at building his fortune to allow his holdings to fall into the hands of a fribble who would dissipate every penny until the marquessate was flirting with indebtedness as it had done under most of the previous lords. No one currently in the line of succession possessed the intelligence and backbone to manage his holdings—as he knew all too well. He had already rescued most of them from ineptitude—some more than once.

Mark had helped him acquire his new wealth by allowing him to share the services of his extraordinary man of business, a financial wizard who had multiplied his fortune many times over. He would do nothing to jeopardize those gains. To increase the odds that his heir would be competent, his wife must be both intelligent and strong-willed. Only love would prevent such a one from becoming a managing harridan.

"Damnation!" he muttered as a horseman dressed in the maroon and gray Carrington livery pounded up the drive. Who needed help now?

His position as head of the Avery family was more of a bother than an honor. He had acceded to the title at age fifteen, his determination and maturity standing out in a family long cursed with weak wills and poor judgment. Averys muddled through life from crisis to crisis, averting disaster only by soliciting outside help—which had been his role for eighteen years now. At first it had felt odd being consulted by uncles and cousins who were thirty or forty years his senior, but it did not take long to realize that he had inherited the only backbone in the family. He had addressed many crises over the years, from financial embarrassments and unsuitable attachments to personal conflicts, potential scandals, and estate problems. He had discharged dishonest servants, introduced girls and boys to society, patched up a long-standing quarrel, and bought colors for three young cousins. What would it be this time?

Mark brought the letter outside ten minutes later. "Bad news?" he asked as Richard groaned.

"It could be worse. It's from my Aunt Mathilda."

"Have I met her?"

"I doubt it. I've not seen her myself in several years. Uncle Gareth died back in May, naming me guardian for his two children and trustee for the estate until Terrence is five-and-twenty."

Mark grimaced. "How old is the lad now?"

"Twenty. At least the estate will be solvent. Gareth was the wealthiest of my father's second cousins, and my aunt had a substantial dowry. I should have gone there instead of here, I suppose, but I was not in the mood to cope with her histrionics. Not after wasting a month on Reggie's love life." His cousin Reggie was the greenest lad he had ever introduced to society. The boy's father had contrived urgent business elsewhere to avoid the job himself, then thrown a fit over the results.

Mark chuckled.

He glared. "You wouldn't laugh if you had been the one to face Uncle George with the news that you supported his son's desire to marry a chit who had not even made her bows to society and whose guardian was half a step in front of the tipstaffs."

"Did you mention that you approved it to prevent the girl from compromising you?"

"Of course not! And I would never have allowed her to do so, in any case. But all is now well. Her guardian has accepted a governorship in the Indies, which will take care of his financial problems. And knowing his conniving wife won't see London for a few years pleases me no end. Reggie will wed at Christmas and live on Uncle George's estate, where he is unlikely to get into trouble. At least I will no longer have to bear-lead him in town. I never saw a greener cub."

"Nor I. So what does the excitable Aunt Mathilda want?"

"More cousin trouble. Terrence has fallen into the clutches of an unscrupulous seductress."

"Not another one!"

"Fortune hunters lie rather thick on the ground just now," he agreed. "And Terrence has enough blunt to attract them. I have a very bad feeling about this."

"You had best make haste, then," urged Mark, frowning. "I've never known one of your feelings to fail."

He nodded. All his life, he had exhibited an uncanny sense of trouble, both for himself and for his closest friends. It had saved him from harm when he balked at accompanying a group to Richmond—the subsequent carriage accident badly injured all passengers. It had proven prescient the day Mark's daughter had disappeared. Mark heeded the warning and dispatched several search parties, finding Helen in a collapsed cave before she succumbed to her injuries. Now the feeling was back.

Mark returned indoors. Frowning, Richard reread the missive. Were his aunt's fears exaggerated? Despite her confused agitation, her terror seemed genuine, but she included few details.

You must help! she had scrawled untidily. *Poor Terrence has succumbed to the blandishments of an unscrupulous seductress and believes himself in love. All nonsense, of course, but those unspeakable farm girls will stoop to anything to get their hands on his inheritance. They've nothing of their own. Come soon! I fear he will elope, for he claims that I am plotting against him.*

There was much more, but he set the recrossed page aside. He despised fortune hunters. Instead of the classics, schools should teach young men the dangers lurking behind the seductive smiles and other wiles that women inevitably employed to mask their plots. There ought to be a law against allowing young cubs into mixed company without intensive training in how to recognize traps. Not one of them was capable of rational thought when they first arrived in town. Poor Terrence. The lad was at least as green as Reggie.

Pray God he would be in time to stop the scheming jade!

Resigned to spending the rest of his life rescuing incompetent relatives from their own unwitting mistakes, he strode into the Abbey, his mind already churning out plans—his secretary must join him to help check the books; he would need his own horses, for Gareth Avery had never been complimented on his stables; a wardrobe suitable for a house in mourning . . .

Half an hour later, the messenger returned to Carrington Castle, a sheaf of orders tucked into his pocket.

Chapter Two

Richard tooled his curricle along the lane that led to Tallgrove Manor, if that ostler had his directions straight, which he thought highly unlikely. Nothing had gone right for days.

He had left Bridgeport Abbey at dawn, expecting to arrive at Tallgrove shortly after dusk. He would not have attempted to make the journey in a single day in winter, of course, but August days were long and Mathilda's demands were urgent.

So much for planning.

A rainstorm had blown up from nowhere, stranding him at a derelict inn. Even worse, his baggage coach was far behind, so he had no change of clothes or even a razor. After enduring two days of a damp, lumpy bed, nearly inedible food, and the company of what he suspected was a band of cutthroats, he left. But the roads were in pitiful condition. Even the turnpikes were rutted, while country lanes remained nearly impassable. He had run into further delay when one of his horses cast a shoe.

What abominable timing! His groom was with the baggage coach, for he had wanted to be alone with his thoughts. Leading the animal to the next inn and finding a new team had taken nearly four hours, and the only horses available were the worst he had driven in years—slow, unmatched, and nearly unresponsive. If the horses were so bad, could he trust the ostler's directions?

Memories had taunted him as he slogged through the mud—his mother's admonitions; the loneliness inherent in being the sole arbiter of family problems; Mark and Elaine locked in each other's arms the moment they thought he was gone; female voices proclaiming him cold, harsh, and solemn. But he wasn't really! And his own inconsistency bedeviled him as well. Though he condemned the girls' temerity in criticizing a lord, he despised toad eaters. His head swirled.

He wrested his thoughts back to Tallgrove. What calamity lurked there? His premonition had grown with each delay until this sojourn loomed as the pivotal point of his life. Only life-threatening situations had triggered this feeling in the past, a fact that had lodged his heart in his throat ever since the summons arrived.

He negotiated a sharp corner, grimacing at the unkempt hedgerows that blocked any view of the countryside. Six feet tall, they narrowed the lane until two carriages could not pass in many places. He preferred the open vistas around Carrington Cast—

"Bloody hell!"

In sudden panic, he jerked the miserable team hard enough to risk ditching his favorite curricle, averting that disaster only because their tough mouths made them slow to respond. But he was unable to escape an accident. The peasant woman he had spotted too late flew into the ditch, a splash of water and crash of breaking pottery nearly drowning her scream.

"Oh, God! No!"

Snubbing the ribbons, he leaped to the ground, some of his panic subsiding when he realized that she was already trying to rise. But his apology froze on his tongue.

"Infernal, cow-handed fool," she muttered to herself even as her struggles sank her deeper into the mire. "Why can't gentlemen pay attention to what they are doing? If he is in such a hurry, he should have stayed on the turnpike."

He suppressed his temper, for she was not really addressing him. "I *was* paying attention, but I hardly expected to find someone walking down the middle of the lane," he growled in his own defense, grabbing her arm to help her out of the ditch. The mud was reluctant to release its hostage. When it finally surrendered to his superior force, she slammed against him, nearly knocking him down.

"Thank you—I think." She wrung out her dripping mobcap, using its cleanest edge to wipe her face. "As to paying attention, honesty compels me to point out that you were driving far too fast down the wrong side of the road."

He barely heard her. Every inch of his body had registered her shape. Young. Firm. Voluptuous. He could still feel the impact of nipples peaked from cold water. His gaze caught on her torn bodice, where her breasts fought to burst free of the tight gown. Heat exploded through his loins. He had encountered such a bosom once before. A wave of longing wafted him into the past. . . .

A hand suddenly flashed up to slap his face. Appalled, he realized that he had unconsciously caressed one glorious bud, brushing his palm wonderingly over its tip.

"My God!" he choked, rapidly backing several paces. "I—"

"Lecher!" she snapped, following him across the lane. "Cad! Unprincipled rogue!" She accompanied each word by a blow to his shoulders with her sodden cap.

He struggled to breathe, shocked into speechlessness by his unwarranted conduct. He had never assaulted a woman. Even in his heedless youth he would not have dreamed of such an uninvited advance. His head swirling in chagrin, he took in her appearance.

She was tall—nearly his own height—and slender, which only emphasized her generous breasts. Her dripping gown clung to long legs and rounded hips, sending a new wave of unaccustomed lust rampaging into his loins. Flaming hair encompassing shades from chestnut through copper to antique gold escaped a prim knot to frame her head in a nebulous halo. More than her bosom looked familiar. He had seen that combination of sapphire eyes and red hair before, though these highlighted a freckled oval rather than a porcelain heart. And she neither simpered nor flirted. Every muscle quivered in fury as she abused his character, his conduct, and his ancestry.

Not until he tripped over his curricle did he overcome his vocal paralysis. "Enough, ma'am!" he declared in his voice of authority—the one that never failed to command respect from inferiors. "It was only a touch, and unintentional at that. I believe you have amply avenged any insult. Perhaps in future you will walk on the verge and save yourself some trouble."

She ignored his tone. "Are you blind? I *was* on the verge! You were driving down the wrong side!" She whacked him again.

Anger exploded through his head. He grabbed the mobcap

and hurled it into the ditch. "Don't blame me for your own stupidity. I'll have you know I have excellent eyesight. And I never drive on the wrong side."

She stared at the crest that gleamed on his curricle. "Dear God! Another arrogant lord!" she snorted, throwing up her arms. "One would think a man of your age would have outgrown reckless driving."

"There is nothing reckless about my driving," he swore. "I belong to the Four-in-Hand Club. My skills are unmatched."

"By a two-year-old perhaps, though even that is doubtful. Only your conceit is unmatched. No man of sense would race around a blind corner on an unfamiliar road. Did you forget that this is a public thoroughfare? Men of your stamp seem to believe that the world exists solely for their own pleasure."

"So quick to judge when you know nothing about me." He fisted his hands to keep from strangling her.

"I know enough, sir. You are a pompous, conceited lecher who belongs in Bedlam for expecting an apology because I failed to die at your hands. Why don't you go to Spain? With your talent for creating mayhem, Napoleon wouldn't stand a chance."

"How dare you insult your betters? Has no one taught you your place? But who can expect propriety of redheads?"

She laughed, the carefree peal sending his temper flaring even higher. "You lack anything approaching intelligence, a misfortune confirmed every time you open your mouth. You recklessly run me down, assault me, blame me for your own misdeeds, and then claim to be my better? You really *are* insane."

"Termagant!" He stepped forward, fists raised.

"Go ahead. Hit me again! I'm not armed. Maybe you can break a bone this time instead of merely destroying a batch of pottery."

This had gone too far already, he decided, ruthlessly suppressing his fury as he climbed into his curricle. "We are both unharmed," he stated coldly, "so there is no need to stand about quarreling like fractious children."

"You started it! The least you can do is pay for the damage. How am I supposed to put food on the table if I have to replace these myself?" She pointed to the basket still half buried in the ditch.

He grimaced. "And what inflated price do you claim that trash to be worth?"

"Supercilious, as well." Her eyes sparked dangerously. "This trash, as you call it, may never grace your table, but that does not diminish its quality. It commands considerable respect from those who must earn their own living and cannot afford to dine from golden plates or sip from crystal goblets. But a man who never lifts a finger to provide for himself can hardly understand that. Give me your direction, and I will send an accounting— unless you care to wait while I do an inventory? It won't take long."

"This should cover it." Not trusting his control if he remained a moment longer, he pulled out his purse and threw a handful of coins at her feet. "What is your name?"

"Penelope Wingrave." She glared.

"I might have known such a harridan would be named Penelope." He snatched up the ribbons. "Is this the road to Tallgrove?"

"I might have known you were a friend of *those* people," she growled, matching his disdain. "You would be better served by leaving the district at once. But if you insist on calling there, tell your hosts to mind their own business and stay away from me and mine!"

"I can't imagine they would have anything to do with you. Even the lowliest Averys have some standards." He whipped the horses to a gallop and escaped. Insufferable female! How dare she brangle with a lord? He despised temper fits, and she had just treated him to a pattern-card tantrum. He reviewed her words, his fury growing at her temerity. He would have to be more careful what he wished for. Simpering, fawning widgeons looked considerably better after this brush with Penelope Wingrave's brand of candor. So why was his body still painfully aware of hers?

But within a mile his conscience rebelled against his mental diatribe. In retrospect, his own behavior had been insupportable. He had never in his life behaved so dishonorably. Publicizing this fracas would permanently damage his reputation. He may have rued being thought cold, stodgy, and hard to please, but a suggestion that he assaulted strangers would be worse.

What had come over him? Lust was alien to his nature. He had needs, of course, and satisfied them discreetly—so discreetly that only Mark was aware of his mistress. But never before had he been overwhelmed by desire. And lusting after a sharp-tongued peasant was ridiculous, especially one caked in mud from head to toe who dripped water every time she moved. Devil take it! She was a mess!

He glanced down at his caped driving coat and grimaced. The wet patches on his shoulders were bad enough, but clearly imprinted on the front was a muddy female shape, easily recognizable to the dullest intellect. He shuddered, reliving every detail of the impact. Pulling to a halt, he tore it off and stuffed it under the seat. Arriving in such damning evidence would seriously undermine his authority.

Perhaps his reaction was rooted in terror—and the galling knowledge that she had been right. He had indeed been driving too fast. Exasperated over the delays, his aunt's summons, and his growing sense of danger, he had pressed the horses to their limits to relieve his tension. His heart had nearly stopped when his negligence tossed the woman in the ditch in seemingly fatal fulfillment of his premonitions. His euphoric relief that she was intact had destroyed his usual control. He forced himself to believe it and to ignore the lingering heat where her breasts had pressed into his chest. He was the Marquess of Carrington, not some drunken lout ready to tumble the nearest tavern wench.

Had he injured her? Caught in the emotions of the moment, he had neglected to ask. He had seen no sign of damage, but the nearside horse had hit her. He should have escorted her home. At the very least, he should inquire after her in the morning— and apologize.

The idea left him shuddering. Whatever malady had afflicted him was still very much in force. His groin strained against his pantaloons, sending new heat racing through his blood.

Enough! Suppressing memory of the encounter, he braced himself to greet his aunt. The accident had not been the event he feared after all. His presentiment of danger was still alive and growing.

* * *

Penelope watched the infuriating lord disappear before bursting into tears. When her knees could no longer support her, she sank to the road and rested her head in her hands.

The incident had been ridiculous from first to last. When the curricle had appeared, she had been carrying a basket of cups home from the pottery. Not only was he moving too fast for safety, but he had swung wide on the corner. And she had jumped too late. A sizable bruise was already forming on her thigh.

She tried to forget the ensuing brangle. How could she have behaved so outrageously? She was known throughout the district for her serenity, good sense, and practical reactions to trouble. No one was better able to keep their head in a crisis. So how could she explain her utter loss of control? He had looked concerned when he stopped, yet she had allowed her mental imprecations to emerge into the light of day, then fallen apart from a simple caress.

She shuddered. It was not the first time she had been touched. When she was nineteen, Jeremy Jacobson, son of the squire, had professed his undying devotion, spending half an hour nuzzling her in the garden during the local assembly. His adoration had not survived her lack of dowry, of course. Or her responsibility for raising her siblings. He had returned from Bath the following winter with a giggling bride whose fortune excused having more hair than wit. That had been a lasting lesson. Without assets and encumbered by her siblings, she was unmarriageable—except to one aging lecher who was so desperate to find a mother for his six children and a replacement for his housekeeper that he would have accepted a dozen siblings and a mountain of debt. If she had been beautiful, she might have surmounted those obstacles, but she was not. Men did not admire red hair or tall women. They seemed to like her overgenerous bosom, but only because they thought it denoted loose morals. This odious lord was merely the latest example.

She had donned spinster's caps within a month of Jeremy's return, claiming they increased her stature with tradesmen. His scorn for her eccentricity incited enough anger that she had thrown off self-pity. And he had continued his ridicule long after the neighbors ceased noticing the change. Perhaps his antagonism covered guilt for choosing money over affection.

Imbecile! she chided herself. Only a hopeless romantic would cling to such a fantasy eight years after the fact. The truth was painfully obvious. Though she possessed a body that men lusted after, she was not a woman any gentleman could genuinely care for. She thickened the barrier around her heart that allowed her to flirt without risking emotional involvement—as with Sir Francis, who did not even pretend serious intentions. She enjoyed their lighthearted repartee and had even allowed him to kiss her once, but she had never been in danger of losing herself in his arms.

What a horrible thought! She jumped to her feet. Surely she had not lost herself to the arrogant stranger! His caress had been insulting, clearly that of a libertine. She could not possibly regret cutting it off before he could draw her back against that hard-muscled body. Flames flickered on her cheeks until she feared the heat would cause scars. Tingles emanated from every spot that had touched him. Her knees collapsed, depositing her back on the road.

"How could you?" she scolded herself.

He was certainly nothing to look at. His face was filthy and sported several days' growth of stubble. His coat had been dirty even before the accident, and his boots were caked in mud. The odors clinging to his body—horse, sweat, stale beer, and more—would have taken awhile to build up. A gypsy sleeping in cow byres and under hedges could not have looked worse. In fact, if not for the crest, she would never have pegged him as a lord.

And his behavior was insulting. She was firmly on the shelf and was wearing the old cap and gown she used at the pottery. Both were now dripping mud and water. So either his attack was meant to chastise her for being in his way, or it was yet another example of arrogant conceit. Did he think his touch would compensate her for her injuries? Or had he expected to drive the memory of his idiocy from her mind?

"Ass!" she muttered darkly, adding some even less ladylike epithets for good measure. "Libertine!" The man must be the most notorious rake in the realm to have affected her so strongly. At least his driving coat would never be the same.

She giggled, diverting her attention to business. The pottery was a total loss. Fury returned as she gathered the scattered coins. Condescending toad! Two pounds ten—three times what the cups were worth. Another insult. He had not even bothered to count the money. Now she must discover his name. Never would she accept charity—especially from him! His behavior was even more provoking, more insolent, and more unwarranted than Lord Avery's had been, may the late viscount roast for all eternity. And now Terrence was sniffing around Alice. Was he determined to continue his father's odious plots?

Tears again threatened. She had barely managed to deflect the father. How was she to counter the son? Winter House was all Michael had.

"Guess what, Penny!" exclaimed Alice the moment Penelope entered the house. "You'll never guess in a million years! Oh, I cannot believe it."

"Calm down, Allie," she urged, setting her basket in the corner and pulling her muddy shawl closer to hide the rip in her gown. His gray eyes had darkened as he gazed at that tear, the pupils blurring very strangely just before he had touched her. Her breasts tightened. Appalled, she thrust the memory away.

"Good heavens! What happened?" demanded Alice, taking in her sister's appearance.

"I fell in the ditch. Perhaps I should change before we talk. A least it is warm enough that I needn't fear a chill."

"As if you ever would!"

She hurried up the stairs. Her reluctance to describe the encounter was as irritating as the meeting itself. He deserved to have his improprieties known. Spreading the tale might allow other girls to avoid his pawing. But she did not want to douse Alice's obvious excitement. The girl had so few pleasures.

She washed and donned another gown, grateful that the bruise was not as bad as she had initially thought.

"What happened?" she asked Alice half an hour later when they were ensconced in the drawing room with a tea tray. Michael was supervising the peach harvest, throwing himself enthusiastically into estate work as he always did when he was home from school. Every year he was able to take on more. Soon he would assume complete control. Pride in his achievements battled a flash of jealousy and an unaccustomed terror at the rapid passage of time. She was already feeling old.

"Terry wants to marry me!" Alice burst out, a smile almost consuming her face. "He loves me as much as I love him. Oh, I never dreamed that he could actually return my feelings."

"Surely he is young to consider settling down," she managed, stunned into near silence. "He is only twenty."

"I know, and he must get permission from his guardian, who is due to arrive any day now, but that is a mere formality."

She took a long sip of tea while she groped for a response. Such an alliance was appalling. Terrence could not truly want to wed Alice—not that she was unlovable. She was beautiful and sensible beyond her seventeen years, but even love did not justify a mésalliance, so he must have other reasons for ignoring the rules of his class. Yet Alice would not believe ill of him. Her eyes were clouded by infatuation, seeing only what she wanted to see.

She should have expected this maneuver. By bypassing Alice's guardian, Terrence hoped to force acceptance of his suit before discussing financial questions. He could then demand Winter House as her dowry by threatening to jilt and ruin Alice if they refused. Had the previous Lord Avery contrived this plot, or had Terrence concocted it on his own? More importantly, why did the Averys want the estate? It was barely self-sufficient and would hardly enhance Tallgrove's prestige. Yet the previous viscount had gone to great lengths to persuade her to sell and even greater lengths to force that sale when she refused.

Over her dead body! Alice's happiness was paramount, of course, but she would never find it at Tallgrove. Not only was Terrence's affection suspect, but Lady Avery hated all Wingraves, disseminating false rumors and demanding ostracism that estranged them from much of local society. Any hostess choosing whether to invite a viscountess or a former clergyman's daughter wasted little time pondering the options. She would never countenance placing her sister in proximity to the woman.

But speculation of the Avery motives could not distract her from Alice's other statement. Her obnoxious assailant had asked the way to Tallgrove, so he must be Terrence's guardian. And that was good. His arrogance would condemn Alice out of hand. Not even Winter House could compensate for such a match. She normally despised blind judgment, but this time it was a blessing. With his opposition virtually guaranteed, she need only postpone any decision.

"I am delighted that you have found someone you care for," she said calmly. "But it would not be wise to jump into a betrothal just yet. Terrence must return to school in another month. A formal decision can wait until he finishes his studies."

"Are you implying that he will change his mind?"

"Of course not. Nor am I doubting you. But you are both young. There is no rush to marry. Since that would not be possible for at least a year, I would prefer to keep the attachment nonbinding until a later date. After all, he has been home for less than a month. His last visit was all of three years ago. You need more time to make sure that his character is what it appears to be."

"You don't trust us!"

"Fustian! I merely want to assure your happiness. He seems to be a personable young man, but there are things he has yet to learn. His father let their estate fall into considerable disrepair. How does he plan to address that problem? Are his finances able to cover both improvements and the acquisition of a wife? What will his mother and sister think of this match? You will all have to live together. Even if his mother moves into the dower house, you still must deal with her. Does he understand about your dowry? These are all serious questions. We needn't rush to get the answers, but all must be addressed before you commit yourself to the union. You know you would fret over a husband who ignored his duty to his tenants as Lord Avery has done for so long. Terrence has yet to show that he is any different. By taking the time to consider all aspects of his character, you will assure your own happiness. Even love cannot counter some defects."

"He knows I have no dowry, but that makes no difference. Millicent will not be a problem—and she will marry in a year or two, so she can do little to affect my future. It is true that his mother dislikes me, though that is rooted in general dislike of all of us, so I believe that as she comes to know me, we will reach an accommodation."

Dear Lord! This had gone farther than she had expected. How much time were they spending together? Never had she cursed the lack of a governess more, but she managed to smile. "I see you have discussed serious topics already, and that is good. Continue to apply your good sense. You must agree that haste is unnecessary."

"I suppose so, but I love him so!"

"I can see that," she agreed, inwardly wincing at the pain Alice would suffer when Terrence rescinded his offer. But there was nothing she could do. And she still questioned his motives.

Why did this problem have to arise now? she grumbled even as she turned the conversation to other topics. The last thing she needed was an unsuitable romance. A month of scrimping put her no closer to meeting the next mortgage payment. And she dared not mention the problem to Alice now that she knew the girl's feelings. Alice would tell Terrence, who could use the information to pressure the bank into foreclosing.

Where would she find the money? The pottery was gaining a market, but slowly. An expanded flock would improve the feather harvest, but not enough to cover that unfortunate gaming debt. They badly needed a new ram, for only half of the ewes had conceived this year. But there was no money. And now their neighbors had an arrogant lord in residence who would not scruple to run roughshod over her. She had a very bad feeling about the coming weeks.

Michael returned from the orchard, passing a subdued Alice as she left the drawing room. "Josh is ready to leave for Exeter," he reported, naming their man of all work.

"Good. How are the peaches?"

"Delicious." He grinned. "The rain did some damage, but not as much as you feared. Mrs. Peccles rescued most of the windfalls for making jam and wine."

"Perhaps the storm will drive up prices. Our trees are more sheltered than most."

Michael's face twitched at the mention of money, but he said nothing. After his first week home, she had banned further apologies.

"How is Ozzie?" she asked, changing the subject.

"I was on my way down there. We will be cutting hay next week, so I thought to clear a spot for the stack."

She nodded, proud that he was planning ahead without her prodding. "Take him any of the peaches Mrs. Peccles cannot use, but remove the pits first. They did not agree with him last time."

"Right."

She headed for the kitchen. Mrs. Peccles would need help with the peaches. Without any pottery to decorate, she had time.

Chapter Three

~

Richard was still reproaching himself when he pulled to a stop before Tallgrove Manor. The house had been built from one of Inigo Jones's Renaissance designs, though he doubted Jones had participated in its construction. Myriad panes twinkled in the afternoon sun from a stone facade liberally sprinkled with leaded windows.

"Lord Carrington?" The butler's voice barely formed a question despite the fact that Richard had never visited Tallgrove. "Her ladyship is in the drawing room."

"Has my luggage arrived?" he asked, hoping that Kesterton had passed him while he was searching for a new team, but the butler was shaking his head. "Very well. Send up warm water. I will attend my aunt later."

Even without fresh clothes, he needed to clean up. His boots were caked with mud. A sizable puddle just inside the gates had spattered his pantaloons and ruined his jacket. He would have done better to wear his driving coat until he was in sight of the house. But before he could escape upstairs, Lady Avery burst into the hall.

"Thank heaven you are here at last!" she exclaimed, tears evident in her eyes. "How could you delay so long when you know the danger that threatens poor Terrence? Those awful people are leading him about by the nose, determined to ruin him, and I can do nothing to stop them. Terrence ignores every word I say. His insolence is driving me mad!" She broke into choking sobs.

"Control yourself, Aunt," he admonished, appalled by her outburst. Half a dozen servants were drinking in every word. The butler did not even pretend a lack of interest. Nor did he make any effort to send the lower servants away. "Let us retire to the drawing room, where we can discuss this in a civilized manner."

"Of course, my lord. You must forgive me, but these past weeks have brought one horror after another. Nothing has gone right since my dear Gareth died." she turned weeping eyes to his face.

Knowing her penchant for endless complaint, he quickly steered her out of the hall.

"If only you had come immediately! Terrence ignored my summons to the funeral! Cited his studies, of all the frivolous things. Now he runs wild, eschewing propriety. And Millicent hasn't mourned as she ought. I cannot understand how she can be so flippant. The girl lacks all sensibility. What did I do to deserve so unnatural a daughter?" She dabbed at her tears with a wisp of lace. "And Mrs. Gudge complained only this morning that Scott had not checked the household accounts. What does she think I can do about it? No lady understands figures, so why anyone expects me to do sums, I do not know. That is Scott's job, for why do we pay him if not to run the estate? But everything will be all right now. You will send those horrid creatures packing and return Terrence's attention to his duty."

"Hush," he ordered as the door handle jiggled. He was in no mood for complaints, and if she aired her woes before the servants, the entire county would know that she exerted no control over her children—if they were not already aware of that disgrace.

The butler delivered a tray containing tea, wine, and an assortment of biscuits and sandwiches. Richard's glare managed to keep Lady Avery quiet until the man reluctantly departed. He accepted a glass of wine and took up a position before the Italian marble fireplace, where his muddy clothes would inflict minimal damage.

"You must save my poor boy," she wailed, giving him no chance to speak. "Gareth's death has addled his wits. How else can I explain his behavior? I have warned him against those vulgar schemers since he was in short coats. They are base-born mushrooms who have long looked to rise above their station. The girls are no better than they should be. And that boy! Do you know that he had the audacity to apply to Eton! They have no notion of how to go on in the world, engaging in activities I swoon merely to think about. But what can one expect from people whose mother was a courtesan and whose grandfather was in trade?"

He stiffened. "I cannot believe that Terrence is so deceived," he said soothingly, setting his empty glass on the mantel. "He is barely twenty. Even if he is suffering an infatuation of the moment, it is of no account. He will not do anything stupid."

"That's all you know!" countered his aunt. "He has no experience of the world. And that insufferable chit is angling for marriage. She has bedazzled him and will do anything to compromise him, playing on his naïveté by appearing helpless and pure. Yet all the time she is a scheming jade who wants nothing more than to be mistress of this house. I won't have it, I tell you! I won't! She will not usurp my position and drag dear Gareth's name through the mud!"

He missed the rest of her increasingly strident diatribe as disturbing memories teased his mind. There had been another girl who had perfected the art of appearing helpless and pure. He had come within a hairbreadth of succumbing to her blandishments. Even ten years had not dimmed the memory. Penelope Rissen, with her red hair, sapphire eyes, and voluptuous bosom. He hated her very name. If fate had not revealed her purpose, he would have languished in misery every day of his life. He forced his attention back to his aunt.

"And that sister of hers is even worse!" she was saying. "Why, the woman actually runs the farm herself. What more proof does one need of low breeding? Terrence saw her last month supervising sheep dipping, of all the outrageous activities. Mrs. Jacobson swears she works in the fields alongside men who don't even wear shirts! Yet Terrence accepts every word she utters as gospel." Again she dabbed her eyes. "And those horrid birds! Even the lowliest tenant would eschew such business. Yet she has the audacity to claim a place in society. And she has Sir Francis Pelham so besotted that he actually invites them to dinners and card parties that by rights should be reserved for decent folk. You've no idea what I have been made to suffer. Sir Francis actually cut me in Exeter only a week before poor Gareth died. Two women who I thought were friends laughed, and a total stranger turned her back. Sir Francis is the one who should be cut. By ignoring class differences—to say nothing of common decency—he has confused poor Terrence until he actually believes that those harpies are as good as we are! Gareth must be turning in his grave. To think that his heir could be so heedless of what is due his title and breeding!" She succumbed to inarticulate sobbing as one hand waved a vinaigrette beneath her nose.

"Rest easy, Aunt Mathilda," he urged, pouring himself another glass of wine. For all its size, the drawing room was suffocating him. He hated scenes. "I will talk to Terrence and remind him what he owes his position. And I will inform these girls that they are no longer dealing with a green youth. Where do they live?"

"About two miles north of here," she sniffed. "Winter House, they call it, though that is too grand a name for the place. It is nought but a tumble-down hovel unsuited even for pigs. Go immediately! I live in hourly fear that they will succeed in trapping poor Terrence. He is so unworldly!"

"Tomorrow morning will be sufficient." He could hardly appear in public in his present condition. "I must first recover from a lengthy journey and speak with my ward. But you need not worry. Fortune hunters are all alike. As soon as these discover that Tallgrove is under my control, they will seek an easier target."

"Of course!" exclaimed Lady Avery, her expression lightening in relief. "I had not considered that point. I only wish you could have gotten here sooner. It was cruel to delay when you knew how upset I have been."

"I came as soon as I could. I was not at Carrington Castle when your letter arrived, and the weather has been most uncooperative. But everything will soon be in order. What is the name of this family, by the way?"

"The Wingraves."

He stifled a gasp. He might have known. Fury again engulfed him even as the certainty of imminent disaster overwhelmed all reason. Every moment of that meeting in the lane returned to taunt him. But perhaps it was well that he had seen her without her public mask. She might have fooled Sir Francis with a facade of sweet humility and breathless adoration, but he had seen her true colors. He had no doubt who was the moving force behind this scheme. Her game was obvious. Though she was firmly on the shelf herself, her sister could provide entree into higher social circles, so she had foisted the girl onto an impressionable lord. He could count on her to make unacceptable demands the moment a marriage was finalized—money for herself and other indigent relations, introductions into society for any number of unsuitable sprigs, perhaps even control of Tallgrove. He ground his teeth. Never!

Her grandfather had been in trade. She was also dabbling in trade in the form of a pottery. She must have picked up some tricks from her mother as well. That would account for his reaction. And she was running the farm. If those overgrown hedgerows were any indication, she was not doing it well. Little wonder that she had set her sights on her wealthy neighbors, but how did she expect to carry off a charade of innocent respectability? Her scandalous business ventures alone would bar her from polite society even if she managed to hide her immoral past. It was a point he must make very clear to Terrence. Regardless of any physical attraction—and if the sister looked like Penelope he could understand an attraction—Terrence must take a wife from his own class. A mésalliance would destroy his own standing and impair that of his offspring.

But he would prevail. She was now dealing with a wily gentleman who had earned a reputation for judging people to the inch. No woman was entirely honest, and experience had taught him that redheads were the most pernicious liars of all.

His aunt was again bemoaning the trap her son had stumbled into. He repeated his assurances half a dozen times. Earlier noises hinted that his baggage had finally arrived. His skin crawled with the need to bathe. But before he could leave, the door burst open to admit Terrence.

It had been three years since Richard had last seen his cousin, and he nearly groaned. Terrence reminded him all too much of Reggie. The boy was enamored of the more flamboyant of the dandies, flaunting exceedingly tight biscuit pantaloons, a close-fitting peacock jacket, and the gaudiest waistcoat he had seen in years. His brown hair was cut in the Brutus, though it was even more disheveled than was common for that style. But his face stood at odds with his dress. Instead of the *ennui* that was *de rigueur* at the moment—especially in the dandy set—he was bursting with starry-eyed excitement. Brown eyes glittered and a mobile mouth stretched from ear to ear. Indeed, he seemed on the verge of exploding from ecstasy.

"Thank heaven you finally arrived!" Terrence exclaimed, hurtling across the room to grasp his hand and pump it furiously. "I could hardly wait until you got here, for I know you will love Alice—though not as much as I do. Nobody could possibly do that, and I would call out anyone who dared, but she is the sweetest, most wonderful girl who—"

"How can you be so foolish?" wailed Lady Avery, interrupting the flow of words. "She has bewitched you, for you know as well as I do that she is beneath contempt despite the airs and graces she dons in your company."

"Fustian!" retorted Terrence. "You have never even met her, so how can you judge? This baseless hatred must stop! Your absurd claims do nothing but undermine your own standing. She will make me the perfect wife—capable, intelligent, demure."

"Aren't you rushing things?" put in Richard. "You have years before you need to set up your nursery. Enjoy them, for life will never again be so good."

"Don't go all fusty on me," begged Terrence, some of his excitement evaporating. "Wait until you meet her. You must agree that she is everything a gentleman could ever want. I still cannot believe that she loves me as much as I love her."

Lady Avery gasped. "I told you to stay away from her until your guardian had spoken to you. Perhaps then you will see the sense of what I have been saying. I won't stand for that mushroom usurping my place. It is too much for any lady of quality to tolerate."

"There is no sense in any of your words, madam," said Terrence coldly. "You frequently take unreasonable dislikes to people based on no more than twitterings and flutterings in your own head. Our neighbors laugh at you behind your back, parodying your tirades and ridiculing your intransigence. I prefer to judge people for myself, based on my own observations and on the reports of those I trust. Alice is the kindest, gentlest girl I have ever met, far more worthy of being a viscountess than you. Get used to the idea, madam, for she has already accepted me. As for your place, it has been in the dower house since the day your husband died."

Lady Avery uttered a strangled squeak and fainted dead away.

Richard jumped to catch her, laying her on the couch. "You reveal your inexperience in every word you utter," he snapped. "No one of your tender years is capable of judging others, particularly females. They are natural deceivers who master the art of seeming fragile while still in the schoolroom. In reality, they are nought but calculating hypocrites, always alert for a greenling they can exploit."

Devil take the storm that had delayed him! The disaster was far worse than he had expected. He now faced an appalling fight that would ultimately cost a small fortune. How much would these jades demand to drop their claims? Had anyone witnessed his half-witted cousin's proposal?"

"Where did your offer take place?" he asked sharply.

"Not that it is any of your business, but just now when we were walking by the stream that divides our properties."

"Did you tell her sister?"

"Not yet. Miss Wingrave was not at home this afternoon."

He sighed in relief. Of course she was not. She had been abusing him in the lane. "Good. There is no witness, so she can prove nothing. That precludes a breach of promise suit. She will undoubtedly claim seduction, but there should be little evidence for that as well. It will be no problem to buy the pair off."

"Buy her off? I intend to marry her."

"Of course you will not marry her," he swore. "Such a mésalliance would ruin you."

"What lies is Mother spouting now?" demanded Terrence. "The one about the nonexistent merchant grandfather? The slander about her mother? Or was it the claim that Penelope runs a bawdy house? Ridiculous stories, every one. You are the one who is naïve if you believe a word Mother says. There is nothing wrong with Alice's breeding. It is true that she has no dowry, but I have enough to support us. As for Mother, if she will not remove to the dower house, I will have her committed. I'll not have her spite disrupting my family."

"Aunt Mathilda is right. You are bewitched. But no ward of mine will make such a mistake," he thundered. "You are far too young to consider matrimony. And I will never condone an alliance with Miss Wingrave. You will not see the girl again. I will explain their miscalculation to them. The word of a marquess will be enough to make them mend their ways."

"How dare you storm into my house and throw your title around? Do you really expect me to obey a man who issues decrees without checking a single fact?" shouted Terrence, his face alternately white and red. "You will not ruin my life! I'll take Father's will to court and have you declared incompetent to supervise even a privy! You are the worst excuse for a gentleman I have ever met." He whirled toward the door.

Fury again exploded through Richard's head. "That is enough, young man!" His voice whipped Terrence in the back, halting him in his tracks. "You betray your youth with every word. Even your manners are sadly lacking. You will go to your room and contemplate the world in which we both live. If you examine Miss Wingrave's actions, you will discover that she has been grossly misleading you, playing a part for the sole purpose of attaching your title and wealth."

"And you betray your ignorance with every word," Terrence countered sharply. "How can you claim to be reasonable when you judge without even meeting the people involved?"

"I have met her sister. That is enough."

Terrence tried to interrupt, but he continued without pause. "I will never countenance association with that family. You will forget this nonsense at once. I control your inheritance until you turn five-and-twenty. How long do you think she will consider you a catch when she learns that you will have no allowance for the next five years?"

"I should have believed the tales," Terrence murmured, half to himself. "You have a reputation for icy arrogance, but I truly thought that you would at least investigate before making a decision. How wrong I was! You are a close-minded fool, my lord, and I deplore being in your power. But I will manage. Keep the inheritance. Transfer it to yourself if you want. I care not. Alice and I will find a way."

So saying, he threw himself out of the room with even more energy than when he had entered.

Damnation! What a day. His head swirled, threatening his balance. Lady Avery was showing signs of reviving. Turning craven, he summoned a maid and escaped.

He tried to hold thought at bay while he washed and changed, concentrating instead on his old-fashioned room. Deep red velvet hangings and dark furniture gave it a glowering look that fit his current mood. Fate had bounced him from crisis to crisis, hardly allowing him time to react, let alone consider his options. And his reactions left him feeling exceedingly uncomfortable. He had not shown to advantage this day.

A giggling girl raced past in the hallway—his other ward, the sixteen-year-old Millicent. Another prick of uneasiness tickled his chest.

Chapter Four

❧

Richard's curricle swept through Tallgrove's gates and turned toward Winter House. Waiting until morning to visit the scheming Miss Wingrave had given him time to repair his appearance, but it had done nothing to improve his mood—or his discomfort at the coming confrontation. He deflected his tension by recalling the previous evening.

Dinner had been another harrowing experience. The footmen clattered utensils and dripped sauces on both table and floor. The food was cold, tasteless, and mushy. He recognized barely half of the offerings, but his companions seemed neither surprised nor distressed. He could only conclude that the meal was normal, raising questions about his aunt's supervision of the household. Despite poor lighting, he could see dust on the sideboard, tarnished silver, and a spider crawling lazily on the chandelier. Neither Terrence nor Millicent could be ready for society after being raised in such an environment. And their manners were execrable.

Terrence pouted through the entire two-hour meal, responding only when directly addressed, and then in a sullen monotone. His scowl changed to blazing hatred whenever their eyes met. With every passing minute the lad's immaturity was more apparent.

Millicent was worse. She chattered enthusiastically, pressing Richard for details of the London Season, society leaders, the latest fashions, and every ball he had ever attended. Her questions masked Terrence's silence, but he did not enjoy the scheming flirtations of London and had no wish to describe them. Yet his evasions merely brought out her petulance.

"Why *can't* I wear gowns like those in *La Belle Assemblée?* "

she demanded. "I am so tired of black! It makes me look ancient—at least five-and-twenty."

"Color has nothing to do with it," he explained with a sigh. "Nor does mourning. You must wait until you are older because the styles depicted in fashion magazines are unsuited to the schoolroom."

"But I am no longer in the schoolroom," she protested. "I am more than ready for parties and balls and pretty clothes."

"Don't flaunt your disrespect," Lady Avery admonished her. "How dare you speak of such things when your father is hardly cold?"

"Be reasonable, Mother," she begged. "He has been dead for three months, and I rarely saw him before that. You know as well as I that he ignored us. Pretend all you want for yourself, but custom allows me to abandon deep mourning next week, and I fully intend to do so. The next assembly will be the perfect place to resume life. Everyone will be there. How I wish I could wear a stylish gown—something blue to match my eyes, or perhaps pink."

"Unnatural child!" gasped her mother.

"Hardly. I know custom restricts me to dreary gray or lavender for another three months, but nothing can stop me from thinking about pretty clothes. Or about silly rules. Why is wearing hideous dresses thought to show respect for the dead? Unless knowing one looks like a hag makes the pretense of grief easier to carry off. But I will contrive. Even lavender can be persuaded to appear fashionable. I am determined to be the belle of the ball. Gentlemen will vie for my favors."

"Hah!" snorted Terrence.

"You are just envious," she retorted. "When word of your infatuation sweeps the neighborhood, you will be a laughing-stock. I must build enough credit to overcome your reputation. How else am I to have London at my feet."

"Fustian! You are no diamond, Millie," said Terrence dampingly.

"What do you know? Every gentleman I meet tells me I am beautiful. Watch me at the assembly. You'll see!"

"Conduct is as important as appearance," Richard reminded her, cursing the new problems she represented. "High spirits are not tolerated in town. Nor is contradicting a gentleman, even if he is your brother. Well-bred young ladies approach the Season with *ennui*."

"This subject is too distressing," said Lady Avery before Millicent could respond. "All this talk of assemblies and Seasons is absurd, for she has no chaperon. I will not emerge from mourning for months, if then. Dear Gareth! How can your own children turn from your memory? And you, my lord, are worse. How dare you encourage impious frivolity by expounding on London fashion?"

"It is a guardian's duty to look to the future," he reminded her. "Girls must prepare for their come-outs with care lest they ruin their chances with unacceptable behavior."

"She has plenty of time to consider the future, for it will be at least two years before I am sufficiently recovered to present her to society," she countered. "In the meantime, she can engage in a proper period of mourning. These past weeks should not count, for she has not grieved."

"You wish me to support your hypocrisy, madam?" snapped a white-faced Millicent. "I would rather be honest. You know very well that Papa cared not a whit for any of us—not even you. Rather than mourn his passing, I intend to get on with my life."

Lady Avery erupted into a tirade that put her earlier hysterics to shame. Richard tried to ignore the resulting brangle by signaling the servants to leave and concentrating on the unappetizing food. But when ten minutes had passed with no abatement, he changed his mind.

"Enough!" His fist slammed onto the table. "Never have I been treated to such rank vulgarity," he continued when three openmouthed faces turned to him in astonishment. "If this is your idea of proper conduct, I can allow none of you within a hundred miles of London. You would call censure upon the entire family."

Millicent paled. Terrence glared. Lady Avery dabbed at her eyes with the corner of her napkin. "Pardon me, my lord. You are right, of course, but if you knew what insults I have endured from such unfeeling chil—"

"Not another word, madam," he interrupted coldly. "If you raise this subject at the table again, you will eat from a tray in your room for the remainder of my visit."

Lady Avery gasped, but lapsed into silence. Millicent took one look at his icy face and followed suit. As soon as the ladies withdrew to the drawing room, he excused himself from a seething Terrence and retired for the night.

But sleep did not come easily. Though he occupied the best guest chamber, the bed was uncomfortable, its thin coverlet doing little to keep out the chill and damp. Dust tickled his nose from the hangings. Yet it was his encounter with Miss Wingrave that kept him awake. The woman was a menace. Flaming red hair, a temper to match, and clothes that blatantly flaunted her charms. Again those stiff-tipped breasts floated before his eyes, fighting to burst free. Voluptuous. Enticing. Begging to be stroked and fondled and kissed. His breathing quickened. The temperature no longer bothered him. If Alice was like her sister, he could understand how Terrence had been trapped. The lad had not yet learned to distinguish lust from the finer emotions.

He tossed and turned, rising at dawn to pace the floor while he considered his next step. It would be best to confront the schemers immediately, to let them know that he was wise to their game, and to demonstrate that they were now dealing with a man of the world who was impervious to charm and adept at recognizing lies. And so he had called for his curricle the moment he had broken his fast.

Winter House was ancient, built of weathered gray stone with a slate roof that showed significant sagging. It was larger than he would have expected for a farmer, but its condition explained why no one of better breeding would keep it. Though it was not quite the hovel described by his aunt—being a little too good for housing pigs—he doubted that it had seen any significant repairs in many a year. One window was boarded up. Another was cracked. The trim had remained unpainted for so long that he was hard-pressed to discern its color. No servant appeared to take his horses, so he tied them to a post.

A disheveled maid accepted his card and showed him into a shabby drawing room. It had originally been decorated in the French style, but its elegant design had long since been adulterated by a pair of heavy chairs, a Chinese vase, an Egyptian claw-foot table, and other anomalies. Ill-fitting chintz covers and threadbare draperies proclaimed the poverty that must have prompted their scheme.

A portrait of a man dressed in the manner of thirty years before hung above the fireplace, his cheap good looks belying his aristocratic pose. It must have been painted by one of the itinerant artists that drifted about the countryside—and one of the less-talented at that. Did the father have ambitions to become a country squire?

His fury revived.

The entire merchant class was becoming a plague and a nuisance. When would they learn that nothing would make them acceptable to polite society? Only last year a coal dealer had actually tried to buy a membership in White's, even going so far as to marry his daughter to an impoverished baron in a vain attempt to improve his standing. It wasn't the first time that an ambitious tradesman had tried to cross that sacred portal. People had no respect for their betters these days. And now he must depress the pretensions of yet another upstart.

Penelope glanced at the calling card Mary brought to the breakfast room and sighed. Though the name meant nothing, she knew who was waiting in the drawing room. Memories of his attack had kept her awake for much of the night, assisted by her growing bruises.

Lord Carrington was a perfect example of aristocratic arrogance. She could deduce his character all too easily—conceited, uncaring, and determined; a man who relentlessly pursued his every desire with no thought for those he crushed in the process; an ignorant wastrel who ruthlessly exploited his dependents to support an idle life; a flagrant lecher who callously appeased his appetites on the nearest female. She would have to make sure that Alice never left the house unaccompanied while the marquess was in residence. If he could vent his lust on a bedraggled spinster whose own father had disdained her appearance, what would he do when he beheld the delectable Alice?

But that did not matter at the moment. He had come to discuss Terrence's infatuation. Surely they could ignore their antagonism long enough to decide how to end their wards' attachment. At least that was one topic on which they must agree.

The sooner they accomplished that goal, the sooner he would leave Devon in peace.

"My lord," she stated coolly from the doorway of the drawing room.

He was every inch the aristocrat today, from his fashionably short black hair, impeccable cravat, and form-fitting blue coat, to the tasseled Hessians that graced muscular legs encased in tight gray pantaloons. He had cleaned up better than she had expected. While not handsome, he *was* compelling, with a craggy face, broad shoulders, and slender hips. The cut of his clothes and his obvious fitness proclaimed him a sportsman even without his boasts in the lane. But his temper had not improved one iota. Stormy gray eyes glared at her greeting. His long fingers curled into claws.

"Good morning," he snapped.

"Rather early for calls," she commented, gracefully seating herself on a settee and motioning him to a chair.

"Only in the polite world." He ignored her gesture, remaining in stiff solitude before the fireplace. "I will not prolong this visit. Your game is herewith canceled. Lord Avery may be an impressionable youth, but you are no longer dealing with him. I am his guardian and would never, under any circumstances, permit an alliance with a girl of inferior breeding. Don't try to claim a compromise, either. No one would accept the lies of a farm wench over the word of a gentleman born. I would not even bother to pay you off, for the only reputation you could hurt would be your own. And forget about talking him into an elopement. I have sole control of his inheritance for another five years. If you expect him to forego his allowance, think again."

She was so furious that she had been unable to utter a word during his incredible diatribe. But she finally found her voice. Rising to her full height, she glared at him. "You are insufferable!" she snarled. "And incredibly stupid—as I should have deduced after your conduct yesterday. Anyone with an ounce of brains would at least discover the facts before making accusations that trumpet his ignorance. Do you want to be a laughingstock?"

"How dare you!"

"I cannot ignore what stands before me. But here is a dare for you, my lord. I dare you to emulate Diogenes. Are you man enough to seek the truth? Talk to Sir Francis or Squire Jacobson. Or anyone in the village, for that matter. Even the most cursory investigation will expose your charges for the foolishness they are."

"I learned everything I need to know from my aunt," he declared. "Why should I waste time talking to your dupes?"

"As I thought." She glared. "You are a coward, my lord. A craven coward so afraid to discover that dishonor resides in your own family that you blind yourself. You are more in need of Diogenes's lantern than I thought. If you persist in your delusions, you will have to rusticate for years to hide your embarrassment. People will howl in scorn at the sound of your name." She was so angry she hardly knew what she was saying, wanting nothing more than to lash out. "Alice is the perfect wife for Terrence, and I will do everything in my power to assure that they find the happiness they deserve. He needs her guidance and common sense after so many years of living with incompetent relatives. Frankly, I am amazed that he has grown into a personable young man. It proves his strong character, so if you think your opinions will deter him, you are even more stupid than I suspected. As for money, Terrence will always be welcome here. I expect he would starve before accepting a groat from so despicable a guardian. I cannot understand how Lord Avery came to name you to such a post, unless he truly did despise his children. You are the farthest thing from an acceptable trustee that I can imagine! Or did you coerce him into appointing you so that you can loot his estate to support your dissipated revels in town?"

"I should have expected such accusations from a scheming redhead." Carrington glowered through eyes that had turned nearly black. His hands clenched into fists as they had done in the lane. "Fortune hunters always try to drag the honorable down to their own level. Either give up your plotting, or I swear I will break you."

"Break me? What a mature reaction. So very gentlemanly!" She made her voice as goading as possible. "Is that your answer to opposition? Ride roughshod over those who thwart your current whim?"

"Your vulgarity is showing."

"You dare to call *me* vulgar?" She pulled herself even taller. "You knock me into a ditch by speeding down the wrong side of the road. You assault and insult me. You improvise all manner of false charges, then threaten me if I do not agree with them. Your behavior is worse than vulgar, sirrah. It is mad."

"Quit trying to change the subject," he snapped. "Your game is up. Abandon your schemes, or I will expose you and your sluttish sister to ridicule by every man, woman, and child in England. You picked the wrong target to finance your dreams of indolence." Without another word, he slammed out of the room.

She collapsed onto the settee, shaking like a leaf. What had come over her? She could not afford to antagonize anyone in a position to destroy Michael's inheritance. Lord Carrington had the power to do just that—to say nothing of bottomless coffers—and she had now given him ample reason to try. She dropped her head into her hands, cursing herself for losing her temper.

How could she have claimed to support a match between Alice and Terrence? Alice would be miserable tied to such a family. Aside from Lady Avery's antagonism, the late Lord Avery's obsession, and Lord Carrington's arrogance, Terrence was too young, too immature, and too unreliable to provide the security that Alice needed.

Yet she had just vowed to promote it. If she did not do so, the insufferable marquess would know that she had been lying. But how could she jeopardize Alice's happiness?

The drawing room door banged open. Skirts akilter, Alice rushed in, her mouth stretched by a wide smile.

"I knew you approved!" she exclaimed.

This was all the day needed. She sighed. "You overheard?"

"I was in the dining room. Thank you! I can hardly wait to tell Terry. He will be ecstatic."

"Not so fast, Allie," she begged. This was going to require some tricky backtracking if the situation was not to tumble out of all control. "Don't do anything rash. My earlier comments still hold. Terrence is young and has not yet finished school. And I will have little to say in the matter. Lord Carrington thinks you beneath contempt. You must have heard his vow to cut off Terrence's allowance. How would a penniless husband support you? Even if you lived here, we would be hard-pressed to cover the extra food and clothing."

Alice sighed. "In fact, the situation is nearly hopeless."

"For the time being. I should not have lost my temper, but his charges were so base that I could not remain silent." Just thinking about them sent fire racing through her blood. And they cast further doubts on Terrence's character. If his own guardian believed him to be a weak-willed pawn easily exploited by schemers, how could she even consider consigning Alice to his care?

Alice laid a hand on her shoulder. "Do not take the blame, Penny. I doubt he listened to a word you said. He began his diatribe before you even opened your mouth. But it is all of a piece. Terry warned me that Lord Carrington is impossible to please. And now we see the truth of it. But I will not despair. Somehow we will find a way." Smiling, she left the room.

Penelope shook her head. Youthful innocence. How were they to weather this crisis? She glanced heavenward. *Please help Alice survive when Terrence's interest shifts elsewhere.* She knew too well how painful the rejection would be.

She shivered. Carrington's compelling presence still ruled the drawing room, driving away most of the air and all of the warmth. His words continued to reverberate. *Inferior breeding . . . farm wench . . . sluttish . . .* She had heard the charges before, of course. They formed the core of Lady Avery's claims. Even an arrogant lord would accept as gospel anything his own aunt uttered, regardless of his normal judgment. What would it take to bring him to his senses?

She snorted. Did she want to correct his misconceptions? On the one hand, making him see reason might deflect him from resurrecting Lord Avery's plots, especially if Terrence's affections were honest. But if he recognized Alice as the jewel she was, might he not decide to promote the match himself? Alice would be good for Terrence—she had spoken truly about that— and Carrington's backing might even deflect Lady Avery. But Terrence would not make a good husband.

Did Terrence know why Lady Avery despised the Wingraves? The woman's hatred had first surfaced on Penelope's tenth birthday. The housekeeper had taken her into town to buy ribbons for a new gown—her stepmother had been confined to childbed at the time. They had shopped, giggled over a traveling puppet show, and eaten cakes at the pastry shop. Then Lady Avery had spotted her, turned stark white, and uttered an awful epithet before deliberately crossing the street. Others followed suit, but she would not have recognized the cut without the verbal insult. The housekeeper had been furious, but she could do nothing but hurry the girl home. No one could imagine the cause, but Lady Avery's antagonism had not waned in the seventeen years since.

Sighing, she headed for the bookroom. Somehow she must find the money for the next mortgage payment. It was due in barely a month. The corn harvest would not begin until afterward, but with Carrington's vow to break her family, she could not afford to ask for a postponement. Thus she would have to sell something, a stratagem she had employed before but which she had thankfully abandoned six years ago. What must go this time? Another Shakespeare first edition? The Chinese vase Uncle Oscar had brought home from his travels? Her mother's pearls?

She heaved a deeper sigh and picked up her pen. The pottery was showing ten pounds more profit than she had counted on. But the slight increase in the price of peaches did not offset the weather damage, canceling the pottery gains. If only they did not live so close to the edge that a few pounds could destroy them.

Richard vaulted into his curricle and sprang the horses. If he did not escape Winter House, he was likely to do something unforgivable—like break a few windows, burn the place to the ground, or choke the life out of Penelope Wingrave. Never had he been so furious.

Insufferable wench! How dare she continue her lies even after he had discovered the truth? Did she think she could seduce him into ignoring facts?

A picture of flashing blue eyes and a heaving bosom blocked his view of the drive. Heat poured over him. His groin tightened. Today's gown had also emphasized every inch of her bosom. His hands could feel the weight of each breast, feel the tips hardening into his palms, feel the . . .

Harlot! How could she incite such lust in a man who never

lost control of his emotions? At least he had not done so in the past. But he had needed all of his strength and backbone to keep from throwing her to the floor and ravishing her on the spot, which would have given her even more power over him. The image of her gloating in victory was what had tipped the scales in favor of restraint.

Cursing, he wrenched his curricle back onto the drive, narrowly missing a tree. What kind of spell was she casting to turn him into a witless, rutting bull? Somehow he must discover a counterspell, for the effect was too potent to ignore. Her sister must have done the same to Terrence. How often had he succumbed to his lust? The pain in his groin increased as his mind conjured up images of Terrence and a younger Miss Wingrave in meadows, in haylofts, on the floor of the Winter House drawing room . . .

He groaned.

Whipping through the Tallgrove gates, he drove directly to the stables. His groom looked at him askance, taking in the grays' heaving sides and foam-flecked mouths. His anger inched up another notch. Never had he abused an animal in his life. Yet if the distance between Winter House and Tallgrove had been any greater, he would have foundered his best team.

Turning away without a word, he strode to the house.

"This arrived just after you left, my lord," said Barton. A small package lay on the butler's silver tray.

"Thank you." He frowned as he entered the library, unfamiliar with the writing that addressed only "Terrence's guardian," but as he scanned the note, fury again choked him.

My lord,
    If you had remained another five minutes, you would
have discovered that the damage you inflicted was worth
but fourteen shillings. Your change in enclosed. I will
never accept charity, especially from so arrogant a man.

                        Sincerely yours,
                        Miss Wingrave

Despicable wench! She must have hoped that this gesture would hide her poverty. The enclosed coins bounced off the wall, scattering in all directions.

She had made a mistake by invoking Diogenes. That archetypical cynic would be sure to recognize her inherent dishonesty. Oh, but he would love to expose her vices to the world!

Chapter Five

❧

"I must regain control."

Richard's whispered words reverberated around the library, seeking out nooks and crannies before bouncing back to batter his ears. He shivered. Shafts of afternoon sunlight slanted through the windows, but he remained hunched over the desk, his head in his hands, ignorant of the warming rays. Had anything gone right since he had received Lady Avery's summons? Bad weather. Poor judgment. More emotional confrontations in two days than in his entire life. Where were his logic, understanding, and good sense hiding? Why had his perceptivity and finesse fled? He had been swept along by events with no chance for reflection or analysis. Yet even Miss Wingrave's provocation did not excuse his own mortifying behavior. And she was not his only problem. The day had gone from bad to worse.

Kesterton had regaled him with complaints. Servants were normally even more conscious of status than their masters, but Terrence's valet had refused to concede his place at the table despite Kesterton's higher rank—not only did he serve a marquess rather than a viscount, but Carrington was Terrence's guardian. Richard soothed his man's ruffled feathers, but not before enduring a diatribe on the Avery household's shortcomings. The housekeeper was inept. One of the maids was carrying on with the head groom. The butler was shirking his responsibilities. Cook ran a slovenly kitchen. Lady Avery exerted no oversight on the staff, having abandoned even the pretense of caring before Millicent's birth.

But the servant problem was not what had sent him into seclusion in the library. Terrence was nowhere to be found. The boy must have slipped off to meet Alice despite orders to avoid her. He could not recall when anyone in his charge had flouted him.

Terrence's absence had triggered another of Lady Avery's hysterical monologues. She had decried the unscrupulous Wingrave girls, imploring him to halt their plots, and bemoaning the death of Lord Avery, who would never have allowed the liaison to begin. Millicent parroted every charge against Terrence even as she goaded her mother for rewriting the past. By the time he had escaped, his head was pounding.

And so he slumped in the library, cursing his uncle for dying when his household was so disordered. Lady Avery was worthless. Her solution to any crisis was hand-wringing, hysterics, and tearful exhortations that somebody do something. She was incapable of conducting even her own business. His trusteeship promised to be as onerous as his guardianship. First he must hire a new housekeeper and cook who could whip the staff into shape. Then he must check on the steward. That overgrown hedgerow stood on Tallgrove property.

But that could wait until tomorrow. Today he must confront Terrence. He had left orders that his ward attend him as soon as he returned. And this time, he meant to control his temper and enforce his will with precise logic and immutable fact.

His thoughts had swung full circle, back to his own inexplicable conduct. Scenes were so foreign to his nature that his recent loss of control frankly terrified him. A gentleman governed himself with propriety at all times, regardless of circumstances. A perfect example had occurred the previous Season. A lord arrived home to find his wife entertaining a lover. He issued a challenge, the lover accepted, and the wife departed for the country, all without any loss of composure. Richard had seconded the duel, which had proceeded smoothly to a satisfactory conclusion. Nothing at Tallgrove embodied even a fraction of the passions that had arisen during his friend's confrontation, yet he had exploded into rage four times in twenty-four hours.

His head shook as he reviewed the incidents. A minor accident that had done little damage; an unexpected betrothal announcement; a dinner table argument; a confrontation with a fortune hunter. Why had any of them prompted him to abandon his training?

Her charges echoed. *Mad . . . a laughingstock . . .* She was the one who was mad. His reputation embraced propriety and sober sense, though he winced at how stuffy that sounded. Surely he did not wish to become a loose-screw! *Insufferable . . . stupid . . .* Never! How could she expect him to ignore society's standards? One could not countenance a mésalliance. Nor could one allow the blood of the merchant classes into the aristocracy. *Coward . . . craven coward . . . I dare you . . .* The taunting voice would not go away. Why should he waste time verifying facts he already knew? Her challenge was nought but manipulation, directing him to men who had already succumbed to her wiles.

Yet that did not excuse abandoning his breeding. Not even unbridled lust could pardon his behavior. Fate had tested him and found him wanting. His position among the highest of the land seemed almost fraudulent. Not that it should. He was no longer a fifteen-year-old boy being asked to mediate disputes between people old enough to be his grandfather. He had felt like an impostor when his family first feted him as a modern Solomon, but that had been understandable. By the time he turned eighteen, all doubts had faded. He truly was the only man capable of handling his family's affairs. More than once he had returned control to incompetent relatives only to face resuming his oversight when they bungled even trivial tasks. He had learned to trust only himself. So why did he suddenly feel like that lad again?

Terrence finally rapped on the door. He drew in a deep breath, releasing it slowly to force relaxation on his tense muscles. This time he would conduct a gentlemanly discussion.

"Enter."

"You wished to speak with me?" Terrence asked, barely controlling a raging temper.

"Yes. Let us forget that yesterday's meeting took place. None of us managed it with aplomb. Serious discussion is difficult when emotions are high, and Lady Avery's hysteria did not help. I hope that today we can acquit ourselves like responsible gentlemen, for we need to clarify the facts."

"I thought I was perfectly clear." Terrence's voice was sullen.

"If you wish to be treated like an adult, you must first act like one," Richard stated coldly. "Tantrums, pouting, and threats are hardly mature behavior. As I was in a temper myself, I will overlook your lapse of decorum, but do not expect me to do so again. Have a seat."

Terrence appeared ready to explode, but he drew in several deep breaths. "Very well." He took one of the leather wing chairs that flanked the fireplace.

Richard poured wine for both of them before settling into the other one. "You have little experience of the world, Terrence," he began, forcing calm into his voice. "One of the lessons you have not yet learned is that poor country lasses constantly look for any opportunity to marry up, even if they can do so only through trickery. Thus they lie and scheme. You cannot trust them for a moment."

"I fail to see your point, my lord."

"It should be obvious to even the meanest intelligence. The Wingrave chits are far beneath your touch. You are too young to see past the sweet face girls are so adept at showing the world."

"You are misinformed." He set his glass on the table with a sharp click. "Alice's father may have lacked a title, but he was the younger son of an earl. Her mother was the daughter of a baronet. I fail to understand how that puts her beneath my touch. Nor would Alice ever indulge in pretense. She is the most honest, sensible girl of my acquaintance, seconded only by her sister."

"Even if such breeding proves true, it matters not," he replied, mentally shaking his head. Terrence was too gullible for his own good. His delusions proved the strength of Miss Wingrave's hold. Lady Avery had lived at Tallgrove for twenty-two years and would certainly know the background of her nearest neighbors. "One cannot trust women," he continued firmly. "Especially those whose finances are suspect and who have little access to society. They will do anything to better themselves. Do not deny my superior knowledge," he added as Terrence raised a hand in protest. "I have encountered many such stratagems in the past and know whereof I speak. Now that you have a title and fortune of your own, you will be in the same situation."

"But you do not know Alice," protested Terrence.

"Nor do you," he countered. "Trust me in this, Terrence, for I long ago earned a reputation for infallible judgment. You have been home for barely a month. How often had you seen her before this summer?"

"Not much," he admitted. "I spent the last several breaks with friends. I saw her occasionally when we were children, but paid little attention."

"As I expected. You know next to nothing of the girl, yet you believe every word she says."

"I have known enough women to detect insincerity," Terrence objected. "Schemers cannot help but overplay their hand. Like Sir Alfred's daughter. She is all fawning adoration and willingness, taking every opportunity to accidentally brush against me, but all she wants is to escape a tyrannical father."

"I know that sort well." He was impressed in spite of himself, for he had spent last Season saving Cousin Reggie from several such chits. In his brief time on the town, the boy had fallen into the clutches of more than one determined miss. Terrence wasn't quite as green as he'd thought. "But not all schemers are so blatant. Miss Wingrave has learned that subtlety works better."

"Why must you insist that all women are schemers?" he demanded hotly.

"Because they are. I have yet to meet a female who does not put her own interests first. Eventually you will learn to translate their words so you can deduce their motives for yourself. Praise for the cut of your coat means they admire the purse that can afford fine tailoring. Compliments on your looks are a request to admire hers. A comment on your efforts in Parliament hides a desire to share your title. Complaints about tradesmen are a wish that you escort her on her next shopping trip. Mention of a jealous husband means you cannot conduct the affair in her home."

Terrence laughed, interrupting the lesson. "What a jaded circle you cultivate, Cousin. Never have I heard such cynicism. You would not recognize honesty if it bit you in the ankle. And you have forgotten that country folk believe in simple truths."

"Only when it is expedient. Examine the facts, Terrence.

Open your mind and think. You know that her family is in financial difficulties."

"Not particularly. They are not wealthy, it is true, but neither are they starving."

"How would you know? I have known many people over the years who were outrunning the constable. None revealed that fact even to close friends, and each one went to great lengths to appear comfortably circumstanced."

"But you have not met Alice," he repeated.

"That is true. Yet I can describe your acquaintance in great detail." The realization that Terrence had not even recognized the poverty that existed at Winter House underscored the boy's naïveté. "You came home for long break, unaware that Alice had grown to womanhood since your last visit. Within a day you met her about the countryside in an unexceptionable way. She smiled sweetly and told you what a fine gentleman you had become. When you protested, she complimented your appearance and some other appropriate attribute—horsemanship, driving, duty to your tenants, and so on. You turned aside from your errand to walk or drive with her. She flirted lightly, but coyly refused to do more than lay her hand upon your arm. She expressed trepidation about the lack of chaperon and begged to return home alone, which you allowed. But her shapely figure stuck in your mind, so when you encountered her again a short time later, you were happy to see her and voiced that delight. Again she played the shy maiden, uncertain about your motives and fearful of your exuberance. But despite her protestations, she spent at least an hour in your sole company. Have I got the story straight?"

"Yes, but you needn't sound so sarcastic. It is true that I ran into her the first day I was back, but since we were both coming home from the village, it was hardly surprising. She cannot have known I would be there, for I had not decided to go until after I left for a ride in quite another direction. I encountered her again the next day along the boundaries of our two estates. Again, it was purely by accident. After that, I looked for her because I enjoy her company. Never has she done the least thing to encourage me. She is only seventeen, completely innocent, and genuinely sweet. Even you must agree when you meet her."

"You have fallen for one of the oldest tricks in the book, Terrence," he declared with a sigh. "It is a trap every titled gentleman must constantly look for. I have avoided it more than once. My first encounter with a serious fortune hunter was ten years ago when I visited an estate in Yorkshire. The neighboring estate belonged to a baron and his four very sweet daughters. The eldest spent a great deal of time out and about the countryside, accidentally encountering me on numerous occasions. She always had a valid reason for being where she was. Most were also commendable, and her behavior was gentle and exceedingly proper. Yet she knew all the subtle wiles for attracting a gentleman's attention that you have not yet had time to learn. She shared my every interest, enthusiastic even over subjects normally eschewed by females. She wore enticing perfume and close-cut gowns that displayed her figure to advantage, then drew attention to her charms with protestations of innocence and constant concern for her reputation. I thought myself in love with her." He squelched the image of Penelope Rissen's voluptuous body, passionate red hair, and sapphire eyes. What a fool he had been. And still was. The similarities between her and Miss Wingrave were what had triggered his current attack of lust. "Fortunately, fate prevented me from making the biggest mistake of my life."

"What happened?" asked Terrence, sounding interested despite himself.

"A last-minute change of plans kept me from going into town one day, so I walked out to inspect the progress of some repair work. As I approached the stream that separated our estates, I heard her talking to one of her sisters on the bridge. But before I could call a greeting, she spoke my name. They say that eavesdroppers never hear good about themselves, and that is true. But I cannot repine. That conversation may have damaged my pride, but it saved me from a lifetime of misery. She despised me, for who could like anyone so dull, cold, and humorless. She prayed she could bring me up to scratch soon because she could not maintain the pretense much longer. Her father had demanded that she attach me. Marriage to a wealthy lord was the only way to keep him out of debtor's prison, so she had agreed. But she was already planning her revenge. She would ruin him the moment her sisters were safely wed, and she expected them to be suitably grateful for her sacrifice. Her only compensation would be a title and the opportunity to live in London, though she doubted whether it would be enough. But with luck, she would provide the necessary heir soon so that she need never endure me again."

"Dear Lord!" gasped Terrence. "What a witch!"

"Precisely."

"But Alice is nothing like that."

"How do you know? The Wingraves are impoverished. One look at the manor tells you that. Even those in desperate financial straits keep at least one room for show, yet their drawing room is the shabbiest I have ever seen. You cannot trust a woman's manner, for girls begin to learn deceit in the cradle and have perfected the art by the time they join the world."

"I refuse to believe that everyone fits the same mold," swore Terrence, clenching his fists. "I know many women who are truthful—as do you, if you would only admit it. Your experience with a scheming jade did more than teach you prudence. It left you so cynical that you cannot recognize goodness when you do see it."

"Think about it," he urged, stifling the image of Bridgeport's wife, Elaine. She seemed to care deeply for her husband. But she had done her share of scheming in her younger days, and he was convinced that she still hid secrets despite Mark's denials. "But whichever of us is right, this is not a good time to consider marriage. You will not even finish school for another year. And you must learn to go on in London society. Only after sowing all your wild oats and acquiring a modicum of town bronze should you consider your future."

"You never sowed any wild oats, from what I've heard."

"I had no choice," he countered. "But that is precisely why you should. Once you take on responsibilities, you can never regain your carefree youth."

"Then why did you support Reggie's betrothal? He is less than a year older than me, hasn't a thought in his head beyond clothes, and wouldn't know what to do if he found himself closeted with the most willing courtesan."

He sighed, wishing Terrence was as malleable as Reggie had been. "It is true that I agreed to approach his father for him— you must realize that the final decision was not mine, for I am not his guardian. The circumstances are nothing alike, however.

Reggie had finished school and had been in town during the Season."

"A month at most," murmured Terrence.

"True. But Reggie is an empty-headed cub who is incapable of sound judgment. Despite her public image, his betrothed is an intelligent, strong-willed girl who will keep him out of trouble."

"But you must know that Reggie falls in and out of love almost weekly. How can you countenance tying him to someone he must rapidly come to resent?"

"You have never met Miss Throckmorton," he reminded his ward, realizing too late that he parroted Terrence's earlier argument. "Reggie's situation is not at all like your own. You are far more intelligent than our mutual cousin, but you lack experience of the world. Turn your intelligence to considering facts. Miss Wingrave's behavior is suspect at best. Her sister's is worse. You have not yet finished school and have no experience with females."

"It is true that I have never been in love before," admitted Terrence. "But I have had plenty of experience with women."

"Very well. I concede that you surpass our cousin in that regard. He looks upon females in almost chivalric ways. But whatever insights your encounters have provided hardly apply to this situation. And one must question Alice's training when her guardian allows her to roam the countryside unescorted."

"Only as far as the village. But where is the harm in that? Millicent does the same. And Alice is not roaming, as you phrase it. She is generally working."

"Another proof that they are indigent. How can you expect a woman who plays at being both steward and guardian to teach anyone how to be a lady?"

"You left out trustee for her brother's inheritance and manager of a pottery," said Terrence impudently.

"Her father must have been mad. No woman is capable of such positions."

"Why don't you reserve judgment until you know her?"

"Enough! You are too young to consider settling down."

"Too young?" Incredulity filled the room. "Too young to manage one small property and one wife? I am nearly one-and-twenty, my lord. You will correct me if I err, but weren't you barely fifteen when you inherited the marquessate, eleven estates, and control of the whole bloody family?"

"Seven titles, eight estates, ten other properties, two plantations in the Indies, and a few thousand dependents," he said wearily. "Plus a guardian who was incapable of managing his own life, let alone mine. How do you think I know how draining responsibility is? You cannot begin to imagine the headaches, Terrence. Finish school and enjoy your freedom like others of your station."

"I have no intention of returning to the university next term," announced the boy firmly. "I have enough classical education to fulfill my birthright as a gentleman. It is time to assume control of Tallgrove Manor. Alice would be of great assistance."

Richard was stunned. "We will consider the question of school at another time. This is no time to think of marriage. You are still in deep mourning."

"For another week only."

"But your mother will not emerge from it for three months, nor will you be free of all restrictions until then. You cannot wish to distress her by flouting convention. Such disrespect will worsen her own grief."

"Fustian! Mother cared not a whit for Father. She merely loves scenes. Her histrionics garner solicitude from people like yourself."

"Show a little respect," he snapped, shocked at the words. But he forced control over his temper. "This discussion is not over, but we would both benefit from a period of contemplation. Perhaps I have been hasty in my judgment. Or perhaps you have been taken in by lies. We shall let the matter rest for the moment. Time will soon disclose which of us is correct. Remember that patience is the mark of a mature gentleman. Do not do anything that will precipitate a crisis, for the one undisputable fact is that I will control your allowance for a long time to come."

Terrence's fists again clenched, but he managed a civil farewell.

Richard poured another glass of brandy and exhaled in an enormous sigh. Misguided youth. Naïve. Immature. Irresponsible. The lad had the bit between his teeth and was trying with all his might to run with it. Could his own superb horsemanship control this most mettlesome beast?

The Wingraves. His thoughts always returned to them. Were they really as well-bred as Terrence claimed? Penelope's voice resounded in his head. *I dare you . . . coward . . . dishonor resides in your family . . .* But his aunt would never make up tales. She must have gotten her facts somewhere.

He sipped his wine, finally deciding that he could believe none of them. Only an independent investigation would provide reliable answers. It was something he normally did before making any decision, but nothing was proceeding normally in this case. Aunt Mathilda and Terrence had pressed him into taking an immediate stand, and he still believed he was right. But his position would be stronger when he could recite chapter and verse of the Wingrave scheming.

He rang for his secretary.

"Cawdry, I want a complete history of the Wingrave household, including breeding back at least four generations, character and reputation of every family member, and an accurate picture of their finances."

"Yes, my lord."

"And be sure to check every rumor about the place, no matter how far-fetched. I want to know the authors of any falsehoods."

Chapter Six

Richard spent the rest of the afternoon going over the estate ledgers. Tallgrove Manor occupied one of Devon's most fertile valleys, yet its income did not reflect its salubrious location. And though most landowners were suffering a decline in profits—the endless war against Napoleon reduced markets and raised prices—the steadily falling revenue from Tallgrove could only reflect poor management. Whether from disinterest or the Avery incompetence, Gareth had exerted little control over his inheritance.

It was all of a piece. Every so often, the Averys produced an anomaly. He was one; his determination and abilities standing in stark contrast to the usual family character. Gareth's grandfather had been another, winning a title for heroism at Culloden, the final battle against the Young Pretender. He had acquired an estate on the verge of dereliction and built it into one of the most prosperous in the area. But his descendants had allowed Tallgrove to slide back into mediocrity.

Not that Gareth had ignored his inheritance. Maintenance records revealed continuing repairs to buildings and fences, a new bull, an expanded orchard, and more. But the steward was planting the same crops in the same fields as he had done every season since his arrival fifteen years earlier. There were no expenditures for equipment or supplies that would indicate Tallgrove embraced agricultural reform. Not only was the steward hidebound, but his methods were old-fashioned even for his own youth.

He stifled a surge of guilt for not coming sooner. He should know by now that attending to matters personally was the only way to assure that things got done right. No one else had his grasp of detail. Bringing Tallgrove up to snuff would be a bigger job than he had expected.

Another restless night and a breakfast of cold eggs and undercooked kidneys left him surly. In no mood for company, he avoided the steward's office, preferring to survey the estate on his own.

Conditions were every bit as bad as he had feared. One corner of the dower house roof leaked. He made a note to tour the building later, then pressed on to the hornbeam grove.

"Idiot!" he muttered.

Wood had been harvested at a rate that new growth could not sustain. Instead of the tenth that would have matured this season, fully half of the trees had been cut back to their pollarded trunks. And three quarters of the oaks that normally shaded the hornbeam had disappeared. All production must immediately cease. It would be five years before regular harvesting could resume. The same was true of the hazel. He frowned. The cutting was very recent, as shown by the lack of regrowth or weathering in the cuts. But the books listed no large sale of timber.

His horse stumbled. The ground was riddled with holes, evidence of an extensive rabbit population. The groundskeeper was another who had grown lazy, or worse, from lax oversight.

A lane led to the first tenant farm. "Good morning, sir," he called to the oldest of the men making repairs on the rotting fence that enclosed the pigsty.

The farmer took in the quality of his mount and the cut of his clothes before tugging his forelock. "My lord."

"You are Mr. Carson?"

"I be, my lord."

Dismounting, he turned Jet over to Carson's son and introduced himself. Carson showed him around the farm, his taciturn voice saying little beyond the necessary. From a nearby rise, he was able to display the bulk of his fields.

"What crop rotation plan do you use?" He frowned at the response. "How about repairs? I notice that the barn roof appears to be leaking."

"True, my lord. We have patched it several times, but the whole needs replacing. Mr. Scott promised to do what he can, but t'will be no money for at least two years. Times be bad, what with the war and all."

"Not *that* bad. What else needs work?" Though he had not yet met the steward, already he loathed him.

"My lads and I can manage here, but t'would be a blessing if you could help poor Briscol. His cottage is in sad repair."

"I will look at it," he promised, impressed by Carson's awareness of others despite having a full complement of his own problems.

Briscol's cottage looked eager to topple in the next breeze. As did his barn. The Briscol farm was the smallest of the tenant holdings. To make matters worse, the farmer had no sons to help him, so he incurred the additional cost of hiring laborers. But he was not one to complain. Times were bad for everyone. He wasn't starving—or so he claimed. His lanky frame seemed almost skeletal.

Four tenant farms later, he was ready to explode. Carson's had been in the best condition due to intelligence, a hard-working family, and the implementation of modern methods despite opposition from Scott. Circling back to the manor's own fields, he snorted in disgust. The corn was thin and sickly, evidence of depleted soil. Orchards were little better.

A raucous screech startled Jet into plunging to one side. Too surprised to react quickly, Richard nearly came unseated. He had hardly brought the horse under control when another screech arched over the six-foot hedgerow that separated this portion of Tallgrove from Winter House land. A mottled gray-brown pole protruded two feet above it, but it looked like no tree he had ever seen. Not until it turned did he realize that it was a thick neck ending in a wickedly powerful beak below enormous dark eyes fringed by ridiculously long, black lashes.

Another shriek assaulted his ears.

"What the devil are you?" His aunt had said something about birds, but he had never seen such a neck.

Trotting along the hedgerow, he headed for the lane where a gate would provide a better view. It took a moment to realize that the head was still next to him, moving at the same speed as his horse. He pushed Jet to a canter. The head remained at his side, only ten feet away. Urging Jet to a full gallop, he watched in shock as the head picked up speed, easily beating him to the corner. Another shriek rent the air, this one clearly triumphant. By the time he turned into the lane, a shorter neck had joined the first. It emitted a low gurgling sound and cocked its head as if puzzled over the newcomer.

"Easy, boy," he soothed Jet, who was growing warier by the moment. Both birds turned at the sound. "You seem inquisitive," he addressed them. "Let us see what sort of beasts you are." He already had a fair idea, having read several traveler's tales. But his mind had trouble accepting the possibility.

"Dear Lord!" Pulling to a halt opposite the gate, he stared. Jet likewise stared before turning a reproachful eye on his rider and sidling nervously.

"Ostriches, by God!" he breathed.

The big male hissed, swelling up to display long white wing and tail feathers. The rest of his body was black. Powerful legs ended in clawed feet. Another hiss from atop the incongruously bare neck completed a picture of defensive antagonism.

"I won't hurt you, fellow," he murmured soothingly.

The beast hissed.

The shorter bird was all brown. After seeing countless feathered hats, he knew that her plumage faded to nearly gray at its soft edges. Half a dozen juveniles crowded around the gate thrusting their heads through the bars to stare in blatant curiosity, their feathers mottled brown and beige with stripes on their fuzzy necks.

"That wretched female is raising ostriches! The woman belongs in Bedlam. What will happen when they escape?"

He shivered, recalling the speed of that big male. A bird that could outrun a horse had to be dangerous. Where had she gotten it anyway? And why? Something must be done before people got hurt—or were scared witless.

But what could one expect? This was precisely the trouble that must inevitably arise from allowing females into positions for which they were not suited. Parliament should expressly forbid any woman from assuming a post as a guardian or trustee. The responsibility was bound to destroy what little sense they had.

Turning aside, he headed for home, pursued by another avian shriek, that note of triumph again clear.

"Lord Carrington's secretary is asking questions about us in town." Michael glared from the drawing room doorway.

"Sit down," ordered Penelope, setting aside the socks she had been darning. "Considering the way Terrence has been dangling after Allie, an investigation is inevitable." Had Carrington accepted her challenge to discover the truth for himself? She doubted it. At best he was looking for new rumors to support his charges.

"Surely he is not serious about her!" exclaimed a shocked Michael. "The cub is only twenty."

"And Allie is barely seventeen, but he wishes to wed her."

"That irresponsible fribble? What happened to her sense?"

"Calf-love," she said dryly.

"I'll—"

"Come back here, Michael," she interrupted as he headed for the door. "Much as you would like to be, you are not her guardian. But I have no intention of giving her to anyone who will not cherish her as she deserves."

"Of course not." He dropped back into his chair. "You turned him down, then?"

"He has not made a formal request, but I told Allie that no decision was possible until he finishes school. The idea should die on its own long before then."

Michael frowned. "But what if it doesn't? Carrington seems to be taking it seriously."

"He has already refused his own permission." She paused to consider how he must have done it. Odious toad! He hadn't the least idea of how to deal with young people and lacked even the rudiments of diplomacy. "Of course his manner undoubtedly set Terrence's back up enough to make him cling to his plans."

"You sound as though you know him."

She snorted. "He paid me a visit yesterday." She described the encounter, leaving out only her own hasty vow to support the match.

"So he believes Lady Avery," he commented when she finished.

"Obviously, which does not say much for his intelligence. But you see why I believe we must accept Allie's infatuation and do no more than postpone a decision. Two powerful opponents might encourage them to do something rash."

"Like eloping? Scotland is too far away."

"But even the attempt would ruin her. And you have forgotten about Guernsey. They require no license and no banns. A boat from Exeter can be there in hours."

"Good God! It is too close to France to be safe."

"Exactly. So we do not want to give them any ideas."

Michael sighed in resignation. "As usual, you have everything under control. I only hope I can be as wise when I am in charge. Should I renew my acquaintance with Terrence? I've not seen him in years. Perhaps I can discover how deeply his attachment runs."

She hesitated. Michael knew nothing of Lord Avery's attempts to acquire Winter House, for he had been away at school most of the time. But he had no need to learn of them now unless she could prove that Terrence was continuing his father's schemes. "That might work very well."

Michael departed, leaving her to her mending and her thoughts.

"You wished to see me, my lord?" asked Scott from the library doorway.

Richard had already decided to give the steward enough rope to hang himself. And he was curious how the man would explain such glaring discrepancies. "After going over the books, I have a number of questions." He motioned the steward to a chair and pulled out the current ledger.

"That is to be expected," murmured Scott. "Understanding the complexities of estate management requires years of study. But there is no need for a gentleman to dirty his hands with the day-to-day operations. That is my job."

"True, but a trustee has a responsibility to oversee the property left in his care. I noticed that the hornbeam was badly overcut," he began mildly. "How did that come about?"

"Lord Avery needed cash." Scott shrugged. "He ordered a second harvest despite my protest. I doubt he grasped the effect it must have on future production."

"Did he explain why the income was necessary?" The tale was ridiculous to anyone familiar with Gareth's investments. Avery had substantial sums in Consols and would surely have sold off a few shares rather than jeopardize his regular income if he found himself in need of money. Besides, the cuttings were less than three months old.

"Something about a debt of honor."

"Ah. So he was a gamester. That would account for his laxity and quick fixes. But why did he not press you to improve production? It is the first step a gamester takes, yet you have not tried any of the methods that Coke has shown to be so effective."

"You are young, my lord, and have little experience with crops and herds. No gentleman can, for the pursuits of your class fill your days."

"You know so much about my class?" he asked in a voice his friends would have recognized as a danger signal.

Scott did not notice. "Enough. Only ignorance can explain such a misstatement. Do not fall victim to Coke's madness," he begged. "While it is true that he has increased yields through his tampering with sound agricultural practice, he will soon face disaster. Even the most fertile soil can support only a fixed amount of growth. By extracting more now, Coke and his deluded followers will face years of failure—just as Tallgrove faces from overcutting its timber. One cannot tamper with the limitations laid down by God. You need look no farther than Miss Wingrave. The ignorant chit took Coke's preachings to heart, doubling her corn yields for several years. But now she is paying the price. Her last two harvests were grossly inferior. Stick with proven methods is my motto. My father and grandfather were stewards of great estates. They learned much about the land, coaxing continuous crops from fields that others declared were unsuitable for cultivation, and maintaining steady production through good years and bad. I have done the same here."

He frowned. Unseasonably cool weather the past two summers had reduced production nationwide. Even Tallgrove yields were down, though they were so low under normal circumstances that the difference did not amount to much. "Yet the corn under your care appears sickly," he observed.

"Not at all. Every soil imparts a unique blend of color, shape, and size to its crops. Tallgrove's corn always looks the same and produces the same. I will get a full harvest."

"I noticed a kiln just past Carson's farm."

"That is more proof of Miss Wingrave's insanity," snorted Scott. "People who leave females in charge of a man's business should be hung. Wingrave was the worst of the lot. He let his daughter run the estate for nearly a decade before he died and then left her in charge until his heir comes of age. The lad won't have an inheritance left by the time she is done. The chit started that idiotic pottery two years ago—to counter the sudden reduction in yields, I suspect. But it only confuses her tenants. How can they keep their minds on their work when she demands they help in the pottery?"

"She has tenants?" He had not expected her holdings to be so extensive. It did not jibe with his aunt's description of her run-down farm.

"Only two. One of the wives helps run the pottery—another sign of her stupidity, for tenants cannot handle such responsibilities. But Miss Wingrave has done worse than that, working in the fields like a man. And those damned birds! Scaring people half to death with their infernal noise, and threatening everyone's peace of mind. I don't know what she hopes to gain by it. Good English sheep would make better use of that pasture. It is no wonder that her estate is on the brink of ruin."

He refused to comment, pursing his lips for some time. Scott was proving to be just the ignorant, old-fashioned fool he had expected. And stupid. While tenants were often reluctant to try new ideas, they were just as capable of understanding them as the more educated classes. And how did the man expect anyone to believe that his depredations had been ordered by his master when no record appeared in the books?

What he had not expected to discover was that Miss Wingrave was following the path that would give her the greatest chance of improving her estate—except for the ostriches.

"There are several entries that puzzle me," he said, pulling the ledger around so both could see it. "Let us start with this one."

"Carson's barn," said Scott with a sigh. "That is a continuing problem. We have to patch it at least once a year."

"I have seen it. Patching seems a waste of money. The entire roof needs replacing."

"Agreed, but the estate cannot afford it."

"Yet the amount you pay each year for repairs is nearly twice what I spent only last month reroofing an even larger barn at Carrington Castle."

Scott flinched. His face remained affable, but wary calculation now filled his eyes. "The difference in station, my lord. Men will do anything to create a connection to a marquess. Undoubtedly your roofer offered you a special rate to get the job. The cachet of doing your work would increase his other business and permit him to raise his fees. Have you never considered how your exalted status affects those around you? Even when you refrain from exercising your power, it exerts its influence. Unfortunately, those of lesser consequence have no such opportunities."

Fustian! He nearly snorted, but caught himself. If anything, tradesmen increased their fees on the grounds that his coffers were full enough to stand the nonsense. He turned a page. "Is the same true for the repairs to Briscol's cottage? According to this, one wall was replaced, yet all walls appeared equally derelict."

"It was the dividing wall between the main room and the bedchamber," said Scott with a shrug. "Perhaps it was not apparent in the poor light. Briscol rarely uses more than one candle, and the cottage is so old there is little other illumination."

"Yes, I noted that it contained but one tiny window." He penciled in a notation and turned to another page. "Where are the rest of the sheep pastured?"

"Rest?" Scott shifted uncomfortably in his seat. "Unless there is an unreported break in the wall, they should all be on Breed's Hill."

"I noted no break, but the hillside holds barely half the total recorded last month." His voice turned hard. "I will not tolerate sloppy bookkeeping, Scott. Whatever my uncle's shortcomings, I am in charge now, and I will expect you to take a great deal more care. Is that understood?"

"Of course, my lord," agreed an ashen Scott.

"Meet me in the stable tomorrow morning. We will survey the estate."

He watched the steward bow himself out. Obsequious fool! Did he really believe that anyone would be taken in by his explanations? Uncle Gareth must have given him *carte blanche* to do as he would. And he had. It would take time to discover all his defalcations, but they would undoubtedly amount to a sizable sum.

By nightfall, he had listed the obvious thefts. He spent the morning riding the estate and listening to more of Scott's slippery lies before arresting him for embezzlement and turning over to the constable. Records in the steward's cottage revealed accounts containing nearly thirty thousand pounds, the deed to a tobacco plantation in Virginia, and plans to emigrate that had been postponed when those impertinent Americans had declared war on England, canceling all shipping.

Sighing, he turned his attention to the future. Conversations with Carson convinced him that the farmer was both knowledgeable and astute. The man's oldest son was capable of taking over the farm, so he offered the steward's job to the father. He ordered basic repairs to buildings and cottages, then installed Briscol as the new groundskeeper. Once the old cottage was replaced, he would bring in new tenants.

But the flurry of activity did nothing to drive thoughts of the Wingrave sisters from his mind. Carson respected Miss Wingrave's abilities and had nothing but praise for her character. Except for the birds, she was managing her brother's inheritance much as he would have done. Yet the way she exploited Terrence's youth reeked of an unscrupulous fortune hunter. Perhaps she was playing a deeper game than he had first thought.

Alice knocked on the bookroom door. "You won't believe what Ozzie was just doing," she announced, face lighting with laughter.

"What now?" demanded Penelope.

"He and Cleo managed to tie their necks into a knot."

"Stupid bird," she muttered.

"They got untangled," Alice hastily assured her.

"That's not what I meant. Twisting their necks together is part of their courtship dance. They strut and pose, displaying their plumes and flirting—much like young people at an assembly. But they seem to have the seasons mixed up again. If Cleo lays eggs now, they will never hatch. Though Ozzie broods the clutch at night, she only shades them—for a good six weeks. It will be far too cold by then."

"I suppose confusion is inevitable. Uncle Oscar told us how different Africa is. Will he ever return to see us?"

"I doubt it. He must be approaching sixty, and his last letter confirmed that he is suffering badly from gout."

Alice sighed. "He is only fifty-five, but twenty years abroad aged him. Do you remember his last visit?"

"How could I not? He gave you two ostrich chicks, and now look where we are." She tried to sound disgruntled, but a chuckle broke out. "A more unexpected souvenir of his travels I cannot imagine."

"And his coachman!" Alice collapsed in giggles.

"The look on the man's face when he opened the carriage door to find the upholstery in ribbons was priceless," she agreed.

"What did he expect after carting six birds around all day?" She shook her head. "For a man who spent two years hunting ostriches, Uncle Oscar is remarkably softhearted. Imagine rescuing a clutch of fifteen newly hatched chicks because he killed their parents—especially since he was scheduled to sail back to England the next morning!"

She laughed. "He spun that story for your benefit, Allie, but it is not strictly true. He collected eggs as well as feathers on his hunts, but the local market was glutted at the time. So he brought them home, hoping to sell them in England. They were two days at sea before he discovered his problem."

"Good heavens! No wonder they accept people so readily. They must think Oscar is their mother." She laughed.

"Poor chicks. And he knew nothing about caring for them. Only six survived the voyage."

"Do you think he intended them for me?"

"Oscar has always had a soft spot for you, and your mother before you, but he brought other gifts for us, you might recall. If he had not wanted to try raising the creatures himself, he would have killed them on board. I suspect he left Ozzie and Cleo here out of desperation. They were already two feet tall with voracious appetites and the speed of a racehorse. I don't think he could face three more days cooped up with them. The other four were more docile—or perhaps they were already sickening. None lived a month after he got home."

Alice sighed. "Why have I never seen Ozzie's courtship dance?"

"He only does it before mating." She shook her head. "If he

and Cleo are setting another clutch, Michael had better renew the sand on the knoll. I hope Ozzie will let me take some of the eggs again. Mrs. Phillips was ecstatic about the shells last time."

"She certainly created some unusual artwork with them. Lady Alderleigh still gets raves over hers. I never thought to see Alder Court painted on an ostrich egg."

"Nor I. Mrs. Phillips has already shown me some new ideas. The shell is so thick, she plans to carve into it and make inlaid designs. She already has orders for three and interest from several other people. We can probably charge double for the eggs."

"Will the younger ostriches ever start producing?"

"Eventually. Remember, Cleo didn't lay her first clutch until age five. The lone survivor was Fluff, but she is only three. I wonder what Ozzie will do as the younger males mature," she added to herself.

But Alice heard. "Will there be trouble?"

"I've no idea, but you know we can't keep multiple bulls or rams together. Males of any species can be jealous, territorial, and ridiculously combative." Flashing gray eyes returned to mind.

"You mean we might have to kill them?" Alice blanched.

"I hope not. White feathers bring in more than brown. But enough of speculation. If Ozzie is courting, we will have to postpone the feather harvest."

Alice nodded and left her to her thoughts.

Chapter Seven

～

"And what are you supposed to be?" murmured Richard, frowning at a badly overgrown topiary beast. "A squirrel perhaps? Or is that curl an elephant's trunk?" He studied the shrub intently, but even such deliberate silliness could not rid his mind of flashing blue eyes.

"Damnation!" He could not get the irritating wench out of his head. Pictures distracted him at the oddest moments, images of her many guises—voluptuous, disdainful, seductive, furious. His body yearned for more contact, oblivious to the mind that knew her faults. She was rapidly becoming more than an annoyance—but only because she looked so much like that other Penelope, he reminded himself sharply. If she had resembled Lady Jersey or Princess Esterhazy or even Lady Bridgeport, he would not be in this fix. Damn Penelope Rissen for leaving him susceptible to blue-eyed redheads!

He had left Yorkshire within an hour of learning her true feelings. It had taken three months on another remote estate to wall off the pain, but he had returned to London a wiser man. Women soon learned that their wiles were useless. He could detect the selfish motives beneath even the most subtle schemes, and he made no pretense about despising both the plots and the plotters.

For ten years he had protected himself from harm. But Miss Wingrave had breached the wall around his core, allowing pain and fury to escape—and an unbridled lust more potent than anything he had ever encountered. And so he must fight and win the battle again if he ever hoped to resume his peaceful existence.

The first step was to engross his mind in something else—

like Terrence. They had just spent another hour together, but he was no nearer making the cub see reason than he had been that first day.

Terrence had all the instincts of a gentleman, wanting to take charge of Tallgrove Manor, improve its productivity, arrange a good match for Millicent, and secure his own succession—all admirable goals. But he had no inkling of how to accomplish any of them.

Only a few questions confirmed that he knew absolutely nothing about estate management, agriculture, or the economic realities of a country that had been at war since the lad was born. Nor did he seem receptive to learning, deflecting suggestions with statements like, "That's the steward's job." But before Richard could point out that stewards needed knowledgeable supervision, Terrence had turned the topic to Millicent's come-out."

"She will make her bows next spring," he stated as if it had already been decided.

"Hardly. Your mother will still be in mourning."

"Alice can chaperon her, and I'm sure Penny will help. She knows everything."

Where should he even start objecting to that statement? Every word was absurd. The subsequent argument had resolved nothing. Terrence obstinately clung to his fantasies, refusing to admit that he had no idea how to launch his sister and knew little of town manners. And he still insisted that Alice was the ideal mother for his children.

He shook his head as the path entered a patch of woods. Eventually it would emerge near a folly overlooking the lake. As with the rest of the grounds, the woods were in dire need of attention. Rustling sounds marked the passage of a small animal through the overgrown shrubbery. Damaged tree limbs endangered passersby.

How could he separate Terrence and Alice? It must be done, of course. Even if she were not as bad as her sister, he could never give Penelope a connection to his family. In retrospect, he had badly mishandled his ward. If he had not been so tired— and so furious—when Terrence announced that he had offered for the girl, he would not have put the lad's back up. He should have known that a newly elevated peer of such tender years would not respond to orders. A title rarely failed to go to a young man's head. He would have done better to welcome a courtship and use the contact to manipulate Alice into revealing her true purpose so that Terrence would abandon the relationship and be thankful to escape her clutches. But he had not. And both he and his ward had now taken stands that would be difficult to repudiate. The fact that Terrence was a tenacious greenling meant that the battle would last longer than necessary.

But the game was not yet lost. Instead of another head-on confrontation, he would try a flanking maneuver. Terrence would never renounce what he considered a betrothal—what gentleman could? Penelope would never abandon her determination to attach the Avery title and wealth. But Alice might be the weak link. She must be biddable to have agreed to her guardian's scheme. Her heart could not be involved, so she might balk at a future of unrelieved agony and call off the supposed betrothal. Even if she had initiated the scheme herself, she was young enough to crack under pressure.

He was turning over ways and means when voices sounded up ahead.

"I must go, my love," murmured a man. "I am already late, but I could not pass a day without seeing you. My heart would surely fail me if I tried."

He frowned. Who was using the folly for an assignation? Not Terrence, for this man sounded nothing like his ward. The accent was wrong for a servant. But perhaps someone was meeting one of the maids. Mrs. Gudge exerted little control over the girls. A strong sense of danger raised his hackles, though the voice was unfamiliar. Should he intrude? The girl's response dispelled all doubts. Fury sent him striding toward the folly.

"Good luck, dearest," Millicent murmured breathlessly. "I will count the hours until we meet again." Fabric rustled, followed by rapidly retreating footsteps.

He rounded the last corner to find a blushing Millicent drifting down the steps. No one else was in sight.

Steady, he reminded himself. *No more mistakes. Mishandling one ward is bad enough. You'll never live down two.* "Enjoying the view?" he asked.

She paled, glancing fearfully toward the path that skirted the lake, but it was so overgrown that her paramour was out of sight. "Yes, this is a most enchanting location."

She was not yet adept at prevarication, he noted in relief. Her face disclosed every thought. He could only pray that her liaison had not moved beyond indiscretion. Perhaps that was why he had sensed trouble in her companion's voice but not in hers.

His own face revealed nothing. "Walk back to the house with me," he suggested. "We need to discuss your future. You have just reached your sixteenth year, have you not?"

"Seven months ago," she replied in exasperation.

"So you will stage your come-out the Season after next."

"I will be out long before then," she countered.

"Hardly. You will have no chaperon next Season, for your mother will still be in mourning."

"That is the most idiotic custom!" she snapped. "Why must we squander our lives weeping over a man who cared not a whit for any of us? It is positively barbaric—punishing the living whose lives are better off without the dead."

"If you wish to be accepted by the society into which you were born, you must learn to control yourself," he said coldly. "Such sentiments will not be well received. No man wants a wife who promises to embarrass him at every turn. Surely your governess taught you better manners."

"She was such a hen-wit, she hardly knew up from down," said Millicent scathingly. "Even Mother derided her. It was a relief when she eloped with Sir Francis's bailiff."

"And no one replaced her?" He put amazement into the words, though he felt only disgust. Both his uncle and his aunt had inherited a full measure of the Avery shortcomings. Gareth should have called him in years ago instead of bequeathing him the mess in his will.

"I am too old for a governess," she snorted.

"Not if you wish to join the polite world. Even the gentry expect proper behavior. And don't think a gentleman will fall so madly in love with you that he will overlook glaring deficiencies in your training. Gentlemen tease and flatter while flirting, but they are hard-nosed pragmatists when it comes to choosing a wife."

She frowned, and he could sense her sudden uncertainty. "You have made your point, my lord. When I reach London, I will be careful. But surely a wealthy beauty can afford a few mistakes."

"Do you know how large your dowry is?"

"Papa's will specified two thousand pounds. That is a fortune."

"Compared to what your tenants must exist on. But to qualify as an heiress, it would have to be ten. And excusing gauche behavior would require twenty. But even the most fabulous fortune would attract only impoverished wastrels unless your manners matched your breeding."

Millicent gasped as his words sank in. He walked in silence, allowing her to digest the harsh reality of the world in which they lived. Rank and privilege guaranteed a congenial life only to those who followed the rules. Ostracism awaited any who refused. There were plenty of eccentrics, of course—England prided herself on them—but eccentricity was accepted only in the old or in those who cared nothing for society.

They reached the house and settled into the library. Despite her bravado, Millicent appeared ill at ease.

"Are you telling me that we are not wealthy?" she asked at last.

"You are comfortably well off. You will not need to pinch pennies, but neither can you waste them. What made you believe otherwise?"

"Mother always described Father as a wealthy lord."

"Is her judgment sound?"

"Heavens, no!" she exclaimed, then flushed. "I have been a fool, I see. Knowing that she is deplorably ignorant, incapable of grasping numbers, and prone to flights of fancy, how could I have accepted her word for our financial standing? Especially since Papa complained so often of prices." She shook her head and fell into contemplation.

He said nothing. Both of his wards had now disparaged their mother. His heart sank to his toes.

"Who was the gentleman by the lake?" he asked abruptly.

"What gentleman?"

"Do not deny it, for I heard you speaking to him. He left via the lake path. Who was he?"

She bit her lip before answering. "Mr. Darksmith. He is staying at the King's Arms in the village."

"How long has he been here?"

"A fortnight."

"And how did you meet this gentleman?" He put enough dubiousness into the last word that she bristled.

"Of course he is a gentleman! How dare you impugn someone you do not even know?"

"Regardless of breeding, a gentleman does not speak to a lady of quality unless he has been properly introduced. A gentleman does not make assignations with innocents," he stated coldly. "Nor does he hide his presence from their families."

"Fustian! How can he call when we are still in deep mourning?"

"How could you have met him since you are still in deep mourning?" he countered. "Who introduced you?"

"We met quite accidentally shortly after he arrived. I was returning home from the village, and he was enjoying a short walk."

"Where was your maid?"

"I never take a maid to the village," she scoffed.

"If you wish to maintain your reputation, you will never leave the grounds unaccompanied," he reminded her. "You are too old to get away with hoydenish tricks. Are you trying to blacken your name before you even make your bows to society?"

"Of course not—"

"Then never appear in public without a chaperon," he interrupted firmly. "And never strike up a conversation with a strange man!"

"It wasn't like that!" she swore, tears gleaming in her eyes. "He said, 'Good day,' and I nodded. Then he asked if the lane I had just passed led to Squire Jacobson's residence. It did not, so I gave him directions. He thanked me quite prettily and introduced himself, so I was obliged to do the same. Then we parted. It was an unexceptionable meeting, I assure you. Since then, I have occasionally seen him about the countryside, for he is researching his mother's family—some point concerning an inheritance."

"Then what was he doing in the folly?"

Her eyes shifted. "He was cutting across the estate to return to the village and happened upon me."

"Do not take me for a flat. You will ruin yourself by keeping assignations," he said. "How old is he?"

"Seven-and-twenty as of last week," she replied promptly, her precision revealing more than she would have wished of her relationship.

"Old enough to know better. Where is his home?"

"Yorkshire."

"Does he have an estate there?"

"I believe so," but uncertainty put a tremor in her voice.

"You mentioned that his mother had connections here. To whom?"

"Mortimer did not say. After all, business is not a subject gentlemen discuss with ladies," she parroted smugly.

"Don't be pert, Millicent," he admonished. "What do you talk about if not business?"

She blushed, confirming his worst fears. "My father's death, the weather, the beauties of the day." Her color deepened.

His thoughts churned furiously. Mortimer Darksmith sounded like a practiced seducer bent on securing an heiress. Millicent had probably claimed great wealth—not to make herself interesting, but because a man of his ilk would be certain to ask. And she would have believed every word he said up to and including those false protestations of undying love. She was even more naïve than Terrence. But it would be a mistake to condemn Darksmith out of hand. The last thing he needed was to precipitate an elopement.

"This friendship is not at all the thing," he said gently. "At the very least, Mr. Darksmith's actions call his breeding into question, for no true gentleman would countenance secrecy— and do not again claim the exigencies of mourning, Millicent. Your own deepest mourning will be over in two days. If he truly wished to cultivate the acquaintance, he could have waited and called upon you in the usual manner."

"You understand nothing!" she interrupted him, storming to her feet. "You are the coldest, most supercilious man I have ever met. Have you any idea what I have suffered in recent months? How can you expect me to sit idly by twiddling my thumbs and staring at the walls? There is nothing as boring as this house, what with Mother carrying on in endless scenes and Terry off on his own business. Why don't you chastise *him* for ignoring mourning? Why don't you call *him* on the carpet for arranging assignations? Or is it acceptable for men to gallivant about the countryside while I must wither away without a reasonable soul to talk to?"

"Sit down and behave like the lady you pretend to be," he ordered. "I suspect you have a fair amount of intelligence, so perhaps you would care to use it. I don't make society's rules, Millicent. I merely enforce them. Your brother's behavior or lack of it is not your concern. We are discussing your own at the moment."

She dropped back into the chair but kept her lips compressed in a tight line.

"Thank you." He deliberately relaxed, leaning back in the desk chair while one hand toyed with a letter opener. "If you had refrained from this childish outburst, you would know that I do not wish to condemn Mr. Darksmith out of hand. He may be a perfectly acceptable gentleman who succumbed to temptation. Or he may be a scheming rogue or an unscrupulous fortune hunter. I cannot say until I know him. Nor can you, for his behavior would be identical in any case, and you cannot claim sufficient experience to distinguish his motives. That is one of the benefits you derive from following the rules. Chaperons and proper introductions help weed out fortune hunters and seducers."

"Mortimer is neither!"

"In that case you will not mind introducing me. Send him an invitation to call the day after tomorrow. Your mother cannot receive him, of course, but I will stand in her place."

Her face lit with excitement. "Oh, thank you, thank you! You will adore him, I know. He is a most handsome man. And so personable."

"I am sure he is. In the meantime you must conduct yourself in a more acceptable manner. Even a minor *faux pas* can tarnish your reputation. If the polite world discovers these assignations, you will be cut. Word that kisses passed between you will be grounds for ostracism."

"That is absurd!" She was so caught up in horror that she forgot to protest the mention of kisses.

"It is the way of the world," he continued ruthlessly. "If you wish to remain in it, you have no choice but to conform. We will see what sort of gentleman Mr. Darksmith is. Though his actions to date make his intentions suspect, I will accord him the benefit of the doubt. But do not press my good nature, Millicent. If you continue behavior that you now know is unacceptable, then I must conclude that neither of you is well-bred."

Millicent had tears in her eyes as she left the library. He pondered her tale, fingers drumming absently on the desktop. The girl had no friends with whom she could talk openly—the same problem he had suffered in his own youth. Even Mark, whom he had met at school, was not the sort to share confidences. And duty created barriers between him and his schoolmates. By the time they had started experimenting with sensual delights, he had been too engrossed in the marquessate to join them. Ignorance had left him susceptible to Penelope Rissen's scheming. Millicent would be equally vulnerable.

Lady Avery was too concerned with her own megrims to bother controlling her daughter. The liaison with Darksmith might be nothing beyond a need for admiration and attention. After all, she was bored, naïve, trusting, and unsupervised— ripe for getting into mischief. Or Darksmith might have tapped a more troubling tendency toward loose behavior. The girl was an untrained hoyden who would instantly draw the wrath of the *ton* upon her head if she appeared in London. It was a deficiency he must address.

He summoned his secretary, ordering him to look into Darksmith's background, financial position, and reason for visiting Devon. Then he went in search of his aunt.

Lady Avery presented a portrait of Frail Tragedy. She reclined in the drawing room, desultorily waving a vinaigrette beneath her nose as she dabbed at her eyes with a scrap of black-edged cambric, her widow's weeds stark against the crimson upholstery. She sniffed loudly.

"What has overset you now?" he asked, suppressing an unsympathetic surge of annoyance.

"Terrence, of course. He is hard-hearted, undutiful, and refuses to consider my sensibilities, insisting that he will wed that ill-bred hoyden. Why have you not shown him the error of his ways?"

"I am working on it," he replied with a grimace. "But other problems also need our attention."

"Not now," she begged, waving the salts faster. "I cannot think when I am distressed."

"Pull yourself together, madam," he ordered sharply. "I have no tolerance for megrims and no patience with incompetence. Your tricks do not affect me, so put them aside."

"Cruel!" her fading voice charged.

"But true. Your household is in deplorable condition. How can a lady of your breeding accept such a state?"

"How dare you blame me, my lord?" Shock energized her enough that she actually sat up. "I try to order the staff, but they ignore everything I say. Why only yesterday Mrs. Gudge refused to change the dinner menu as I requested!"

"And you accepted such impertinence? You should have turned her off without a reference."

"Cruel and cold! Gareth would be appalled to learn your true nature."

"I leave to differ, but it is of no matter. Since you refuse to run the household and appear incapable of performing even the least of your duties, I must assume the job myself. Barton has the makings of an adequate butler, but without supervision, he has grown lazy. I will give him the chance to improve his performance. Mrs. Gudge is venal as well as lazy. The household accounts disclose pilfering to even the most casual perusal. The reported breakage is many times the usual amount, and the wax candles used each month would light every room as bright as daylight around the clock. I have located an excellent housekeeper who can start immediately. She will answer to me."

"How dare you bypass my authority?" she demanded weakly.

"You exercise no authority. By your own admission you cannot do sums, command no respect, and do not wish to be bothered by household problems. I will not allow the manor to deteriorate under my charge. Having abdicated your responsibilities, you have no say in the matter."

"My palpitations!" she sobbed, clutching her chest.

He grimaced. "Enough! I warned you that such stratagems won't work with me. I am not Aunt Olivia, who goes into panic every time someone sneezes—you had her waiting on you hand and foot the last time you visited the castle. Nor am I Uncle Edward, who so fears scenes that he will give in at the slightest hint of opposition. That is how you wound up with his late wife's Sèvres china, isn't it? But you cannot manipulate me." He rose to pace the floor. "We must do something about Millicent. The girl lacks all training."

"Her governess was deplorable."

"Then why did you employ the woman for eight years?"

"Gareth hired her, but he refused to discuss the servants."

"That is no excuse. If you ever hope to find her a husband, she must learn decorum. I will enroll her in school. There is an excellent institution in Surrey that specializes in girls with deficient upbringings. If she applies herself, she will be ready to make her bows when she turns eighteen."

"Surrey! That is so far away!"

"The distance matters not. She would return home only for breaks regardless of the school's location. Consider how much she has to learn. Her deportment is deplorable, her understanding questionable, and her accomplishments on par with the average eight-year-old. She wanders the countryside unaccompanied and sees nothing wrong with such behavior. She knows little of the world and is incapable of running a household. All of that must change. I will not bring her out to have her embarrass the family with her antics. You did her no favors by allowing her to forego proper instruction."

"Do what you will," she said with a sigh, reclining with one arm draped over her eyes. "I am sure I cannot make so many decisions."

Shaking his head, he left his aunt to her megrims.

Chapter Eight

Penelope frowned, deaf to the boundary stream gurgling nearby as she pondered the latest setback. Barring bad weather, the haying would be done in two days, so they could start the timber harvest on Monday—not that it would improve their finances. Consecutive cool years had stunted the hornbeam. But overcutting would make next year even worse. Her only hope was that the more affluent landowners would curtail their own harvests to allow their trees to reach full size, creating a scarcity that might drive prices up.

In the meantime she must tackle the tangle of underbrush that had grown since last year's harvest. Her father had sold the oaks whose shade should have kept down the shrubs—his last attempt to avoid mortgaging the estate. But the trees had never been replaced, leaving her without the security such costly hardwood could have provided and forcing a constant battle against brush.

Enough! There was no point in ruing what could not be changed. The facts were clear. A reduced timber harvest left her short even more than the hundred pounds Michael had lost. Covering the deficit would wipe out her last insurance against foreclosure.

A shod hoof struck stone, drawing her eyes across the stream. Lord Carrington emerged from Tallgrove's apple orchard and glared.

"Good morning." The words sounded more like a challenge than a greeting.

"My lord." She nodded formally, noting that his black horse matched his hair and provided the perfect foil for his green coat, buff breeches, and polished top boots. The effect was deliberate, of course. London gentlemen chose everything for appearance. When a ripple of thigh muscles effortlessly curbed his horse's nervous sidling, she forced her eyes back to his harsh face.

"Calculating your harvest?" he asked cynically.

"As a matter of fact, I was. We will be cutting next week."

Another ripple urged his horse forward. Hooves splashed in and out of the water, scattering sparkling droplets. "Those trees don't look ready."

She bristled. "Those of us living near the River Tick must cut our tithe or starve. Only the wealthy can skip a year in deference to the weather." She immediately regretted her bitter tone, but it was too late to recall the words.

"I am not surprised that the job overwhelms you. Estate management is too complex for females. A proper steward could make this place pay." His face conveyed disdain while his eyes teemed with antagonism, anger, and determination—clearly declaring war.

Refusing to surrender, she assumed her most supercilious expression. "Like the steward who has run Tallgrove into the ground?"

He had the grace to blush. "Scott had his deficiencies," he admitted in unbelievable understatement.

"Among which were greed and dishonesty. How dare you question my management when your own is so lax that he was able to strip an estate supposedly under your control?"

"How was I to know the man was a thief?" he countered sharply. "I have many responsibilities more pressing than Tallgrove."

"For three months?" Her incredulity scored a hit. Guilt flashed across his face, which he quickly suppressed. "Even if responsibilities kept you elsewhere, a competent trustee would have sent an underling to check the books and judge the steward."

"Perhaps," he grudgingly conceded. "But the problem is resolved. Scott is awaiting trial, and we recovered all his booty."

"Hardly."

"What is that supposed to mean?" He dismounted, those revealing eyes now blazing with irritation, though curiosity ran a close second.

Her own emotions were less calm than she would have liked. His compelling masculinity was doing strange things to her stomach. She shivered. But her hatred for dishonesty burned stronger than her distrust of Lord Carrington. She owed him any information that might help prosecute Scott.

"He was so anxious to wrest every possible guinea from Tallgrove that he threw caution to the winds, selling many crops for prices far below market value—the cherry and hay, for example."

"What?"

"Did you not know about those?" she asked sweetly. "Surely you did not believe that the missing cherry trees had died! How did he account for losing thirty-five prime trees when no other landowner lost more than one or two? He sold them to a cabinetmaker in Exeter for half their value. He did the same with all of the hay Tallgrove cut six weeks ago and doubtless had similar plans for next week's cutting."

"How do you know?"

She knew of the hay because she had considered buying some of it, but in the end she had decided that the hedge against a long winter was not worth the cost. Michael's news the following week made her thankful for that decision. But she was not about to discuss her own business with this arrogant lord.

"Unlike you, my lord, I make it my business to learn everything that might affect my brother's estate. Any competent trustee would do the same." She fought to keep her face passive as he loomed over her, his eyes clearly furious. The fact that he stood uphill enhanced his menace, for it made him a full head taller. His heat burned through her thin gown to scorch her skin. He was deliberately intimidating her, she reminded herself, ignoring the sparks that sizzled along her nerves as a breeze enveloped her in the scent of horse, sandalwood, and male.

Richard glared at Miss Wingrave. She was not wearing a cap today. Sunlight turned her hair to flames, the sight burning through his mind to brand his soul. Had she deliberately left it off to lure him into another indiscretion? But fairness acquitted her of that ploy. She could not have known that he would ride this way. He had not known it himself.

Wrenching his thoughts from her bare head, he concentrated

on her words. How dare she imply that Scott's defalcations were his fault? Somehow she had turned the tables, twisting his words to make him appear incompetent. How dare she! He had been supervising estates since he was fifteen. No Marquess of Carrington in history had done it better. No Avery had even a tenth of his ability to recognize and solve problems. In fact, every man, woman, and child in the family turned to him for leadership and advice. *She* was the one who should never have been left in charge of an estate. *She* was the one whose every action mocked a woman's rightful place in society. *She* was the one who was plotting to trick his ward into marriage.

Her eyes sparkled with contemptuous challenge. He lowered his gaze to her neck—resisting the urge to wring it—then forced his eyes away when they noted its slim elegance. Immediately they collided with her bosom, which was again straining against a tight gown. Did the woman own no decent clothes? His loins stirred.

Enough! Her words hinted that she knew more about Scott's thefts than he did. Much as he despised the idea, he had to ask for details. His responsibilities to Tallgrove demanded that he uncover all pertinent information, no matter how infuriating he found the source.

"Scott comes up for trial next week. I do not want to miss any charges. Will you tell me what you know about his activities?"

"Certainly, but only because Alice's comfort will be in your hands until Terrence turns five-and-twenty." She flashed the most insincere smile he had ever seen.

Chasing a lizard from a rock, she sat down just far enough away that he must again absorb the full effect of her being— voluptuous body, blazing eyes, red curls tickling the side of her alabaster neck. . . . He paced the bank so he needn't look at her, scooping up a pair of pebbles that he rolled gratingly in his palm. A breeze rustled the trees, subsiding when she began to speak.

"In the past three months, Scott has overcut all timber, sold half the sheep and a third of the cattle, and rescinded an order for seed that should have been planted in those two fields across the lake from the manor. I also suspect he removed items from the dower house. You might wish to consult the latest inventory."

"Is that all?" he asked sarcastically.

"I already mentioned the cherry and hay. His other crimes predate your involvement by years."

"You knew of embezzlements but did not tell my uncle?" He stared at the sunlight winking on those fiery curls, forcing his feet to resume pacing when a wave of lust caught him. If he did not control this obsession with her body, he would reveal his foolishness, destroying his reputation as an impartial resolver of crises and his image as a man of good sense.

"Lord Avery cared nothing for his estate, my lord. And he had an unpredictable temper, especially toward anyone who brought unwelcome news. Half the county knew of Scott's predations, but few dared mention them. The last man who hinted that Tallgrove was ill-run mysteriously fell down a flight of stairs, breaking an arm."

Typical Avery, he fumed in silence. Why was he cursed with such an ill-bred family? And how galling to hear such truths from the lips of an unfeminine harridan. His groin protested the description, but he ignored it. "Do you know specific charges, or is this nought but innuendo?"

"I do not know all the ways he cheated, my lord, for I have never examined the books or questioned the tenants. But for years he has turned a blind eye to three poachers who frequent the woods and park around Tallgrove. More than once I have seen him drinking with them in the village. I suspect they split the profits from selling game in Exeter. Tallgrove's deer are long since gone. As are pheasant, partridge, and doves. Then there are repairs. My own tenants often mention the poor conditions endured by Tallgrove's dependents, despite Scott's boasting of his meticulous upkeep. And I doubt the family knows that he doubled the rents two years ago, though nothing warranted such an increase."

"My God!" He did not question her charges for an instant, though he was furious that she knew the details. It spoke of a long-standing plot to entrap Terrence. She must be planning to take charge of Tallgrove. And why would she not? His ward knew nothing and would welcome her involvement. She could have doubled or tripled his income while still diverting significant sums to herself. "I will thank you to keep your nose out of my business in future," he growled.

"I should have known better than to expect thanks for answering questions about how your employee was bilking you," she murmured. "You are another who would prefer to kill the messenger so you can ignore the message."

"Manipulative baggage. I wonder if I can believe anything you say?" he muttered. "After all, females are incapable of understanding, accepting the most lurid gossip as gospel. Your father must have been out of his mind to leave you in charge of two children."

"On what do you base your prejudices, my lord? Stupidity? Or the arrogance that decries that I can handle a task at which you have already failed?"

"Jade!" He whirled to glare at her, rolling the pebbles faster. "I have never failed to perform a duty in my life."

"Then you have remarkably odd ideas of what constitutes duty. Under your guidance, your wards are running wild and your steward robbed you blind."

"Be fair," he growled. "Scott's thefts predated my arrival. I uncovered them and arrested him."

"Ah." She smiled with even more insincerity. "I understand now. You always carry out your duties. But they only become duties when you feel like addressing them."

"Confound it, woman!" She had done it again. Twisted his words to put him in the wrong. "Keep your greedy sister away from my ward. And if you care a fig for your brother, find a steward who can make this place productive again."

She rose to glare at him, her heaving bosom scrambling his wits until he could hardly recall what they discussed. "Why don't you follow your own advice and keep your nose out of my business? This entire exchange is absurd, for your mind is closed."

"Words may lie, but deeds tell a truer story. And your deeds proclaim your incompetence. Anyone stupid enough to waste land on ostriches that could be better used for sheep cannot be trusted to run an estate," he sneered.

"Never have I met anyone so anxious to trumpet his ignorance to the world," she declared with scathing disdain. "What did I invest in my ostrich flock? How much income do they produce? What would it cost to convert that land to sheep? Which flock would return the most, both in absolute pounds and percentage return on investment?"

"I can't—"

"Of course, you can't say! You have never even considered the questions, let alone the answers! Yet you dare to stand there and tell me how to run my business. Foolish, foolish man. But even if you knew what you were talking about, you have no control over me or mine. Face it, my lord. Even a wealthy marquess cannot force others into the mold he considers proper."

"I don't make the rules," he snapped. "You cannot move into the world you covet without conforming to its expectations."

"You are insane! Why would I wish to consort with hypocritical fribbles like you and your friends?"

"Drop the pretense, Miss Wingrave," he ordered. "We both know your game. But you are deluding yourself if you expect to win."

She laughed, sending his temper even higher. "Delusions are your vice, my lord, not mine. Do you think you are God that everyone must bow and scrape and do your bidding? The great Marquess of Carrington! Bah! I refuse to bandy words with a close-minded fool who mistakenly believes he knows everything."

"I will not allow you to sidestep the truth again," he swore, the pebbles clicking as his hand repeatedly clenched. "You forget that I have already learned your true nature from my aunt."

"And you believed her? That alone proves your incompetence. Your judgment has dry rot, my lord. Why else would you believe the ravings of a vindictive, prejudiced harridan?" She stalked away, leaving him by the stream.

"Don't you dare leave in the middle of a discussion," he growled.

"Discussion?" She glanced over her shoulder, showering him with scorn. "You rant and rave without listening to a word I say. That is a tantrum!"

"Jade!"

The pebbles sprayed dust on her hem before bouncing into a tree. He jerked her around to face him, throwing her off balance and slamming her into his chest. But his apology froze on his tongue. Soft skin burned into his hands. Long legs pressed against his thighs. Hard nipples stabbed through his jacket. Groaning, he lowered his lips in a kiss of raw need. She tried to protest, but only gave his pillaging tongue across to her mouth.

More than access. Mastery. He ravaged its moist recesses, exploring, teasing, and finally thrusting brazenly into its depths. He lost contact with time and place, washed away by waves of heat and desire the likes of which he had never before experienced. Was this what had driven Mark to raking? This overwhelming urge to plunder and possess? To challenge and conquer? To force submission while eliciting an equally powerful response? Never had he felt such exquisite agony. He shifted his arms.

She freed a hand and slapped him. Shock loosened his grip, allowing her to slam one knee into his throbbing groin. "Lecher! Cad! And you dare to call yourself a gentleman!" Both fists rammed into his shoulder. Already doubled over and off balance, he sprawled to the ground. Stars flashed before his eyes. "Is the truth so painful that you must deflect it by ravishing innocents? How can you live with yourself?" Tears streaming down her face, she fled.

Dear God! What had he done? He pulled himself to his feet and leaned against a tree, fighting nausea. Defeated by a lowly female. Jackson would bar him from his saloon forever. Every Corinthian in London would pillory him. He grimaced as new pains exploded through his abdomen. If word of this leaked out, he would become the laughingstock of the century, never able to live down the ignominy.

He staggered to his horse. Riding was going to prove difficult, but walking would be worse, for his knees would hardly hold him up. How could he have lost control so badly?

Her charges echoed as he painfully mounted Jet. She was not a woman who could be bested by bluster, verbal attack, or male arrogance. Admitting that he had employed such tactics at all was humiliating. As was the ease with which she had pricked his pride. Her points had merit. Next time he criticized her, he had better be prepared to back up his arguments with facts. And if he could substantiate her accusations against Scott, he owed her his thanks. The idea both annoyed and excited him.

Jet picked his way across the stream as he shifted to find a more comfortable position. At the very least, he would have to apologize for his latest attack. No matter how low her morals may have sunk, she had not invited that kiss. Nor could he believe that she knew much about full-blown ardor. She had responded—he had no doubt of that—and in a way that confirmed she harbored all the passion her flaming hair implied. But she had not yet experienced it. He had sensed fear just before she slapped him. Was she afraid of his greater strength—not that he would ever force her, he assured himself through a wave of guilt. In fact, that burst of fear was what had slackened his hold and allowed her escape. But perhaps she feared that she might succumb to her own nature. Yet that implied that she remained innocent, contradicting Lady Avery's sworn statements.

Setting aside her fear, he relived those few moments of bliss when her soft lips had parted, molding to his. She had tasted of peaches and honey and warm summer sunshine, her breath sending fire into his veins hotter than any dragon's. And her tongue! Its first tentative tickle had changed to a bold, seductive sweep, turning his knees to jelly. In three-and-thirty years he had never been so affected. The witch!

Penelope closed the door to her room, thankful to have slipped upstairs unnoticed. Her face was still streaked with tears. Lord Carrington was becoming more than just a problem. He was a menace—to her reputation, to her family's future, and to her peace of mind.

Horrid man!

Why had he kissed her? The caress in the lane might have reflected his normal behavior, but that could not explain this kiss. He knew who she was and showed every sign of despising her. Was he trying to compromise her so that he could overturn her father's will? A court might accept immorality as an excuse to appoint a new trustee.

She paced the floor, forehead furrowed in thought. Such a course could only matter if he applied for the position himself, but even his arrogant assumption of omnipotence would hardly prompt him to take on an estate and wards unconnected to his family.

So he must have another scheme in mind. If her banker ever doubted her competence, he would demand a steward. And she would have no choice but to comply, though they could not afford such a luxury. Hiring a steward would prevent Michael from finishing school and could force them to sell the estate.

Lord Avery had wanted Winter House. She had sometimes wondered if he wished to get rid of the ostriches, for he had often questioned her sanity in raising the birds. But his first offer had occurred fully six years after Ozzie and Cleo arrived, by which time most of the neighborhood had grown accustomed to her eccentricity and had ceased worrying that they would all be murdered in their beds.

Memories of those early battles made her smile. She had been able to counter the worst fears by pointing out that ostriches were native to the holy land and by getting the vicar to admit that they were mentioned in the Bible. People had still looked at her askance, but at least the lower classes no longer considered her an agent of the devil. Moving the birds to an out-of-the-way pasture once they outgrew the barn had also helped. As did the fact that their field was surrounded by an ancient hedgerow so choked with thorns that even songbirds could not penetrate it. Jeremy Jacobson had been the most vocal critic. The chicks had arrived just after he had sworn his love, undoubtedly contributing to his change of heart.

But ancient memories of Jeremy could not withstand Carrington's overpowering masculinity. He posed a serious threat. And not just to the estate. If he continued his assault on her virtue, he might easily win, for she found his touch all too enticing. The sensations remained—instant warmth when he pulled her into his arms, well-muscled legs pressing against her own, strong hands stroking her back, the bulge that had noticeably thickened as he dragged her closer.

"Enough!" she gasped, fighting for breath as new heat swirled into the pit of her stomach. But her treacherous mind refused to listen, instead reliving how his mouth had ravished hers with the intensity of a condemned man suddenly faced with reprieve. She staggered to the washstand to splash cold water on her flaming face. Had she responded?

She had.

Her knees collapsed. An experienced lecher would have noticed so mortifying a truth. It had taken well over a minute to summon the will to pull away. Her fury had been aimed at herself as much as at him. But he could not know that, and he would never forgive those humiliating blows. It did not bode well for their next encounter.

She should not chastise herself for responding, she decided, pacing the floor in an attempt to stiffen her knees. It was a natural reaction to his expertise. And she was not proof against such attentions. Her world had rarely contained even the pretense of affection. Her mother had died when she was four. Her father had ignored her existence. Only after she assumed charge of her siblings did he occasionally greet her.

And so it was natural that Carrington's kisses would awaken a desire to be loved and cherished, held and petted. But he was not the man to do so. At best he wanted her for dalliance during his stay in Devon, but she would be no man's mistress. More likely he was preying on her sensibilities to force her either to abandon her support of Terrence's betrothal or to sell Winter House.

She could never admit that she had lied about her support, and she would never sell, so she would have to circumvent his plot. To start with, she must never again be alone with him. Awakening even mild desire could only hurt her.

Other problems finally drove Lord Carrington from her mind. She might oppose a match with Terrence, but Alice was of marriageable age. Somehow she must amass a dowry. And then there was the mortgage. To negate Carrington's schemes, she must make this quarter's payment immediately.

Composing her face and straightening her hair, she headed for the bookroom, resigned to selling her first editions. With luck, her mother's pearls could wait until the next crisis.

It was hard to admit that the children she had raised for fifteen years were nearly ready to step out into the world. Alice would soon be gone. Michael was so much older than his years that he would probably marry young. And she could not disapprove, for he needed an heir. But a shiver tumbled down her spine as she pictured the inevitable future—Michael in charge of Winter House, his wife running the manor, Alice happily ensconced elsewhere, and Penelope—?

Where would she be? Playing aunt to various nieces and nephews, most likely. And biting her tongue when those in charge of the house or the estate made decisions different from her own. She shuddered. Or perhaps the pottery would expand enough to support her in a cottage. Running a business full-time would bar her from local society, but she had no future there anyway. She was already firmly on the shelf with no dowry and no prospects. Even without Lady Avery's antagonism, the polite world would never accept her, for she lacked beauty, fortune, and feminine accomplishments, had acquired a markedly blue education, and had long engaged in unacceptable pursuits—Carrington was right about that. Years of doing a man's job left her dangling between classes while belonging to none. She might as well resign herself to life alone.

Chapter Nine

Choking out renewed sobs, Lady Avery raised accusatory eyes to Richard's. "Have you no respect for the dead? How dare you invite a stranger into my home with poor Gareth still warm in his grave? If only he were here to berate you for tormenting me. You care nothing for my feelings." She sniffed, again dabbing at her eyes. "How am I to survive without my dearest husband? I suffer, but you care not, rejoicing in my sorrow and gloating at my grief."

"That is quite enough, Aunt Mathilda," snorted Richard. "You should consider a career on the stage."

She sobbed harder. "What can I expect from the son of my odious brother? I am surprised you have not thrown me out on the highway, though forcing me to entertain an uncouth stranger is nearly as bad."

After his morning confrontation with Miss Wingrave, the last thing he needed was another scene, but Lady Avery had neatly trapped him in the morning room. He sighed. "No one expects you to join us. But I want to see what manner of man your daughter has befriended."

"How pointless! Forbid her to see him and that will be the end of it. You are her guardian, so she must obey you."

"Hardly," he snapped, ignoring her recourse to smelling salts. He had humored her megrims too long already. If only he had recalled her manipulative frailty earlier, he would have handled her differently. Terrence was right. She was pretending grief to garner attention and ignore her responsibilities. "Millicent has learned nothing in sixteen years. Does she obey you? Did she obey Gareth? Of course not, though you are her parents. She would ignore any strictures and slip off to meet with him anyway. Is that what you want?"

Anger flashed in her eyes, momentarily banishing tears and weakness. "There is nothing wrong with her training. It is the same as my own, the same that any gently bred female receives."

"Hardly. I cannot imagine Grandfather hiring incompetent governesses and ignoring your behavior. Whatever his shortcomings, he was a stickler for propriety."

"Don't blame me for Millicent's intransigence. She has always been willful. Was any lady ever cursed with such unnatural children?" she wailed rhetorically, regaining her pathos as she dabbed her eyes with well-rehearsed abandon. "They have no sensibilities. That callous girl ignored the death of her own father. Ignored it! Not a single tear did she shed for him. I heard her laughing with a maid not twelve hours later. Cruel! And Terrence did not return home for six weeks, preferring to cavort with his friends rather than grieve. You care nothing for my loss, either!"

"I would never mock genuine grief, Aunt Mathilda," he said on a long sigh. "But society does not expect children to mourn as long as a wife would. Children look to the future, easily setting the past behind them. And that is good, for living in the past is suited only to the elderly. Millicent's period of deep mourning is over. Moving into half-mourning will ease her back into the world. Receiving afternoon callers in no way insults the memory of her father."

"That may be, but the wretched girl has been wandering the countryside for weeks, as you yourself admitted. Her rightful place was at my side, comforting me for my loss, not arranging assignations with unsuitable gentlemen."

"If she had been properly trained, we would not have to deal with such misbehavior." The steel in his voice raised another flash of anger in her eyes. "She will leave for school in two weeks. In the meantime we must end this friendship, and the best method is to discourage Mr. Darksmith, something I cannot do until I meet him."

"Then go to his lodgings," she demanded. "Millicent is too young to receive gentlemen callers. You corrupt her by playing out this charade."

"Corrupt her?" he demanded incredulously. "She has been receiving a gentleman caller for at least a fortnight without even a chaperon in attendance, a fact that will ruin her if it becomes public. She has wandered the countryside unescorted since her governess eloped nearly a year ago. Were you even aware of that, madam?"

Her white face was all the answer he needed. "All the more reason to prevent this unacceptable liaison," she countered. "You should call on him and warn him away."

He had considered doing so but preferred to observe Darksmith and Millicent together. A fortune hunter would have much to worry about during this proposed call, for he would share the room with two people who must be treated quite differently. "The arrangements are made," he told her with finality.

"You care nothing for me," she wailed, again breaking into sobs. "How can you invite a stranger into my home during my mourning?"

He had endured enough histrionics. "Madam, you forget yourself. This house belongs to Lord Avery. Like his sister, he is no longer in deep mourning and is looking to the future. If you must continue to wallow in the past, perhaps you should remove to the dower house."

Leaving her gasping in shock, he headed for his room. The idea of moving her was not a new one. She must eventually make the transition. Though sparsely furnished, the dower house was a charming Restoration structure that remained in excellent condition. Terrence would not marry for years, but he had no real need to keep his mother in the manor. She was doing nothing to order the place. Of course, she would be equally inept at running her own establishment, so it might be better to keep her where she was. The new housekeeper answered to the steward. Terrence and Millicent would be away at school.

He nodded. The dower house would remain closed. He was well on his way to resolving the problem of Millicent, which left only Terrence. Miss Wingrave would soon abandon her plots. Despite her blustering, she was too astute to wait five years for any financial rewards. So he need not fear that Alice would elope with his ward. The relationship would die a natural death. But Terrence was nearly as nonsensical about women as their cousin Reggie had been and would undoubtedly fall top over tail for some other chit. Thus a servant must keep an eye on him when he returned to school. As long as Terrence held the romantic notion that he could live without an allowance, he could be counted on to behave stupidly.

He shook his head, praying that no one could see past his reputation. He would never really cut the boy off, even if he eloped with the scheming Alice Wingrave. Pushing the admission aside, he summoned Kesterton and changed for tea.

"Mr. Mortimer Darksmith," announced Barton.

"My dear Miss Avery," Darksmith gushed, lifting her hand to his lips and bringing a rosy glow to her face. "You rival the sun, the moon, and the stars combined, that golden gown providing the perfect setting for a diamond of the first water." Richard frowned at the realization that Millicent was not even wearing half-mourning this day, but Darksmith's effusive words swept on. "It is stunning but cannot do you justice, my dear. You should be arrayed in silk and satin, not simple muslin. But we will speak of that another time. Your invitation overwhelmed me with delight. I trust you are well today."

She simpered. "Of course, dear sir. And I am pleased to entertain you properly at last." She poured tea.

Darksmith's face twisted into sadness at this reference to mourning. "The recent months have been difficult for you, as I well know. And for me also. Your father was a good man who will be sorely missed. But it is time to move on, to face the future free of tears, to take your place in a wider world than this small corner of Devon. Entertaining callers such as my poor self is but the first of a string of social triumphs, for you will surely put London's top hostesses to shame."

"How kind of you to think so, but no occasion will mean more than today. No gathering can surpass one that includes you," she responded boldly, sending Richard's spirits into his boots. "My dearest Mortimer, allow me to introduce my guardian, the Marquess of Carrington."

Richard acknowledged the visitor coolly. Darksmith was clearly trouble. The man was handsome, though his clothes were flamboyant enough to make Brummell cringe—a close-cut blue coat with hugely padded shoulders and enormous lapels, a gaudy blue-and-red striped waistcoat, skintight buckskin breeches, and gold-tasseled Hessians. Seven fobs dangled from his waist, and his cravat pressed his shirt-points dangerously close to his eyes.

But if dandyism was not a crime, his expression should be. A green chit like Millicent would interpret it as all-consuming infatuation. But a more experienced eye saw an oily rogue of great cunning, a poisonous snake who lived by his wits, a determined trickster who would allow nothing to divert him from his goal.

What did the man want? Darksmith's eyes roamed the room as he exchanged light talk with his host. But they displayed no sign of greed. They were looking for something—and not marriage. He might enjoy dalliance with Millicent—she was bold and good-looking—but that was not his primary purpose. Millicent's claims aside, he must be well past thirty and would not enjoy the charms of a sixteen-year-old for long.

Richard made another bland observation on the weather while he considered his guest. Eloping with an heiress or expecting an irate guardian to buy him off did not fit the man accepting a slice of seedcake from a blushing Millicent. So Darksmith was not the usual fortune hunter. But that left only the more sinister motives. Perhaps the man hoped to injure Gareth's family by ruining its daughter. He knew of nothing that might invite revenge, but he was not well-acquainted with this branch of the Averys. Or maybe Darksmith wished to gain access to the house for the purpose of theft. But Gareth possessed nothing of value, and Darksmith would be the first suspect if anything went missing.

"You are in the area on business, I hear," he commented when they had exhausted the usual drawing room subjects and Darksmith had put him off his food with flowery effusions comparing Millicent's beauty to a spring day, her freshness to dew-drenched violets, and her charm to any number of well-known society ladies—some of whom possessed so little charm that the man could not possibly have met them. Millicent basked in the insincere words, preening and simpering like a besotted fool.

Darksmith donned a somber expression. "It is most distressing. My uncle recently died, leaving me his estate. But I cannot yet take charge of it, for a stranger swears that it actually belongs to him. It threw my aunt into hysterics, as you can imagine. His claim is clearly preposterous, but proving it is becoming a tedious chore."

"Is the estate in Devon?"

"No, no. It is in the North Riding of Yorkshire. A small estate that I would not expect you to know, my lord. Our ancestors purchased the land from an Exeter family who now deny that any sale took place. Lord Avery was helping me prove the transfer."

He raised a quizzical brow. A solicitor would be far more qualified to handle a legal matter, but he held his tongue. "I would not have thought my uncle was either canny enough or philanthropical enough to have done so, but I obviously do the man an injustice."

He nodded.

"But where is your own home?"

"I told you he came from Yorkshire," sputtered Millicent, irritated at the inquisition.

"It is a large county."

"Very," agreed Darksmith. "But a beautiful one, whose rolling hills and quiet moors are nothing like the inhospitable wilderness that looms like a curse over Devon. Ours are green and refreshing, the perfect antidote to a weary soul. You would thrive there, my sweet," he said to Millicent with a seductive smile. "One feels a zest for life that cannot be found in other parts of the country and an exhilarating vitality one can only savor. I cannot describe it, but must allow you to discover it for yourself."

"It sounds wonderful," said Millicent with a sigh.

"You live near Fountains Abbey, then?" Richard asked.

"A few miles south, though I was not born there, moving in with my aunt when I was orphaned at age seven." Millicent laid a sympathetic hand on his, removing it only after Richard glared. "But the abbey is a remarkable place, its soaring ruins lifting the soul until one expects to come face-to-face with God Himself. One can spend hours contemplating the nature of the universe or man's relationship with heaven. A more humbling location I cannot imagine. Are you familiar with it, my lord?"

"By repute only," he lied, for he owned an estate only five miles away. Both his estate and Fountains Abbey were in the West Riding. But he did not wish to discuss his own property, for it was there that Penelope Rissen had nearly trapped him into marriage. His last visit to the abbey had been in her company. "I hear it is good sheep country."

"Acceptable." Darksmith shifted slightly in his chair. "We have always done well. Our breeds are different from those you run here, of course. The harsher winters require sturdier animals. But the principles are the same."

"Indeed. How did you meet my uncle? Yorkshire is not a place he normally frequented."

"At a fair. We were bidding against each other for a ram. Unfortunately a third gentleman was willing to pay more than either of us, but we fell to talking. When he learned of the claim against my uncle's estate and my family's connections to this area, he invited me to visit."

The answer was glib—and wholly unbelievable. He could not have known Gareth well if he thought this fabrication would work. After all, Gareth was the man who had paid so little attention to his estate that Scott had been able to embezzle thousands with impunity. "Your problem must have arisen long ago, then," he commented. "How is it that you have been unable to resolve it?"

"Long indeed. It has been fully six months since the first claims. I sent to Exeter for copies of the transfer, but fire had destroyed the records. It was not until I met Lord Avery that I decided to investigate for myself. He insisted that secondary sources must exist that would mention the sale."

"If only Papa had not died, you could have stayed here," said Millicent on a sigh. "He would have been horrified to see you in that awful inn."

"Your sympathy touches me, my dear," replied Darksmith soothingly. "But you must not think that the inn is neglecting me. It is true that the food is less abundant than I prefer, and the meat overcooked, but meeting you compensates for any hardships. Had I known what beauty awaited me in Devon, I would have come long since merely to gaze upon your exquisite face.

Even the frustrations of your father's untimely death fade when I bask in the pleasure of your company."

"Have you been able to find the references you seek?" asked Richard, interrupting what looked to be a lengthy accolade.

"Not yet. The information can only be found in the seller's estate records. Lord Avery had hoped to examine them himself. I have little hope of doing so."

"Surely they would not prevent you from searching!" exclaimed Millicent.

"You forget that they claim the sale to be false," he said gently. "And they are reclusive, barring the doors to all but their few friends. I had hoped that one of those friends would assist me, though I have not yet found one who is willing. But I will persevere."

"Who is contesting your claims?"

"No one you are likely to know, my lord. And there is nothing you can do to help. This is my own affair."

"Possibly, but with Lord Avery's death, I would have expected you to move closer to Exeter," he said, employing a bored sarcasm calculated to set Darksmith's back up.

"There are other sources of information here," he stated. "And once I met Miss Avery, I could not bring myself to move on. Surely fortune smiled upon me that day. To raise my eyes from the road and perceive such loveliness is an experience I will never forget."

Terrence joined them. "Sorry to be late. Is there any tea left?"

"Of course," said Millicent. She poured for her brother and offered him a choice of cakes and biscuits. At least her handling of the teapot was correct. "Have you met Mr. Darksmith? He is staying in the village. Mortimer, my brother."

Terrence's eyes narrowed. "Didn't I see you skulking in the woods yesterday?"

"Possibly, though I would hardly call a walk in the Devon air skulking. I wander this way quite often, as would anyone susceptible to beautiful ladies," he added with another smile for Millicent.

That smile brought a frown to Terrence's face. Turning away, he retired to the far corner of the room and stared out the window.

"Forgive him, Mortimer," begged Millicent. "I cannot imagine what can have overset him so."

"It is nothing, my dear," he replied promptly, patting her hand while casting a furtive glance at Richard to assess his reaction.

Conversation continued. Richard tried to pin down the man's parentage, but could get no answers. Darksmith used a deprecating smile to declare that his own background was far too insignificant to be familiar to the Marquess of Carrington, while continuing his effusive compliments of Millicent, who was clearly infatuated. But there was no evidence that Darksmith returned her regard. Nor did it appear that he was using her to counter boredom. But that was no cause for rejoicing. The mere fact that she had been sneaking off to meet him was enough to compromise her reputation. That Darksmith had not already seduced the obviously willing Millicent was of further concern. What was his game? He was clearly cultivating her, yet he seemed to have no designs on her virtue.

The question remained unanswered when their visitor took his leave.

"Is he not the nicest man?" exclaimed Millicent, her face aglow with excitement. She had risen to bid Darksmith farewell and now danced about the drawing room as if her feet had wings.

"Perfectly polite," agreed Richard quietly. "And now that you are no longer in deep mourning, you should meet him often as you make calls about the neighborhood. A respectable gentleman will be welcomed in all the best houses. But you must watch your own behavior carefully lest you sully your reputation. Never leave the house unaccompanied. Society condemns such hoydenish tricks. What would Mr. Darksmith think of a girl who was not received by her own neighbors?"

"But who would ever know?"

"Enough, Millicent. All it takes is one lady observing a lapse in decorum. She would write to a friend who would confide in another, and before the cat could lick its ear, you would be at the center of a scandal without ever having set foot in town." He stared at her long enough to make sure she understood, then headed for the library.

* * *

Terrence watched in fury as Carrington departed the drawing room. He had remained silent since turning his back, but every minute had increased his tension. Why had the marquess accepted the odious Darksmith after repudiating the angelic Alice? Their caller was a blatant blackguard whose intentions were dishonorable at best. Yet Carrington had treated him as a favored guest. He had not even forbidden Millie to see the fellow. It wasn't fair.

"Where did you meet your oily friend?" he demanded, not allowing her to leave the room.

"What do you mean by oily?" she snapped. "Mortimer is the kindest, most understanding gentleman of my acquaintance."

"He is a hypocrite who lies through his teeth every time he opens his mouth. You can see it in his face—the sly calculation, the greed, the exhilaration at tempting fate. If you cannot recognize it, then you have no judgment."

"He loves me."

"Hah!" Terrence stared in amazement. "Your attics are to let. He must be all of thirty. No man of thirty falls in love with a girl of sixteen whose manners are so lacking that she arranges secret trysts."

"What are you talking about?"

"I know very well that you have been sneaking off. I did not think that you were stupid enough to fall into the hands of a smarmy trickster, or I would have said something earlier. It has to stop."

"Why do you hate him so? He has done nothing to harm you."

"He is leading my only sister down the road to ruin," he countered. "That is reason enough. Trust me on this, Millie. I have seen many gentlemen woo females. Some genuinely cared. Most merely wanted a quick tumble. The eyes always reflect their owner's goal, despite the false smiles and lying flattery. Darksmith's eyes speak to me. He wants something from you, but it is not marriage."

"Hateful boy!" she shouted. "What can you know of life? Your words are nought but conceited boasting, as empty as yon fireplace." She flung a theatrical arm toward the yawning hole that would not hold flame until winter returned. "How dare you command me to give up my dearest friend? Even Lord Carrington—who knows far more about the world than you—has not demanded such a sacrifice. I won't do it. He is the only one who cares about me, who understands me, who supports me through this odious farce an unfeeling world demands I endure. Who else am I to talk to? Mama does nothing but weep and wail over the death of a man she spurned every day of our lives. You might as well have stayed in school for all we see of you. No one calls, and I am not allowed out. Can you blame me for enjoying the friendship that fate has provided in my hour of need? Mortimer salvaged my sanity. For that reason alone I love him dearly. Leave me! Go see that fubsy-faced farm wench you have been dangling after. You have no right to condemn me for doing less than what you do every day, and you certainly have no right to question my judgment when your own is so lacking."

Glaring in fury, she stomped out of the room, leaving an open-mouthed Terrence behind.

"Your excellent understanding of men is balanced by a deplorable ignorance of women," commented Richard from the doorway.

"What is that supposed to mean?" He glowered at his guardian, still burning with fury over the man's inequity.

"Did you enjoy being told that the object of your infatuation was a scheming wench who wanted only your title and money?"

"How dare you—"

"Be quiet," Richard interrupted him grimly. "One can usually deal with a gentleman by discussing a problem calmly and rationally. Women are trickier—something you will learn once you've been on the town for a while. You have put her back up and hardened her resolve, assuring that she will accept the truth about Darksmith with even greater reluctance. Thus my job is now even more difficult. I will thank you not to meddle again."

"We are talking about my sister," he objected hotly. "My family. My responsibility. How dare you invite that odious snake into my home?"

"I dare because I am in charge of this home and the people in it. I must discover the man's weakness and exploit it. He is no gentleman—you judged him very well. I doubt he can even claim gentle breeding from the wrong side of the blanket, but it will be easier to expose him in genteel surroundings, and Millicent will accept his scheming more easily if she observes it for herself. You have a long way to go before you are worldly enough to plan such a campaign. Leave it to me, and set your own affairs in order. Perhaps this demonstration of how badly you mishandled a female will convince you that you have also misjudged Miss Wingrave."

As silently as he had appeared, Richard was gone.

Chapter Ten

"I have the report on the Wingraves, my lord." Cawdry laid a sheaf of papers on his employer's desk.

"Is Terrence being duped?"

"No, sir."

Richard frowned, motioning Cawdry to a chair. "Explain."

"Lord Avery's characterization is correct. Lady Avery, on the other hand, has waged a baseless campaign against the Wingraves for seventeen years despite being repeatedly told that her claims are false. She ignores facts and cuts anyone who tries to correct her misconceptions. Her intransigence has eroded her reputation, inviting ridicule from her neighbors. Yet her vitriol continues."

"Why?"

"No one knows. The Wingraves were already here when she married Lord Avery. In the beginning she treated them no differently than other untitled landowners. Her attacks began quite suddenly about five years later, but even the most determined gossips have not discovered why."

Richard paced the library in silence while he considered Cawdry's words. *Your judgment has dry rot* . . . Sucking in a deep breath, he resumed his seat.

"Tell me about the Wingraves."

"The Honorable Lucinda Winterbottom married the Honorable Walter Wingrave in—"

"They were both honorables?" he interrupted. Terrence had claimed that Mrs. Wingrave was the daughter of a baronet.

"Mr. Wingrave was the fourth son of the seventh Earl of Marleigh. I doubt you knew him, for the Marleighs have always lacked the resources to visit London, and his health was poor for several years before his death. Walter grew up on his father's estate in the Midlands, eschewing both the military and government to enter the church. He was installed as curate to a parish in Hampshire whose living was under the auspice of Viscount Winterbottom, another impoverished lord who never goes to town. The viscount's youngest daughter Lucinda formed an attachment to the new curate, but they had no hope of marriage, for neither had the means to support even a cottage existence. Lord Winterbottom tried to find her an acceptable suitor, but with no dowry, the only offer he got was from an aging lecher. To the man's credit, he turned it down. A year later, Lucinda inherited Winter House from her great-uncle and immediately married Mr. Wingrave. Walter gave up the church and moved here to administer the estate."

"So what gave my aunt the idea that the Wingraves were descended from merchants?"

"I do not know," admitted Cawdry. "I have uncovered no one connected with trade. The great-uncle was another Winterbottom. The viscounts have always chosen brides of impeccable breeding despite their own lack of fortune. But to return to the Wingraves, Lucinda produced one daughter, Penelope. Over the next four years, she suffered a stillborn son and a miscarriage, ultimately falling victim to influenza. Walter remarried when Penelope was nine. His second wife was Laura Higgins, the oldest daughter of Sir Oswald Higgins."

"Another gentleman I do not know." But here was the baronet.

"Many families avoid London, my lord. He lives secluded in Somerset, as much from inclination as from lack of funds. That marriage produced Alice and Michael, but Laura did not survive the second birth. I have spoken with villagers, tenants, and the local gentry. All agree that Mr. Wingrave was exceedingly attached to his second wife, falling into a serious decline after her death. No one saw him for over a year. Twelve-year-old Penelope took over running the house and raising her half siblings. It was quite a job for a girl who was still a child herself— even then they had few servants—but she managed."

"Any connections to trade on the Higgins side?"

"None, though one of Laura's uncles was an adventurer, traveling to China, India, and Africa. He is no nabob, but he managed to stave off starvation."

"What happened to Mr. Wingrave?"

"When Penelope was seventeen, he was diagnosed with a wasting sickness. That was when he relinquished control of the estate, caring about nothing from then until his death two years ago. His will appointed Penelope guardian and trustee."

"There cannot be much there. The house is in tatters."

"Their finances are precarious, but not hopelessly so. Laura Wingrave was extravagant, forcing Walter to mortgage Winter House. But Penelope is an astute manager. The estate is solvent. Its productivity has steadily improved, for she puts every spare shilling back into the land. And she has never missed a mortgage payment. The bankers are satisfied with the arrangement. Sir Francis Pelham offers effusive praise, though I suspect he harbors a *tendre* for the lady. But others also admire her, with the sole exception of your aunt."

He frowned. Cawdry was a painstaking investigator who always produced accurate reports, so he could no longer reject the truth. But Cawdry could not know the state of a person's mind. Miss Wingrave might have better ancestry than he had believed. She might have worked miracles in improving her brother's legacy. But her very determination would force her to grab every chance for security—and Alice would be her most valuable asset. A woman performing a man's job was dangerous, for women eschewed the code of honor that governed gentlemen's lives.

But he could not lower himself to her level. Her plotting did not excuse his own mistakes. He had known since she left him by the stream that he must apologize, despite what publicly admitting errors could do to his image. Cawdry's report made it even more imperative—and more difficult. He would have to confess faulty judgment as well as blatant lechery. His temperature rose at the remembered feel of her pressed against his length, raising an uncomfortable mixture of excitement, shame, and disgust at himself. He had always left lust to society's rakeshells, preferring discreet liaisons with well-paid courtesans.

"What about those damnable ostriches?"

Cawdry chuckled. "Eccentric, aren't they? People shake their heads over the birds, but they have grown accustomed to them. They actually belong to Alice—a gift from the adventuring uncle—but it was Penelope who figured out how to keep them alive. They make a tidy sum from selling the plumage, which allows Michael to attend Eton. One adult bird produces about the same income as half a dozen sheep."

Richard grimaced. He didn't know how much she was spending on the birds, but if they paid for Eton, she must be doing well with them. Again he had made a cake of himself. Dismissing his secretary, he skimmed the report. It contained a wealth of details but no further revelations. Yet it raised as many questions as it answered.

Why did Lady Avery hate the Wingraves? She had not met them socially in seventeen years, for she avoided any gathering that included them. This did not limit her own social calendar, for the Wingraves rarely attended private parties, preferring the public assemblies that Mathilda considered vulgar. She continued her antagonism despite ridicule from her peers, yet none of her charges withstood scrutiny.

He frowned at the last page. Cawdry had been misled on one point. He depicted Penelope as a calm, intelligent, and astute manager, a role she must have played for the bank directors. But he knew from personal experience that she was a tempestuously emotional harpy who would go to any lengths to achieve her goals. Intelligence he would grant, for she routinely tied his logic in knots, but no one who knew her could ever describe her as calm.

He also suspected that her finances were on shakier ground than everyone thought. Just yesterday he had spotted her entering an Exeter pawnshop with a bundle under one arm. Was she supplementing an inadequate income by selling her valuables? Two years of bad crops spelled disaster for anyone living close to the edge. Or some crisis may have demanded more cash than she had. The evidence supported his own view that desperation over growing poverty and incessant mortgage payments had prompted a plot to entrap Terrence.

But she would not get away with it.

Setting the report aside, he returned to cleaning out Gareth's desk. Now that the estate was running smoothly, he was sorting his uncle's private papers, filing some, discarding others. One entire drawer was packed with unimportant correspondence.

Why would anyone bother keeping it? he wondered in disgust, filling one basket and starting a second.

"What the—" In the very back was a beautiful inlaid box. His hand shook as he pulled out a miniature of Penelope Wingrave. Fiery curls brushed alabaster cheeks. Blue eyes sparkled with mischief. His lips tingled at the memory of her mouth softening in response to his pressure, parting at his command . . .

"Idiot!" he growled, shaking his head at the sensual fantasies exploding through his brain. Was he suffering from delayed adolescence? Mark had often urged him to loosen his control and enjoy life more. Or was Miss Wingrave determined to drive him insane? Whatever the cause, he must leash his rampaging emotions.

As he stared at the miniature, almost daring it to make trouble, his shoulders slumped in relief. It wasn't her after all, though the likeness was close enough to make his skin crawl. But the clothing was wrong and the face longer and a little fuller. The box also held a worn journal and a packet of letters. Opening the book, he skimmed random entries, but soon returned to the beginning to read the diary in earnest. The miniature depicted Lucinda Wingrave.

Poor Gareth.

His heart bled for his uncle. The man had found a soul mate such as few people ever discovered. Unfortunately, Lucinda was already married. They fought their attraction for nearly six months, but as her pregnancy advanced, her fears, frustration, and growing love sparked intense emotional storms that only Gareth could control. Inevitably they succumbed to their mutual passion, though their ecstasy was always tinged with guilt over deceiving Walter. Yet they could not stop. The torrid affair lasted the rest of Lucinda's life. Perhaps they would have been happier if they had run away together, but she had been a deeply religious woman who could not abandon all the shackles of morality. And Gareth had responsibilities to his title and estates.

Would they have been as close had they been free to wed? He closed the book and set it beside the miniature. Perhaps it was the illicit nature of their relationship that had fed their boundless passion. But the story plucked a chord in his heart. He could not forget his first encounter with Lucinda's daughter nor his own uncharacteristic behavior.

Absolutely not! He shoved the nebulous thought firmly aside and skimmed the letters. Each was signed *L. W.* Phrases leaped out to torment him. —*need you more than life itself... knew the moment you fell, my love, for I felt you hit the gate... regret harming Walter, but how can I deny our love?... might be late, but I must see you... Walter has damned my soul, but I care not. Your dower house is all the heaven I will ever need...* Envy dragged at his heart. And pity. Why had a benevolent God brought them together too late to love honorably?

Perhaps this had prompted his aunt's antagonism. If she knew of the affair, she might see her neighbors as rivals for Gareth's affections. But that was preposterous. Lucinda had died more than a year before Gareth's marriage. There was no evidence that he had paid any attention to Penelope. She could only remind him of what he had lost, so there would have been no rivalry. Gareth had recorded the day that Mathilda denied him her bed, attributing her sudden repugnance to her new pregnancy. She had never relented.

But the affair might explain Gareth's laxity over Tallgrove. Once Lucinda died, he had taken steps to assure his succession. But he cared little for the estate or his growing family, spending much of his time shut away in the library. Both the journal and Lucinda's notes were thin from frequent handling.

"You are a breath of sunshine, capable of warming the coldest day," exclaimed Darksmith, catching Millicent's hand in his own. He kissed her fingers, drawing them into his mouth and gently sucking. His tongue touched the inside of her wrist, moving seductively up her arm until she was firmly clasped in an embrace that tightened once his lips reached hers. She moaned, arching into him.

"Am I really?" she gasped when he eventually led her to a bench set against the back wall of the folly. He dusted it for her, then assumed a seat at her side.

"No one else glows with such radiance. How have I lived so long without you?" he murmured, sliding an arm around her shoulders as his other hand trailed lightly over her bosom, peaking the breast that lay above her pounding heart.

She shuddered. "We should not be doing this." But she made no move to pull away.

"I know, my love, but it is difficult to restrain myself. You make me feel so invincible, so powerful, so much a man. You are the light of my life, the keeper of my sanity, the hope of my future." He pulled her into another kiss that left her gasping for air.

"Lord Carrington does not approve of you," she whispered into his cravat as his hand softly stroked her hair. "I fear he will prevent you from courting me. Already he has assigned a servant to accompany me whenever I leave the house. I eluded her today, but it will be more difficult in the future."

"It matters not, little one," he crooned. "I can be patient if I must, but he cannot force me to abandon you. He will acknowledge that in the end."

"I hope so, but he is not the sort to change his mind. And he is a power in society. I fear what he could do to you."

He kissed her again. "Set aside your concern, my love. No power can destroy what we share. I can provide for you without help from your family." He straightened with a frown. "Or I can once I defeat the plots of Sir Reginald St. Juste."

"What a curmudgeon he is!" exclaimed Millicent. "But how can he harm you?"

"He is the one whose claims threaten my inheritance. Your father was helping me, as you know. I had hoped to find corroboration of the truth elsewhere, but have been unable to do so."

"Then all is lost." Tears trembled in her eyes that he gently kissed away.

"Not all. I suspect a record of the original transaction exists in one of the Tallgrove ledgers, for my estate and Tallgrove were originally owned by the same man. I was going to ask Carrington if he would allow me to look at them. But you are right to distrust him. If he has taken me in dislike, he would never provide me with the means to support a wife."

"That is easy to believe. He is odious!"

He nuzzled her neck, dropping kisses onto her shoulder even as one hand loosened her gown to push it lower. "Will you find the book I need, my love?" His lips reached her newly exposed breast, his tongue and teeth teasing the nipple until she arched into him, moaning loudly.

Her hands threaded his hair, pulling him closer until his mouth covered her entire breast. "Mortimer," she sobbed, turning so his hand could reach the other one.

He eased back, pulling her against him as he returned to her lips. "We must be careful, my love," he murmured. "In all ways. Can you find the proof of St. Juste's perfidy? Only after the ownership of Belle Noir is irrevocably established can I turn my thoughts to marriage."

"Perhaps."

"The entry should be in the ledger that covers the year 1620, my darling Millicent," he murmured, his breath again tickling her exposed breast. "You will find it either in the estate office or the library. Bring it here."

"I will do my best. Oh-h-h . . . !"

"My future is in your keeping," he finished, moving back to her mouth to muffle her voice. His hand gently replaced her bodice. "Slip it under the cushion, my love. We cannot risk being seen together until I have the right to claim you. As for Carrington, if you comply with his demands for a few days, he will stop watching you."

"How clever you always are, Mortimer." She pulled him back into her arms. After a final embrace, he slipped away.

Millicent had waited impatiently for Lord Carrington to leave the library. None of the ledgers in the office included the year 1620, though the collection extended back to the 1400s. But that only confirmed the importance of that particular book. Her father must have removed it so he could examine it undisturbed.

But after half an hour of searching, she was ready to give up in despair. Had he taken it to his room? Had it been lost? Perhaps Carrington had found it and recognized its worth. Though his demeanor toward Mortimer had been all that was polite, she sensed that he despised the man and would go to any lengths to deny her betrothal. She shivered.

He would not dictate her future. All his talk of governesses and rules was ridiculous. She would make her bows to London society in the spring—as a married lady. Mortimer knew everyone and would introduce her into the highest circles. But first she had to find proof of his inheritance. Dear Lord! How would they manage if it was gone?

But her fears were finally put to rest. The ledger was there, jammed into the bottom shelf and nearly hidden behind a cabinet. The lettering on the spine glowed in the dim light—1608–1623. She was opening it when footsteps sounded in the hall. Thrusting the book behind the cabinet, she skittered across the room to a shelf of novels.

Richard halted in the doorway. "Were you looking for me?"

"N-no." She flinched as his gaze shifted to her damp slippers. "Just for something to read." She grabbed the third volume of *Clarissa Harlowe*.

He stared at her, face creased in a frown. "You seem nervous today. Have you been out?"

"Only to walk in the garden." But she could not stop the heat that seared her face, and knew that she blushed.

"You know you must take a chaperon when you leave the house," he reminded her. "Yet Rose believes you to be in your room."

"Must I be accompanied even in my own garden?" she asked.

"You are no longer a child, Millicent. Do you wish to destroy your reputation by accidentally running into a gentleman?"

She blushed again, then recalled Mortimer's suggestion. "I will always take Rose in the future, my lord."

He nodded and waved her out. She had no choice but to leave, for he settled behind the desk and pulled out a large stack of papers.

What was she up to now? wondered Richard. She must have met Darksmith again, probably by arrangement, but her nervousness hinted at something more. Was she planning an elopement? But he clung to his impression that Darksmith was not truly interested.

His head shook. Millicent was headstrong to a fault and accustomed to getting her own way. Even doubling the watch would not keep her from slipping off on her own. He would need the devil's own luck if he hoped to keep her safe.

* * *

Millicent slipped into the library, a forest green dressing gown hiding her white night-rail. She had despaired of Carrington ever going to bed. Midnight had passed before he finally retired. Using a poker, she fished the ledger out, fighting panic all the while, for the task took longer than she had expected. It had fallen well back, and the cabinet was too heavy to move. Unlocking the French window that led to the terrace, she tiptoed into the night. An hour later she returned to her bed, shivering from cold and from the ever-present fear that Carrington might have learned of her errand.

But no one burst in to accuse her. Within the hour, she had relaxed enough to consider her future as Mortimer's wife. Memories of his kisses filled her mind. Dawn streaked the sky before she slept.

Chapter Eleven

❧

"What does he want now?" murmured Penelope when Mary brought Carrington's card to the bookroom. The last thing she needed was another argument with Terrence's irritating guardian. But that was the direction the day was heading.

While feeding the ostriches that morning, she had noticed a gash on Fluff's neck. More than an hour had passed before Ozzie would allow her close enough to tend the wound. She might have raised him from a chick, but he was very protective when it came to his family. Fortunately, the injury was not as serious as it had first appeared.

But she had barely returned to the house when word arrived from the pottery that an entire batch of bowls had shattered during firing, probably from impurities in the clay. She sighed. Maintaining quality was a problem for most small operations. This was not the first time it had happened, and would not be the last. But the timing could not have been worse. They would have to discard the entire clay shipment and reorder. Despite money being in short supply, it must be done immediately. She could not afford to lose this customer. Would the supplier extend her credit, or must she pawn her pearls?

And now this. Leery of being alone with him, she considered denying her presence, but that would be cowardly. Besides, Carrington was the sort to storm the bookroom if he suspected she was avoiding him. "Tell Mrs. Peccles to set up a tea tray. I will join him shortly."

"Good afternoon, my lord."
Richard turned from his perusal of Walter Wingrave's portrait. Despite her conventional greeting, she was wary, seating

herself in a chair as far from him as possible. And who could blame her? They exchanged comments on the weather until the maid had delivered refreshments and taken her leave.

"What brings you to Winter House?" she asked bluntly.

"I owe you an apology—several, actually." He nearly laughed at her expression.

"You do, but you could knock me over with a feather. I had not expected you to ever admit an error," she conceded, setting her cup on a table as she scrutinized his face.

"Astute of you. Apologies do not come easily to my lips. But this is an unusual situation. My conduct this past week is not at all typical, I assure you. I am not normally considered surly or insulting—or lecherous, for that matter."

"You are not the unprincipled libertine I presumed?"

"Certainly not!"

"Then why have you indulged in such aberrant behavior?"

She wasn't making this easy. "I still cannot explain our first meeting. I have a well-deserved reputation as a deliberate thinker who never acts without careful consideration."

"You?" She burst into laughter. "I find that hard to believe. Or did you decide to throw over the traces, figuring that Devon is too far from your usual haunts for word to drift back to London?"

"Not consciously." He paced before the fireplace, fighting to maintain an image of humility. Any attempt to dominate her would only put her back up again. "Perhaps you cast a spell on me. Or perhaps that accident was the last straw. It had been a terrible journey, leaving me exhausted and angry, but that is no excuse for taking out my frustrations on a stranger."

"What happened?" She retrieved her cup, relaxing as she sipped.

"That storm stranded me for two days in a dilapidated inn with bad service and worse food. But that was only the latest in a long string of mishaps. The last four months have brought nothing but problems."

"Such as?"

He hesitated, but an urge to share his troubles sent words tumbling over each other. "It started last spring when a deluded gentleman challenged my closest friend. Mark won, but his opponent died of unrelated causes less than a week later, prompting a host of malicious stories that accused Mark of murder. He had to retire to the country until the rumors subsided. I joined him."

"Was that so tragic?" she asked, watching emotions chase across a face that he made no effort to control.

"Not in itself, but it meant that I did not hear of Avery's death until nearly two weeks after the fact. Even then I could not assume my duties here, for I was caught up in pursuing the author of Mark's troubles. By the time we unmasked the fellow, Mark's wedding was upon us, and then I had to escort a young cousin to his father's house."

She raised her brows.

"I had been bear-leading the cub. He wished to marry and needed me to convince his parents to sanction the connection." He grimaced.

"He was not too young?"

"Reggie is the greenest cawker I have ever laid eyes on," he grumbled. "If he lives to be a hundred, he will still be too young, but allowing him to run loose would be worse. You wouldn't believe the scrapes he got into in only a month on the town. Besides, the girl will be good for him."

"Unlike Alice." Her friendliness transformed to anger.

"Reggie is not my ward, praise God." It was not an answer, but she said no more. He forced relaxation and humility back on his body. "I arrived home to discover that my mother had arranged another house party crawling with eligible young females. But her latest protégées had even more faults than the last batch, so I returned to Mark's estate. It was there that I received the hysterical summons from Lady Avery that brought me here. What with the storm, a horse that went lame in the middle of nowhere, and a surfeit of demanding relatives—there are times I loathe being head of the family—I was in a flaming temper by the time I arrived. I know I hit you, yet I never even inquired about your injuries."

"They were nothing," she answered his questioning look. "Bruises. No more."

"I truly am sorry. When I reached Tallgrove, my exasperation over everything that had happened made it easy to believe my aunt's ravings about the unscrupulous neighbors who were leading Terrence astray. Not until I had investigated for myself did I realize that her claims were false. Please forgive me for my insupportable tirades, Miss Wingrave. I would very much like to start over and see if we cannot behave like reasonable adults."

Penelope stared into apparently guileless eyes. What was he up to now? There had to be something. Gentlemen did not reverse course without reason. Not even when they were clearly in the wrong. "Very prettily said, but it will take more than words to make me trust you."

He scowled.

"Yet I see no reason to remain at loggerheads," she continued. "You need not fear that I will slit your throat some dark night."

"Had you considered it?"

"Often."

He laughed, lightening his harsh features with a warmth that sent tingles racing down her arms. "I probably deserved it."

"Most certainly. But are you really the only one who can solve your family's problems?"

"Not to sound conceited, but yes. The Averys have long been cursed with weak wills. When anyone of stronger character appears, the others lean on him for advice and assistance. How can I ignore them? If my negligence caused worse problems, guilt would drive me to Bedlam."

"As with Tallgrove?"

"You would bring that up. I admit to more than one vision of you roasting for all eternity."

"It does not sound as if you were as negligent as I originally charged. It seems I owe you an apology."

"Accepted. Truce?" He smiled charmingly.

"Truce."

His face sobered. Forgiveness had come easier than he had expected. Would it last through the next portion of his call? "One of my duties as trustee has been to sort my uncle's papers. I found this." He drew Lucinda from his pocket.

"My mother." She cupped the miniature protectively in her palm. "I hardly remember her."

"You look much alike."

"So people say."

"Do you know how Lord Avery came by the picture?"

"Yes." Her tone was repressive, terminating further discussion. Her gaze remained on her hand, her color rising and fading from emotions he did not even try to identify. It wasn't the reaction he had expected. He debated whether to leave, discuss her mother's affair, or introduce a new subject. But his brain refused to function, so he silently took a seat and turned his attention to the refreshments.

Penelope stared at the miniature, her mind whirling in shock. She had assumed that no one knew of her mother's fall from grace. That the arrogant Lord Carrington did was the worst news she had received in a long while. Many people passed the sins of the parents onto their children. Would he use his discovery to hurt her family? Had his proposed truce been a ploy to disarm her?

The drawing room faded from view. Again she sat at her father's bedside, pitying how his skeletal frame shook with every breath, yet terrified that each whistling wheeze would be his last. But despite his labored breathing, he had insisted on divulging his wife's affair. The knowledge was a burden she could have lived without, though she had not said so. He needed absolution for mistreating her.

"I wronged y-you," he claimed, the words coming slowly, for he hardly had the strength to move his mouth. "You are so like her, Penelope. I could not look at you without recalling her betrayal. But committing new sins does not rectify the old. I should have known that, but as usual, my character proved too weak. But I go now to face the final judgment and can no longer postpone paying for my actions."

"It is done, Father," she assured him, not wishing to see him waste his little remaining energy in talk. "I do not blame you. We need speak of it no further."

But he had insisted. "She was so b-beautiful," he murmured. "I could not believe that she returned my regard. When the means to support us suddenly appeared, I grabbed the chance with both hands. But we had not been married a month before I realized that we had made a terrible mistake. She had been unhappy at home. Her father was poor and begrudged every groat he had to spend on his daughters—unfortunately he produced three girls before siring an heir. Desperate to escape, she mistook infatuation for love and accepted my offer. But I was equally at fault. I had dedicated my life to God's service, yet the privation that curates must endure was so unpalatable that I jumped at the opportunity to become a landowner."

He paused to catch his breath. Penelope laid a comforting hand on his arm, her heart already breaking for the idealistic young people who had learned too late that money did not guarantee happiness. "I did not discover her liaison with Gareth until long after it had begun," he wheezed. "I castigated her, calling the wrath of God onto her head and damning her for all eternity, but she refused to give him up and I lack the temperament that could have forced her. But I could not consider her my wife after such a betrayal. She conceived two children by him, though neither lived. And I counted that a blessing, for I could not have accepted another man's child into my house. You see how badly I failed even in my sworn duty to God."

"Father, do not torture yourself with this," she begged, tears flowing down her face. "God will not condemn you for being human."

"I will soon discover the truth of that sentiment. I have hoped that Lucinda's infidelity was His punishment for revoking my vows to serve the church. But perhaps He expects more."

A cough shuddered through him, so powerful that she feared he would die. But he pulled himself together. "It was not until I met Laura that I understood Lucinda's passion. Love is the strongest force I have ever encountered. My prayers changed then, begging God to forgive her. And I pray you will discover love for yourself one day. My only regret is that I could deny Laura nothing, which has left you in dire straits, and for that I apologize. But I could not help myself, just as your mother could not help herself. Do not hate her for what she did."

"I won't."

Hatred had not even entered her mind. What she felt was sadness, and perhaps a spurt of envy that her mother had found what she could never hope for. Her father's prayers notwithstanding, she was too long on the shelf for marriage, let alone love. And her responsibilities would prevent her from accepting an offer even if one appeared.

* * *

"I thought you should have the miniature," Richard said at last.

Penelope jumped as if she had forgotten his presence. "Thank you, my lord. No other portrait of my mother exists. You say it was with Lord Avery's papers?"

"With his diary."

She bit her lip. "Does anyone else know of this?"

"No one. And I see no reason to enlighten them. I will forget the liaison ever occurred."

"You are kind." She hesitantly smiled.

"You needn't stretch politeness too far," he said dryly. "And this does not mean that I approve a betrothal between Terrence and Alice."

"Why? She is no relation to Lucinda."

He could not admit that he still suspected her of coveting Terrence's wealth. Nor was he willing to reveal his own experiences with scheming women. "Lucinda has nothing to do with it. Terrence is too young to consider marriage. He will be in school for another year and should also spend time in London before making so long lasting a decision."

"My thoughts exactly." He was hiding his real reasons, she knew, though his disclaimer about Lucinda sounded true. But his reticence was obvious to one who had spent fifteen years detecting her siblings' falsehoods. Perhaps he had chosen conciliation to put her fears to rest, thinking the distraction might make it easier to pounce on her estate. But she would not fall for such a trick. She would play along for now because ending the connection between Alice and Terrence would be easier if they worked together. But she must never let her guard down. He was even more dangerous than she had supposed, for he was capable of exerting a great deal of charm.

"But I clearly recall that you supported the match."

She sighed. "Again I must apologize. Please forgive my wretched temper. You infuriated me so much that I had to oppose you, even if that meant lying through my teeth. But it left me in an untenable position. Alice overheard our argument. I had to do some fancy fence-straddling to retreat without making the situation worse."

"You also believe Terrence is too young?"

"Without a doubt. Whatever his feelings at the moment, he

cannot truly know his mind. Boys go through any number of infatuations before they settle down. Especially boys like Terrence who have been coddled since birth. Frankly, Michael is more knowing despite being five years younger. Alice needs maturity and a strong character, not just affection. You have already admitted that Terrence is weak-willed and easily manipulated. That alone makes him unsuitable. But I saw no need to oppose them, instead suggesting that they make no decision until Terrence is out of school. In the unlikely event that they feel as strongly next year, we can either reconsider or resort to playing heavy-handed guardians. But it should not come to that—unless you have already made opposing you a point of honor."

He set his cup on a table and paced the room for several minutes, frowning in thought. "I might have. I mishandled the matter rather badly," he admitted at last.

"You did." He glared, evoking her smile. "Did you expect me to deny the obvious? By coming the odious dictator, you united them in opposition to a common enemy. Regardless of the strength of their feelings, you have made it impossible for them to back down without admitting that they were wrong. I am sure you know how difficult that must be—even for a lad who normally twists with the wind."

"Damnation," he muttered sourly.

"You have little experience with children," she commented.

"True, though I had already realized that my ultimatum was making the situation worse. I tried a different tack with Millicent, but I doubt that was effective, either."

"She is a problem," agreed Penelope. "Girls her age consider themselves grown up. They dream of parties and beaux and fairy-tale romances. But few are ready for the realities that underlie those dreams. Millicent is even less capable than most."

"I am sending her to school for the fall term."

"Good. I presume you know about Mr. Darksmith."

He grimaced. "Does all the world know of that shifty fellow?"

"I doubt it, for he has been discreet, but she cannot go on meeting him on the sly. I do not trust him."

"You do not consider him a gentleman, then?"

She shook her head. "Even his most innocuous conversation

contains evasions. He appeared a fortnight ago, arriving on the stage from Exeter—which itself is suspicious since he claims to have come from Yorkshire." Exeter was in the opposite direction. "He has made no attempt to discuss his business, instead spending all of his time poking about Tallgrove. What might he be looking for?"

Richard was again pacing the room. "I cannot imagine, but I doubt that he wants either marriage or a settlement to leave her alone."

"Astute of you. I would swear that he only discovered her existence after he arrived. And another odd thing." She paused to frown. "I hadn't recalled it until just now when I mentioned Exeter. He was at the Golden Stag shortly before he came here. He nearly ran me down outside the taproom."

"It is possible that he went there first. He claims to be researching an estate that was once owned by an Exeter family."

"Possibly, but I got the impression that he was no stranger to the place. The innkeeper did not treat him as a guest."

"I will have my secretary look into it. He has been unable to trace the fellow so far. Yorkshire is enormous, and I could not pin him down to a specific spot. The closest he came was mentioning Fountains Abbey, but I own a small property near there. He cannot live within twenty miles of it."

"All the more reason to be suspicious."

"I hope I can keep Millicent from doing anything foolish," he said with a sigh, dropping back into his chair to drain his cup.

"What have you done so far?"

"Invited the blackguard to tea. He is slippery as an eel—a nonstop talker who says nothing. But by the time you sift his words to reveal their emptiness, he is long gone. Terrence disapproved of the fellow—or perhaps he is angry over the way I handled it. He cut Darksmith dead in the drawing room and then ripped Millicent to shreds for encouraging him. I called him on it, but the damage was done. I am sure she managed an assignation with him yesterday despite my vigilance."

"Talk to the boy. Explain your reasoning—and your mistake in creating a scene over his own plans. Blame your antagonism on your miserable journey. Or admit that you have so often been pursued for your title that you routinely look for grievous faults in everyone you meet. If nothing else, such a discussion will give you a chance to judge his maturity. Perhaps you can use the opportunity to postpone any decisions until he finishes his schooling. I honestly believe that their infatuation cannot survive several months apart."

He nodded and took his leave.

The visit had gone better than he had anticipated, though what had possessed him to share his thoughts he could not imagine. *I loathe being head of the family.* Dear Lord, where had that come from? It was a sentiment he had not even uttered to Mark! An even bigger shock was Miss Wingrave's assertion that she opposed any marriage between Alice and Terrence. She had sounded so sincere that he began to wonder if he had misjudged her.

But he was not yet ready to discard his hard-earned lessons. Her sincerity merely confirmed her surprising intelligence. She was using guile to lull him into a false sense of security. And she could do it, for she had already demonstrated an excellent understanding of human nature—better than his own if his disastrous handling of Terrence was anything to go by. Even the way she twisted his words proved that she was still waging battle. And so he could not trust her.

Penelope returned to the bookroom in a trance. An apology was the last thing she had expected from the arrogant Lord Carrington. Or was this a new strategy for the same old game? The man was dangerous—and not just because of his charm. Despite his avowed frustration over his family's demands, his sense of responsibility was as powerful as her own. And he could appreciate humor, even at his own expense. When she added a quirky, lopsided smile that removed the harshness from his face, and a wayward curl that dropped over his forehead, her spirits plummeted. Though far from handsome, his appearance was striking. And attractive. He was not merely dangerous. He was lethal.

She could not afford to relinquish her heart. Such stupidity would lead to years of agony, for he was no Jeremy, who could be gotten over in a few months. This man could destroy her. She suppressed her suspicion that such thinking proved she was already treading that forbidden path. The idea was too horrifying to contemplate.

Purging the troublesome lord from her thoughts, she returned to the problem of the pottery. She would have to visit Exeter and arrange to replace the clay. Her pen moved swiftly, listing other errands to complete while she was in town.

Chapter Twelve

~

"Good morning, Miss Wingrave," called Richard, pulling his curricle to a stop. A matched pair of restive grays champed at their bits.

"My lord." She nodded curtly, squinting against the sun. Had he come to pester her banker as Lord Avery had so often done?

"I thought we had agreed to a truce." His voice held challenge.

"So we did. What brings you to Exeter, my lord?"

"Cawdry is checking your hunch that Darksmith is known here. While he quizzes the staff at the Golden Stag, I thought to visit the cathedral and explore the town. Would you care to act as my guide?"

She frowned. "I still have several errands to finish."

"Can your maid not handle them?"

"What maid?"

"Do you mean you are wandering around Exeter unaccompanied?" He scowled. "No wonder Aunt Mathilda disparages your reputation."

"So much for truce," she snapped.

"Forgive me, Miss Wingrave." His voice was much warmer.

She glared. "I am too long on the shelf to need a chaperon, and this is hardly the place to discuss my staff or my reputation, even if either were any of your business, which they are not." She nodded at the passersby who avidly scrutinized the glowering stranger.

"My apologies, Miss Wingrave. Again. Perhaps we should start over. If I assist you with your errands, can you spare an hour to show me the cathedral?"

She smiled ruefully, surrendering to his persistence even as she questioned his motives. "Very well, my lord. My next stop is the linen draper's on Fore Street." She allowed him to hand her into the curricle, reveling in the luxury of driving from stop to stop. Her errands were done in the blink of an eye. They pulled into the yard of the White Hart Inn, where he helped her down yet again.

"Shall we?" He offered his arm and headed for the cathedral. "Do you often come to town alone?"

She tensed, but his tone held no accusation, so she relaxed. "Usually. The others are too busy to get away."

"Even Alice and Michael?" His voice was skeptical.

"Michael is cutting hornbeam today and clearing underbrush. Alice is helping our cook make preserves." She saw shock in his eyes. "My indoor staff consists of Mrs. Peccles and Mary, the maid who let you in yesterday. I prefer to use our income to improve the estate."

"I was not about to rip you up, Miss Wingrave, but I must point out that you are young enough and vibrant enough to need a chaperon. Many dangers lurk in the world, waiting to pounce on the unwary. Ladies wandering about on their own are not safe."

"In London that may be true, but Exeter has never posed a problem—at least until you arrived."

"Truce, Miss Wingrave."

"Of course." She shrugged. "Five years have passed since I last used a companion. No one minds."

They entered the cathedral close. "Magnificent," he breathed, abandoning his inquisition.

"You really are interested." She had thought that he was using sight-seeing as an excuse to learn something to her detriment, an idea his fault-finding amply supported.

"I have always admired cathedral architecture, and this one is unusual in that the twin towers form the transepts rather than the facade, so there is no crossing tower."

She nodded at his observation. "They may have been more traditionally located in the original structure, for they predate the rest by two centuries."

"Which accounts for the extensive use of blind arcading in the towers despite its absence in the nave."

"Precisely, though you will note that the pepper-pot roofs were a later addition."

"From repairs or did construction last into the fifteenth century?"

"Repairs. The cathedral was completed by the mid-fourteenth."

Having established that they shared both knowledge and interest, they abandoned the battle and enjoyed the sights in amity. The Exeter cathedral was impressive, its exterior of gray Beer stone awash in flying buttresses, crocketed pinnacles, and castellated parapets. She thought it contained too much decoration, for the western facade rose in windowed tiers, each level partially blocking the one above. But the interior took his breath away—three hundred feet of uninterrupted vaulting.

"Truly magnificent," he murmured as they paced the nave.

She pointed out the cathedral's treasures—the carved bishop's throne and the oldest complete set of misericords in the country. The sun passed its zenith to hit the western windows, filling the nave with jeweled light that drew their attention to the minstrel's gallery, where fourteen angels played medieval instruments.

"Music is another of my loves," he admitted. "Do you play?"

"Very poorly. Our harpsichord needs new quills, but I've never had the money."

"So Alice is also unmusical."

"She plays no instrument, but unlike me, she has the voice of an angel."

"Are you saying you don't sing?" He grinned, his eyes dancing with silver lights.

"Do frogs sing? Or crows?"

"Surely you are not that bad!"

"I would demonstrate, but lightning would level the cathedral, and the city merchants would doubtless arrest me for malicious mischief when their customers fled in panic."

"Not if I joined you. They would be too busy saving themselves to notice."

She laughed. "Prudence thus begs that we allow others to entertain us. Or do you play an instrument?"

"The pianoforte," he admitted. "But not as well as I would like."

"Perhaps you should let your relatives fend for themselves for a while and spend some time practicing."

"Perhaps."

They returned to the White Hart, where he ordered a light repast. Over the meal they discussed books and ideas, discovering a wealth of common interests. She soon had to force herself to recall that he might be an enemy. She had been right about his lethal charm.

"I've no idea how to keep a rein on Millicent," he admitted once the conversation had drifted to their respective wards. "She is so adept at slipping away that I cannot be sure she is holding to her promise."

"What promise?"

"She vowed to take a chaperon whenever she left the house."

"Was that before or after she last met Darksmith?"

"After the last meeting I know about."

"Did she promise to remain with the chaperon?"

He muttered curses under his breath. "Not in those words. How could I have missed that?"

"You have little experience with young girls," she said wryly. "I have raised both a girl and a boy. There is much similarity when it comes to mischief."

"Were you mischievous in your youth?"

"I wasn't young long enough to find out." She averted her eyes to carefully pour another cup of tea.

Just like me. He frowned at the thought, never having considered his life in those terms. But it was true. His childhood had been both short and lonely. His father was the weakest Avery he knew, eschewing all responsibility by wandering from property to property and vice to vice. His mother had nearly died in childbirth, needing ten years to fully recover. By then he was in school. In another five, he was in charge of everything.

He watched Miss Wingrave drain her cup, struck by her matter-of-fact approach to her burdens. No hint of regret at sacrificing her youth and her future had marred her voice. Something shifted in his heart, raising a desire to replace her lost childhood. He should not have reminded her of that lack, but he had momentarily forgotten her history.

"You are much different than I first thought," he said to turn his thoughts away from dangerous ground.

"Since your aunt's ideas are so lurid, I'm not surprised."

"That is not what I meant. I'm afraid I judged you mostly on looks that day in the lane."

"You keep red-haired mistresses?" she asked, then blushed.

"No, but you look so much like someone I once knew that I assigned you all her faults, especially when I learned you shared a name."

She noted his bitterness and laid aside her pique. "She hurt you."

He nodded. "She was a deceitful fortune hunter who nearly trapped me into marriage. I'll never forgive her."

"But you should—for your own sake. Hatred will harm you more than she did. And it clouds your judgment. You are undoubtedly besieged by young ladies avid for your title, yet I would wager there are others who like you for yourself, but your cynicism prevents you from seeing them."

"I doubt it. My judgment is not that lacking."

"Except when it comes to me."

"Yes, well—" He had the grace to blush. "How do I know you are not another?"

"You will accept it in time. I have too many responsibilities to consider marriage. Besides, I am too long in the tooth and too set in my ways to make an acceptable wife. But I can understand your suspicions. After years of abuse at the hands of your family, I can't bring myself to trust you."

His eyes widened. "What an insult."

"Not at all. I merely apply past experience to present circumstances—exactly as you do."

"I meant the way you disparage yourself. Despite wearing caps and eschewing chaperons, you are nowhere near your dotage."

"What society do you frequent, my lord? I have been an apeleader for years and am now too old, too tall, too boldly colored, too unrefined, and far too independent to ever make an acceptable wife."

"Fustian, Miss Wingrave. You are a beautiful woman and could be even more so with an improved wardrobe. You have a well-formed mind that makes conversation delightful. You—"

"Save the flattery for London," she interrupted. "You will never convince me to accept an appearance that has always cursed me. My father could not bear to look at me. Nor could Lord Avery, though I did not learn the reason until two years ago. You treat me like the light-skirt I resemble—and you are not the first to make that mistake. But I have come to terms with my limitations, and no longer repine. My life is full."

"For now, but what will you do when your siblings leave the nest?"

"I will consider that when the time comes," she answered repressively. "I have too many other problems to waste time worrying about it now." But that was a lie, she admitted as they returned to his curricle. The question nagged at her with increasing frequency.

Both her gig and his secretary were at the Golden Stag, but a surprise awaited them. Cawdry had discovered some leads and wished to track them down, so Richard offered her a place in his curricle. His groom would drive her gig.

The journey back to Winter House passed more quickly than usual. She abandoned her melancholy thoughts. Conversation ranged from books to estate management to his witty but acidic description of the London Season. When he discovered that he need not censure his words for fear of upsetting female sensibilities, he relaxed, enjoying their discussion more than any since visiting Mark. It was a shock to remind himself that she had designs on his ward.

Penelope was likewise basking in their repartee, finding the intellectual exchanges more stimulating than she had thought possible. Hitherto, the most erudite conversations she had enjoyed with men had been financial discussions with her banker and flirtations with Sir Francis. But the growing warmth in Carrington's eyes reminded her too sharply of his earlier assaults. She could not trust him.

"If this war ever ends, I would like to travel," he admitted after comparing what they knew about ancient Rome. He sighed. "I doubt I can, though. There are too many demands on my time."

"You cannot solve everyone's problems," she countered. "Most people can manage if they must."

"Not Averys."

"Even Averys. This family curse you prate about is no more than laziness. It is easier to cry on another's shoulder than to deal with problems for oneself. As long as you are willing to do all their work, why should they bother?"

"You speak from ignorance."

"Hardly. By your own admission, most of them muddle along without falling into debt. If they suffered a genuine curse, they would not be able to avert disaster. But they do. Self-interest overcomes laziness every time."

"You mean—"

She nodded. "Go ahead. Travel. See the world. Explore your own interests for a change. They won't destroy themselves before you get back."

"Interesting theory, but I doubt it."

"Then here is another challenge for you, my lord. Open your mind and review the last ten family crises. Were their short-comings real or had they merely chosen a different approach to life than you prefer? Did you take on their burdens out of necessity or because running their lives makes you feel omnipotent?"

"Of all the uncalled-for remarks—" he sputtered. "Do you honestly believe they turn to me unless they absolutely have to? Most of them are mortified to admit their problems, placing walls between us that prevent any affection."

"Of course there is no affection," she agreed. "They sound like lazy parasites. And you do nothing to change them. If your conduct here is any guide, I would wager that you appear on the scene, assign blame for everything that does not meet your standards, then take control into your own hands, treating the culprits like incompetent children in the process. They save face by declaring that they have no interest in pursuing such drudgery and are grateful for your assistance. But you are becoming overburdened. No man is capable of running the world singlehandedly—as Napoleon must eventually discover."

"You dare to compare me to that monster—!"

"This is not a subject we need to discuss," she interrupted. "You already admitted that you do not confess faults easily. Wait until you calm down. Then think about it. Lending a hand during a crisis is commendable, but unless they learn to stand on their own feet, you have done them no lasting good."

He subsided. When he reached Winter House, he returned to the earlier subject. "Have you ever wished to travel?"

"Of course. Rome. Athens. Even Egypt. But such ideas never move from the realm of fantasy to the sphere of dreams. Dreams have to be at least a little possible."

"And yours are not?"

"I live in England, my lord, not Utopia. Travel requires money. There is no long-forgotten relative who will leave me a fortune, no fairy godmother to grant me three wishes, no pot of gold at the end of a rainbow. I can only work with what I have."

She collected her packages and bade him farewell, wishing her last outburst had never seen the light of day. Baring any part of herself to an enemy could only make his own plots easier to carry out. And recognizing her bleak future did her spirits no good.

Richard alternately smiled and frowned all the way home. The day had almost been a time out of time, a period unconnected with any other part of his life. He shook his head, unable to explain how the cynical and reserved Marquess of Carrington had spent an entire afternoon in lighthearted conversation with a scheming jade—and enjoyed himself. It did not bear thinking on, so he put it out of his mind. Tossing the ribbons to a footman, he hurried upstairs. The rest of his uncle's papers were in the escritoire in the master bedroom. Once he sorted them, he could wind down his visit, though he had no intention of leaving until both of his wards were safely ensconced in school.

An hour later he stretched his aching back before opening the last drawer. Another stack of lists. How could a man who spent so much time organizing his thoughts be so inept at running his life? He scanned the top page, then jerked to attention and read it more carefully. And again. It was a detailed plan to wrest control of Winter House from the Wingraves and push them out of the neighborhood.

That feeling of imminent disaster returned, stronger than ever. *After years of abuse at the hands of your family* . . . No wonder Miss Wingrave decried all Averys and refused to trust him. Much of the plot had already been set in motion. The second page was a list of payments—to a man for sabotaging the pottery; to another for spreading slow poisons in Winter House fields; to a third for injuring her animals; to a fourth for damaging orchards and forests; and to a fifth for setting fire to the stable. Avery's ultimate goal was to buy the mortgage. By that time the estate would be worth so little that even selling it would not raise enough. Gareth could call in the loan and take possession.

Richard totaled the Wingrave's losses. They were sizable, making Penelope's matter-of-fact statements about their finances seem unbelievably courageous. How had she managed to stay afloat? Even selling possessions could not cover such losses. But that might explain her attempt to snare Terrence. She would have seen the boy's interest as another example of the Avery antagonism, perhaps a plot to seduce and ruin Alice. But she could turn the tables by trapping Terrence into marriage and taking control of Tallgrove for herself, thus defeating the Averys at their own game. Yet he did not want to believe that. He had enjoyed their day in Exeter. And he felt guilty about Gareth's scheme even though he had not personally been involved.

Why would Gareth want Winter House so badly? He again skimmed the papers, searching for a clue. Lucinda's name appeared in a margin. Had Gareth's love turned his mind? Winter House had been her dowry. Perhaps he believed that entitled him to the estate. But that was mad.

The phrase *restore ancestral lands* was penciled in another spot, though it made no sense. Gareth's family had not owned Tallgrove very long. He had seen nothing in the ledgers to hint at a connection.

But he knew little of Winter House. Maybe there was something in its history that could explain his uncle's obsession—a Roman villa or druidic temple? But Gareth was no scholar and had cared nothing for antiquities.

When Cawdry returned from Exeter, he summoned him to the library.

"I want an exhaustive history of Winter House," he ordered.

"Yes, my lord."

Richard handed him a sheet of paper. "Find these fellows and put a stop to further action. Get a complete accounting of their activities. Promise them that there will be no repercussions if they cooperate."

"At once."

Trouble again tickled his spine, and he wondered why. The plot was over.

Chapter Thirteen

❧

"What?" Penelope stared at Michael.

"Carrington's secretary was in town this afternoon, questioning the solicitor's clerk about Winter House."

"Damn!" She did not apologize for the profanity. This was the worst news she had received in a long time, for Carrington could not still be researching her family. Thus he must be interested in the estate. Why had she allowed him to lull her suspicions? She had nearly fallen into his trap. Fury brought tears to her eyes—at herself for again allowing a man's sweet words to blind her, and at him for coveting something so insignificant when he already had so much.

"What's wrong, Penny?"

Michael's alarm recalled her to the bookroom. "He is continuing his uncle's tactics."

"Did Lord Avery start maligning us, too?"

"Worse. He spent his final eighteen months trying to force me to sell Winter House." She related her battles with their neighbor.

"Why did you never tell me?"

"He did not resort to underhanded tactics until after you had returned to school last fall. I would have discussed it when you got home, but I thought his death solved the problem."

"Does Terrence know about this?"

"I've no idea, but his sudden infatuation looks suspicious. The most straightforward plan would be to attach Alice's affections and then demand Winter House as her dowry. Have you seen him lately?"

"No. I did not wish to seek him out, but I am bound to run into him in town."

"I don't suppose he will reveal anything useful, but it is worth a try. Carrington seems to be continuing Lord Avery's scheme of forcing us to sell. That way he would not sully the Avery family tree with Wingrave blood."

"Why would he bother talking to Mr. Williams? His firm has never handled our business. I don't even think he works for Tallgrove."

"True, but that means nothing. Carrington must be asking questions elsewhere, too. He is bound to discover how vulnerable we are."

Michael sighed. "How bad is it?"

"Not good." She paced distractedly about the bookroom. "This latest mishap at the pottery will wipe out the entire quarter's profits. I can't understand how that clay became contaminated. The kiln near Plymtree buys from the same supplier, as does one at Whimple, but no one else has reported trouble."

"Could Mrs. Bender have made a mistake with the mixing and be afraid to admit it?"

"Hardly. She is as puzzled as I, and as frantic to find out what happened. Her share of the profits is all that keeps her family out of the workhouse. You know how tiny their farm is. It could never support seven children."

"What will they do?"

She resumed her seat. "If the pottery does not turn a profit this quarter, we will have to negotiate terms for delaying their rent."

Michael nodded. "We can hardly turn them off, but that will leave us in even worse shape."

"We will manage. On the positive side, the income from the ostriches is rising. Now that he is two, Sprite's plumes are as good as Ozzie's, and three of the new chicks are males, which bodes well for next year. Madame Dupres plans to open a second hat shop in London. She has already claimed most of the next plucking. Dealing directly allows us both to bypass the plumiers, reducing her costs while paying us more. It won't offset the pottery deficit, but it will help."

"We found hemlock in the meadow this morning. Several of the sheep are sick," reported Michael. "I set the men to uprooting the stuff, but this will delay the corn harvest by a couple of days."

"Let's hope it doesn't rain."

He nodded. "We must do something about the drainage near the bend in the stream. That field has gotten too boggy to grow crops."

"It has been a bad year all around," she said with a sigh. Her heart broke to see Michael so serious. He should enjoy his youth like other boys instead of filling every waking hour with farming and finance. "I will not allow the Averys to destroy us," she vowed now. "I should have expected them to continue Gareth's crusade." But she had thought that his obsession grew from his affair with Lucinda. Thus she had not taken more aggressive steps to protect Winter House.

"What about the mortgage?"

"I paid it last week."

"How? My stupidity had squandered the funds."

"Several volumes of Shakespeare. I pawned them instead of making an outright sale this time, hoping to redeem them with the pottery revenues."

Michael's head bowed in defeat. "I will never forgive myself for living on your meager possessions, Penny." The books were all hers.

"Enough, Michael. I live here, too. We will survive. But we can no longer postpone finding a dowry for Alice."

"You will let her wed Terrence?"

"No, but she must wed someone. Few men are willing to take a dowerless wife. Now, go secure the outbuildings for the night while I consider how to counter this latest threat."

Why did the Averys want Winter House so badly? The estate only included a three-hundred-year-old manor house in very poor condition, their own farm, and two tenant farms. All occupied marginal land. The estate could not even provide right-of-way to someplace else, for all the surrounding properties had excellent access.

But thinking was useless. She had trod this road too many times before. Their reasons were irrelevant. She had to find a new way to resist them. But the only plan she could devise was to discharge the mortgage. She snorted. Amassing each quarterly payment was hard enough. Where could she find the balance? *Long-lost relative . . . pot of gold . . . fairy godmother.* She was losing her mind.

* * *

Richard stared at the ostrich flock. They were gathered on the far side of the meadow, pecking at a haystack. An old barn offered shelter from storms, though the near wall had collapsed and half of the roof contained holes. The remains of a stone fireplace marked the site of an ancient cottage.

The male's neck seemed pinker than he remembered it, almost as if the beast were blushing. It was definitely brighter than the younger male's. One of the juveniles chased a sibling in a tight circle, squeaking happily. But when they drew too close to their father, he hissed a warning and both instantly froze.

Richard shook his head. If only his wards were so obedient. A chirp from the largest female sent all the youngsters trotting toward the barn. An innocent chick chattered for all the world as if he were complaining about having to pay for his siblings' stupidity. What strange creatures. And they belonged to Alice. If Terrence persisted in marrying the girl, he would have to take charge of the birds as well. Who ever heard of such a dowry?

A gust of wind lifted his hat and carried it over the gate.

"Damnation!" Lock himself had fashioned the curly-brimmed beaver. He should not have worn it today, for it was more suited to Hyde Park than to surveying a country estate. But now it was caught on a clump of sedge ten feet away. The birds ignored it, too intent on eating to bother with a passer-by.

He surveyed the meadow, torn between pique and prudence. They were obviously accustomed to people, for the haystack had not been there on his last visit. And the field was large—a hundred yards by fifty.

Dismounting, he led Jet out of sight and tethered him to the hedgerow. Then taking a deep breath, he slipped through the gate and tiptoed across the short-cropped grass.

Another errant gust picked up his hat and tumbled it into the corner, twenty feet to his right. He followed.

With a suddenness that left him stunned, an eddy whipped the hat into the air, swirling it toward the barn. A female with a cloth wrapped around her neck appeared out of nowhere, gleefully chasing it. But he spared no thought for her. The red-necked male raced, hissing, directly for him, its terrifying speed completing the journey in three seconds flat. He froze, feeling the blood drain from his head. The bird skidded to a stop a yard away, lowered its head to eye level, and spread its wings.

Out of the corner of his eye, he watched the bandaged female pick up his hat, then cock her head as if considering what she had found. Tossing it into the air, she caught it before it hit the ground, then gleefully did it again. He would have laughed if he had not been facing an angry bird two feet taller than himself. Two angry birds. The largest female had joined her mate, gurgling and displaying in turn. Except for the one playing with his hat, the others had followed their youngest siblings into the barn.

The male puffed out his throat to produce a roar much like the lion that had once graced the London Exchange.

"Easy, fellow," he murmured, slowly backing until the hedgerow stabbed his shoulders. All foliage had been stripped from the inner side.

Another roar assaulted his ears.

"I won't hurt you," he assured the bird, trying to make his voice sound soothing and calm.

He sidestepped toward the gate. The male followed suit. They sidled again, and again. And again. Just like a country dance. He chuckled.

But the ostrich was not amused. Its head suddenly butted his arm.

He recoiled.

The female pawed the ground, drawing his eyes to her feet. He flinched. Two toes, one with an alarmingly large claw. A weapon like that could inflict horrible damage. Her legs were more powerful than those of his horse—something he should have expected from an animal with such speed. But he hadn't thought about it. *Stupid!*

The male pecked at his shoulder, ripping his jacket and knocking him into the hedge. He managed to stay on his feet and suppress the oaths that sprang to his lips. Was the bird truly dangerous, or was it playing with him in the same way that the smaller female played with his hat? It wasn't a question he dared put to the test.

The ostriches gurgled and chirped, bobbing their heads as they discussed the intruder. The female's beak widened into an evil grin.

Idiot! he scolded himself. His imagination was running away with him. He would be better served by turning his mind to escape. He sidestepped once more. The male smashed its head into his side.

Damnation! The gate beckoned, barely fifteen feet away. It might as well have been in China. But perhaps if he remained motionless long enough, the ostrich would lose interest. Did birds suffer from boredom?

Ten minutes later, he decided that the question was irrelevant. Whatever the bird's intentions, it was dangerous. Even if it was playing, the result would be the same.

His growing mass of bruises, the gash on his arm, and a possible cracked rib contributed to that conclusion. So did the kitten. It had wandered around the corner of the barn, playfully stalking a windblown leaf. The creature would not make that mistake again. The younger male poked his head outside. The kitten bounded away, but two steps and a kick dispatched the animal, which the bird promptly consumed. Whole. Horror choked him as the bulge descended that grotesque neck.

Dear Lord! He had been incredibly stupid to enter the birds' domain. How could he hide that fact? His position in the family would be badly undermined if this fiasco became known. For eighteen years he had successfully hidden his fears and inadequacies, building a reputation as someone who could always be depended upon to solve any problem. If his facade of competence ever cracked, disillusion would cast every Avery into a morass of confusion.

Which turned his thoughts to Miss Wingrave's insolence. She had actually hinted that his help was sometimes unnecessary. How dare she criticize situations of which she knew nothing? Especially after denouncing him for doing the same thing. Granted he should have researched her stewardship before chastising her, but at least his was an honest mistake. How was he to know the details of raising exotic animals? Which returned his mind to his immediate problem—escaping so he could keep his predicament a secret.

He sidestepped, then bit off an oath as another blow landed on his shoulder. This was worse than sparring with Jackson, for he could make no move to defend himself. At the rate he was progressing, he would be unconscious long before he reached the gate. Any hint of motion invited renewed attack. His waist-coat gaped where buttons used to be. One sleeve of his jacket was in tatters. A long scratch marred his left boot.

"Ozzie!" Penelope's scolding voice exploded across the meadow. "What are you doing?"

Ozzie turned toward the gate, emitting a screech that made Richard jump. The bird glared at him and hissed.

"Don't move, my lord," she warned, striding across the meadow.

So much for keeping this a secret, he grumbled silently, torn between relief and chagrin. But she did not seem to think he was in imminent danger. She walked up to the bird who had caught his hat—which now lay in a mangled heap on the ground—and murmured soothing gurgles. The female promptly abandoned Richard to investigate.

"What are you doing?" he asked, evoking another hiss from Ozzie.

"Be quiet, my lord," she warned as she removed the bandage from the bird's neck. "She is mending nicely," she informed the female, holding up a jar for the bird's inspection. Smearing salve on the injury, she covered it with a new linen strip, then rubbed the mother's neck and scratched her head.

Finally she approached the corner where Richard still cowered. "Enough, Ozzie. You've had your fun. I think we should consider him harmless."

The ostrich hissed.

"He won't hurt you, Ozzie. There is nothing to fear." Draping her arm around the bird's neck, she nuzzled it with her head. "Walk very slowly toward the gate, my lord," she instructed in the same soothing tone. "Do not show fear."

He needed no further invitation. Drawing in a deep breath, he took a step forward.

"Easy, fellow," she murmured, tickling Ozzie's chest.

He sauntered toward the gate, Penelope and the bird matching him step for step.

"Aren't you ashamed of yourself?" she scolded the ostrich.

Ozzie gurgled.

"You should be. It is very bad form to corner a marquess. People have been transported for lesser offenses."

Ozzie emitted a sound that might have been a snort.

"It is true that he is odiously arrogant, but that is no excuse. I expect better manners from those under my care."

Ozzie hung his head to the ground and gently waved it back and forth.

"All right. I forgive you, and he will, too. Particularly as he had no business invading your home without an invitation. Such bad *ton,* but he will never repeat his offense. Slip through the gate, my lord. Then freeze."

Ozzie blinked those long lashes—which at close range proved to be narrow feathers—and stared until Richard's skin crawled. But he did exactly as ordered. With a last rub on Ozzie's neck, Penelope followed.

"Not a word, my lord, until we are well away," she said softly, though her eyes snapped with anger.

He followed her, leading Jet, until they reached Tallgrove land.

She glared. "You are a fool!"

He knew it but was not about to admit it aloud. Especially to someone who already thought badly of him. "My hat blew over the gate."

"Imbecile! What do you know of ostriches that makes you think you can wander into their compound with impunity?"

"They were nowhere near the gate."

"Would you have entered the pasture holding that bull Lord Avery bought last year?"

He reddened, abashed. "Of course no—"

"Of course not," she echoed. "You know from long experience how dangerous bulls can be. I doubt you would wander into a pigsty, either. So what in the name of heaven were you doing climbing into an enclosure containing twelve birds, at least six of which are bigger than you. Ozzie tops out at eight feet and weighs more than twenty stone." Her eyes raked his six-foot, twelve-stone frame with disdain.

He shivered, then exploded in fury over revealing his fear. "Yet knowing their ferocity, you endanger the neighborhood by keeping them. Or will you use them to blackmail Terrence into marrying your sister? Did you threaten to destroy Tallgrove unless he did your bidding?"

"I will attribute your hysteria to your harrowing experience," she snapped. "You have no business trespassing on my estate, and no business bothering my animals."

"I didn't think that—"

"You didn't think. Period," she interrupted his defense.

"They did not seem to bother you."

"They have known me since birth. Yet that does not make me entirely safe. It took more than an hour the other day before Ozzie would let me examine Fluff's neck. You are lucky to have escaped serious injury. The males of most species will attack, especially when they feel vulnerable."

"But these are birds," he objected again, ignoring his earlier impression of a close-knit family group.

"Fool! Have you never been attacked by a jay? Or a gull? Or a rooster? I still bear scars from a childhood encounter with just such a fearsome beast. Think about the difference in size between Ozzie and a rooster."

He flinched, tethering Jet and leaning gingerly against a tree, hoping his relaxed air would blunt her antagonism—though if he were honest, he needed the support. His head swam. Black spots teased his eyes. "You are right. I was a fool to enter unbidden. Thank you for rescuing me. Has anyone else fallen foul of them?"

"No. Few come across them, for they are surrounded by my own land except for the boundary with Tallgrove. I impressed on Terrence and Millicent early on that they were never to go near the ostriches. I would have mentioned it to you, but I thought you had more sense."

"They have never escaped?"

"Never. They could, of course, if they really wanted to. Ozzie is certainly capable of kicking the gate down. He put a hole in the barn when he was barely six months old and became irritated at being confined."

"Out there?"

"No, our current barn. That was when I moved them to the meadow. But as long as they are well fed, they seem content."

"What do they eat?"

"Anything that grows—or moves, for that matter." She rubbed Jet's nose. "They are not particular. Mostly they exist on plants. You saw the hedgerow. And the grass is shorn as short as the sheep leave it. But they also eat small animals and insects. I doubt there has ever been a rat or mouse that survived more than a day in their shelter."

"One of them ate a kitten just before you arrived."

She shrugged. "It is not the first time. Now, suppose you explain what you were doing on Winter House land in the first place." Her eyes again flashed as she abandoned Jet, the ostriches, and her softened tone in one fell swoop.

"Curiosity," he admitted. "I came to watch the ostriches."

"Curiosity?" she echoed skeptically. "And is it curiosity that made you poke your nose into my other business?"

"What—"

"Don't lie," she snarled. "I know you have been investigating our finances, our ancestry, and now the estate itself. Did you think that exerting your considerable charm in Exeter the other day would lull my suspicions and give you an advantage? Well, be warned. I spent years countering your uncle's plots. I won't succumb to yours, either."

"I have no wish to force you out."

"Pardon me if I don't believe that, my lord. You have yet to speak the entire truth on any subject. Nor has Terrence. He must have seen Alice as the means to coerce us into giving up the estate. It wouldn't be the first time it has been used as a dowry. But I won't even consider it."

"Terrence believes himself to be in love and knows nothing of his father's activities. I only found out about them a couple of days ago. I don't approve."

"Of what? My refusal to sell?"

"You are hysterical," he charged, leaving the support of the tree to loom over her.

She stood her ground. "Not at all. You so-called gentlemen are all alike, willing to say anything in the pursuit of your goals."

"Damnation, woman! Quit transferring your understandable pique at my uncle onto my shoulders. I have no idea what he was trying to accomplish, but I cannot condone any part of that plot. Nor can I rest until the estate has repaid every shilling of the damage he caused."

"What rot! Are you trying to buy me off so I won't sully your name by telling the world what a bounder Lord Avery was? Well, forget it! Get off Winter House property and stay off! And keep your ward away from my sister. Next time, I'll let Ozzie deal with you without interference."

She stalked toward home, leaving him to stare after her in puzzled thought.

He could no longer question her opposition to a match between Alice and Terrence. After everything Gareth had done, she would never believe that Terrence was ignorant of his father's affairs. She would move heaven and earth to prevent a match that might make Alice miserable. Her siblings were more important to her than her own life. Never had he seen such maternal passion.

Rubbing the shoulder that would be purpled with bruises by morning, he mounted Jet, uncomfortably aware that his thigh was nearly as bad. And his ribs, and his arm . . .

He would repay her, of course, though he had never dreamed she might see the money as a bribe. How was he to counter that? He did not care if she made Gareth's deeds public. The man deserved no better.

But he did care, he admitted as he repented pushing Jet to a trot and pulled him back to an amble. Why did he spend so much time rescuing relatives from censure if not to keep his family name clean? Disgusting as he found the idea, she had been right to challenge his motives. They surpassed both altruism and duty. If he did not take control, the inept Averys bungled even simple jobs. Inefficiency annoyed him even more than stupidity, so assuming their chores kept him sane.

Males will attack when they feel vulnerable. As he had just done. Miss Wingrave was dangerous, for she knew too much to his detriment. Never had anyone crawled far enough under his skin to discover his weaknesses—and certainly not far enough to induce ungentlemanly conduct. How could he keep her from exposing him to the world? She was neither dependent on him nor beholden to him. He felt like a gauche young fool, armorless and helpless.

Perhaps he could trade his silence about her mother's adultery for her promise to forget Gareth's plot and his own misbehavior. But he balked at stooping to blackmail. Besides, she would never accept his vow. She already considered him an unscrupulous schemer. *Exerting your considerable charm.* The strain of raising her siblings, running an estate, and countering

Lord Avery had subverted her reason. Why else would she accuse him of turning a nonexistent charm on her? Unless she, too, was attacking to cover vulnerability. She had lied once before when angry. But whatever the truth, she would never believe his word long enough to strike a deal. Nor could he propose one. He had already promised to forget that affair, and could not honorably renege.

The ride home was slow, interrupted several times as he paused to adjust his seat. Self-preservation alone should keep him away from Winter House in the future. These painful return journeys made his head swim. And he could not blame Miss Wingrave. Even her attack by the stream had been entirely his fault.

Reining in again when he reached the dower house—whose back door stood open—he dragged his aching body from the saddle, only to have fury overwhelm his pain. The inside was a shambles—paneling destroyed in room after room, pictures flung to the floors, mirrors smashed. What had happened? And when? No one had been in the building since the roof had been repaired a week earlier.

That feeling of doom was growing. It could not have been a robbery, for items of value remained in every room. Nor would the Wingraves have vandalized the place, even if they knew the full extent of Gareth's plots. What was going on?

Chapter Fourteen

~

"Good morning, Mr. Wingrave." Terrence remained polite even though Michael had bumped into him as he exited the King's Arms.

Michael blinked. "Pardon me, my lord."

"How are your sisters?"

"They are well."

He noted the repressive response. Michael must be another who did not approve of his betrothal. Unexpectedly irked, he was trying to formulate a set-down that would not worsen his own position when Michael turned the subject.

"How is your new steward working out?"

How like Carrington to remain silent about estate matters, Terrence fumed, ignoring the voice that chastised him for becoming so enmeshed in his courtship that he saw little else. Had Scott resigned or had Carrington replaced him? He was tired of being treated like an ignorant child. "One steward is much like another."

Michael frowned in disgust. "Did you not know that Scott was arrested for theft?"

"No." He sighed. "Carrington tells me nothing. What happened?"

Michael listed Scott's crimes. "The new steward is Jeb Carson."

"One of the tenants?"

"A well-informed tenant and able manager. How do you expect to run your estate if you know nothing about it?" Michael's voice had taken on a distinct sneer.

"Unlike you, I need not concern myself," he retorted haughtily. "That is the function of a steward."

"And how do you know if the steward is competent? Or honest?"

His arrogance evaporated under that pitying stare.

Michael continued relentlessly. "Scott feathered his nest for years. Was your father ignorant, or did he not care?"

"He can't have known," Terrence conceded with a sigh. "He was a regular pinchpenny who once had a footman transported for appropriating half a dozen candle stubs."

"Do you wish to spend your life at the mercy of your steward?"

"Of course not, but there is plenty of time to learn. Carrington will tell me what I need to know in his own time. He is not the sort to relinquish control until he has to—but that will be years."

Michael hesitated, finally shrugging. "Come along." He led the way into the inn, taking a seat in a vacant corner of the taproom and ordering ale. "If you are old enough to consider marriage, then you are old enough to conduct your business affairs in an orderly fashion."

"You don't approve of my suit."

"No, I don't," agreed Michael. "I cannot like tying Alice to a man who is ripe for plucking by every sharp in town. You wouldn't hold onto your fortune long enough to provide for her. But I have no say in the matter. All I can do is pray that you are less heedless than you seem."

"I am," he vowed. "But learning about estate management is difficult. Such subjects are not taught at Oxford."

"Of course not," scoffed Michael. "God forfend that a gentleman's education impart any useful information. I am almost glad that we cannot afford the university. I will take over Winter House when I finish at Eton."

"But you will be only seventeen!" he objected.

"So? Penelope took over at that age and managed it much better than our father. She has trained me for years—and will be available to offer advice if I need it."

Terrence shook his head, feeling untutored and naïve despite his greater age. "So she will oppose any match if I do not assume control of Tallgrove."

"Hardly. You have the money to hire a good steward. Leave Alice out of this discussion. You should learn about your inheritance for your own benefit. Only a fool leaves his interests in the unguarded hands of others."

"You have made your point, but we already agreed that school won't teach me anything. Carrington will get around to it eventually."

"Will he? Or is he another who will leave everything to his steward?"

"He has a reputation of being a hard-hearted man who attends personally to every detail. But I suspect that he will postpone any instruction, for he is another who disapproves of my betrothal."

"We are leaving Alice out of this if you recall. Estate management is not something that can be learned in a two-hour tutorial the day his guardianship ends. By then you will be so used to having him in charge that you may well leave him there. You had best train yourself. Penelope taught me everything I know, starting when I could barely talk. That won't work for you, of course, but you might begin by asking Carrington how to supervise your steward. Encourage him to explain Scott's crimes. Then talk to Carson. He will gladly teach you about Tallgrove. Get to know your tenants so they will tell you about any problems they encounter. Read books explaining the latest agricultural discoveries. Eventually you will know enough to judge your employees and discuss estate business without appearing foolish."

"It sounds daunting. If only my father had taught me more."

"How could he when he was so ignorant himself?"

"Perhaps Carrington will agree," he said hopefully. "I have been trying to persuade him to let me stay here instead of returning to the university next term. I cannot face several months of separation from Alice."

"I will be blunt, Lord Avery," said Michael, reverting to flinty coldness. "You will be better served by finishing your education—both in and out of school—and setting your house in order. Penny wants Allie to be happy, but she is convinced that no one of your tender years can provide the security and support Alice needs. She is looking for maturity and reliability, not just infatuation, and will never approve marriage to someone with no experience of the world or how to maintain his position in it."

"Then we must elope."

Michael's fist landed on the table loudly enough to draw the attention of a group of men across the taproom. "Is that the reaction of a mature, responsible gentleman? Do you honestly think Allie would enjoy life as a social pariah? Or do you care nothing for her feelings? You sound like a spoiled, arrogant child who insists on having his own way even at the expense of those he professes to love. Elopement is not acceptable in the worlds in which either of us lives. Guilt would place a barrier between Alice and her family, though we would never turn against her. But society would ostracize her, especially such local high-sticklers as Lady Alderleigh and Lady Harbrough. Even if you could surmount that problem, her life would be far from easy. Your mother has hated my family for as long as I can remember. She would not accept any connection with equanimity, but an elopement would elicit perpetual disdain. How can you subject someone you love to that kind of antagonism?"

He stared at the tabletop for some time, finally meeting Michael's gaze. "You are right. I had not considered the consequences. But I never seriously contemplated eloping, either. Are you saying that marriage is a hopeless dream?"

"At the moment," he answered brutally. "But not forever. All other considerations aside, by the time Alice comes of age, neither of you will need permission, but I don't think it will come to that. Frankly, I believe you have the potential to be a good husband and an enlightened landowner. But you are not ready for either role at this point in your life. Your most pressing tasks are to repair the deficiencies in your education and address the problems of your estate, including what to do about your mother. Once your life is in order, you will have time to consider the future. If Alice truly loves you—and if you truly love her—the wait will harm neither of you."

Terrence cringed at the words, though every one was true. At fifteen, Michael was a hard-nosed pragmatist who understood life's realities better than he did. It was a sobering thought, but it spawned an idea that might convince both Penelope and Carrington. "You are right," he admitted finally. "How did you become so knowing?"

"Living on the edge of poverty provides an incentive to improve one's situation. And Penelope is an excellent teacher.

Never forget that Alice has shared most of my education. She knows a great deal about estate management."

"Would she think less of me if I asked her to teach me?"

"Not if she loves you."

"Thank you."

He bade his future brother-in-law farewell, frowning as he rode back to Tallgrove and thrusting aside his lingering pique, for the message was too important to waste energy resenting the messenger. He owed a lot to young Michael.

Embarrassment heated his cheeks. Alice had asked several pointed questions about Tallgrove that he had turned aside with words that implied such topics were of little interest to a female. She must now consider him both arrogant and disdainful, a judgment too close to the truth to be comfortable. He would have to abandon such poses, at least with her. She was too intelligent to accept being treated like a widgeon, especially by one who professed to love her.

Richard sat at his desk, but he was not working. Instead he stared into space, wishing he belonged to a family of intelligent, competent people. He was so tired of cleaning up everyone else's messes. New problems seemed to crop up every day.

Millicent was a case in point. She had been moping for nearly a week, almost as if she had been jilted. Was it because his watchers prevented her from keeping assignations, or had Darksmith abandoned her? He suspected the latter. If his precautions were thwarting her, she would be angry rather than blue-deviled. And Darksmith must know that he was suspicious. He made a mental note to find out whether the man was still registered at the King's Arms.

But he was not about to relax his vigilance. Perhaps they were feigning a separation. Millicent's current mood could just as easily be impatience. And he could not forget that very odd encounter in the library. She had definitely been up to mischief.

Then there was that strange burglary in town last night. Someone had ransacked the solicitor's office, taking a small amount of cash and a box of documents relating to Tallgrove Manor. The theft made no sense, for the papers were old—Gareth had used the same Exeter solicitor who had served his father. The papers were not even unique, being local copies of ones filed elsewhere.

But his sense of trouble continued to grow. There were too many oddities at Tallgrove—Scott's blatant thievery, Terrence's involvement with Alice, Millicent's liaison, Gareth's plots, Mathilda's antagonism, vandalism, burglary . . . Were any of them related? Maybe Scott had an accomplice who was seeking revenge. Darksmith perhaps? That might explain his reluctance to compromise Millicent. But he had arrived before Scott's arrest.

His head ached. He disliked mysteries, especially when they smelled of danger.

Cawdry appeared in the doorway, a sheaf of papers in his hand. "The report on Winter House, my lord."

"Thank you. Anything more on the missing Tallgrove file?"

"No, and it seems a pointless theft. I examined it last week. The firm has not worked for the estate since it passed into Avery hands."

"Gareth's grandfather acquired it as part of his wife's dowry, I believe."

"No, he inherited it from the third Marquess of Carrington. It was originally the second marchioness's dowry. The burglary is peculiar, though. No one had looked at those records in well over a century until Lord Avery asked to see them eighteen months ago."

Richard frowned. Gareth must have checked that file just before he initiated his plot against Winter House. "Thank you, Cawdry. Do you know if Darksmith is still in the area?"

"He caught the stage to Exeter five days ago. He is well-known at the Golden Stag, though no one knows his direction, and he did not stop there on his return. But Jeremy Jacobson—the squire's son—claims to have spotted him in Plymtree yesterday."

"Do any heiresses live near there?"

"I do not know."

"Find out. If he is stalking someone else, we can forget about him once we warn the girl's family."

"Very well, my lord."

Bidding his secretary farewell, he picked up the Winter House report.

In 1327, Baron Chesterton received Tallgrove Manor from the crown along with his title. Fire destroyed the fortified house in 1498, but the seventh baron rebuilt on the same site. In 1636, the thirteenth lord abandoned the house to his mother and future dowagers, building the larger, more formal manor that served Tallgrove today. Ten years later, he made the mistake of backing Charles in his fight against Parliament and was killed at Naseby. His wife and daughter fled to her parents' home to escape retribution. Cromwell awarded Tallgrove to one of his own supporters.

He frowned, turning the page. This was supposed to be a report on Winter House. The second page seemed even less to the point, being the history of his own family. He skimmed rapidly down the sheet.

When Charles II assumed the throne after Cromwell's death, he granted the title Marquess of Carrington to one of his staunchest allies. Carrington's heir assumed his father's old title of the Earl of Winston. In 1680 Winston married the only child of the ailing owner of Tallgrove Manor, receiving the estate as part of the girl's dowry. Her father moved into the dower house. Five years later Winston needed to house a harridan aunt. Rather than endure her megrims, he built her a residence out of sight of the manor. His father-in-law died the following year, leaving the dower house vacant.

Not long after Winston acceded to the marquessate and moved to Carrington Castle, his fortunes reversed. He was the first of the Averys to exhibit the family characteristics of weak will and financial incompetence. To cover bad investments, he sold the Tallgrove dower house and three small tenant farms to a wealthy merchant, deciding that his aunt's house would make a better dower house if one was ever needed.

He smiled. That explained why Lady Avery thought that the Wingraves were connected with trade. Before her marriage she had researched the Avery family history, which dated back to the Conqueror. She would know that the second marquess had sold Winter House to merchants and would have extrapolated the rest.

The third Lord Carrington was no more canny than his father, but he was proud of his youngest son—who won a viscountcy in 1746—so he willed Tallgrove to the boy.

As for the lost slice of the estate, the merchant did not enjoy his new acquisition. Shortly after the purchase, he died. His son lacked both business acumen and character, losing the property in a card game to Jake Winterbottom, youngest son of a viscount. It was he who named it Winter House. But despite three marriages, he produced no heir, eventually bequeathing the estate to his niece Lucinda, who used it as a dowry when she married Walter Wingrave.

Richard frowned. While the history was interesting, it did not answer the question of why Gareth had wanted Winter House so badly that he had tried to force the Wingraves out. While it was true that it had once been part of his own estate, it had been sold long before Tallgrove came into his family. So why?

He pulled out Gareth's cryptic notes and again read them. But there was no hint. Perhaps his obsession really had grown from his love for Lucinda. Putting the papers away, he stared sightlessly out the window, frustrated beyond belief. He hated mysteries. He hated dishonor. And he hated stupidity.

Which diverted his thoughts to his latest encounter with Miss Wingrave. He had displayed both dishonor and stupidity, precipitating an end to their short-lived truce that he could only regret. He had enjoyed her companionship in Exeter. It wasn't often that he found someone who shared his enthusiasms.

He cringed at his own unthinking arrogance. His charges had been blatantly absurd, arising from terror over Ozzie and a stubborn refusal to accept culpability. Who could blame her for ringing a peal over his head?

Penelope was also ruing her latest encounter with Lord Carrington, and not just because he posed a danger to Winter House. She should not have erupted so harshly. *Fool . . . stupidity . . . stay off.* Her cheeks burned. No matter how serious his transgressions, her castigation had fueled his understandable anger. She should have been more diplomatic about pointing out his faults, but she had been so terrified to find him under attack and so relieved that he was not seriously injured that she had lost control of her temper.

But relief had not been the only cause. She exchanged greetings with Mrs. Peccles, left the newly picked vegetables in the kitchen, then headed for the barn. Carrington's persistent prying into Winter House affairs had hurt deeply. The truce had been his idea. Now she knew it was a ploy. He had turned on his charm in Exeter, treating her with respect and eliciting her help until she had voiced her most secret fantasies. Then he had betrayed her by revealing that nothing had changed. Fury at her own gullibility had fueled her rage. She could not trust him, but neither could she excuse her own wretched tongue.

And so she owed him an apology. Again. She sighed as she scattered corn for the hens. How could one man succeed in oversetting her control so often? She had been trapped in a maelstrom of emotion since the moment they had met.

Dusk was gathering when Michael found a euphoric Penelope in the bookroom. "What happened?"

"We got a new customer for the pottery." Her eyes sparkled. "Look at this! It will nearly double our production."

"Wonderful! But will that not take too much of your time?"

"We will need two additional workers, but the pottery will show a solid profit at last. Perhaps you will be able to go to university after all."

"First we must redeem your Shakespeare. And set aside Allie's dowry. There will be time later to discuss the university. I still have to finish Eton," he reminded her, refusing to get his hopes up.

Despite his words to Terrence, he longed for the freedom to choose his course for himself. School was where gentlemen acquired the friends and contacts that would last them a lifetime. His breeding was good enough to move into society, but he lacked both money and introductions. Yet attending Oxford would force Penelope to carry the entire load for another four years. It wasn't fair. She had already sacrificed too much for him.

He returned his mind to business. Ever since meeting Terrence, he had been nagged by the certainty that he could improve his finances. When the usual thinking produced no new ideas, he let his mind wander into the realm of fantasy. But one possibility did not seem so fantastic. And so, with Penelope's encouragement, he had spent the afternoon poking about the oldest of the attics. They had never examined this particular room, and he hoped to find something they could sell. In addition to Alice's dowry, they needed a nest egg to protect against fluctuations in prices, inclement weather, and bad luck. The Wingraves had lived on the edge long enough.

"True," she agreed, pulling his attention back to the book-room. "What is that?" She pointed to his hand.

"I have no idea but hoped you might know. I moved some other things into the guest room."

"What?"

"A trunk full of fabric that appears to be in good condition; several vases, though I have no way of knowing if they are quality or not; a suit of armor—"

"Heavens! I had no idea we had one. That will certainly be worth something if it is in good condition. The latest rage is to display armor, but many people don't own any. When I was pawning Shakespeare, Mr. Jenkins claimed that the price of medieval armor was rising rapidly."

"That sounds encouraging. And there are several pieces of china, though little of it matches."

"I will look at it later. For now, let's see what you have here."

"It was in a trunk, but I've never seen anything like it."

The apparatus consisted of two poles, each three feet long. The copper sheath protruding beyond the end of one allowed them to be joined into a single rod. A wooden wheel five inches in diameter was attached near the tip of the other. Protruding from one side of its rim were five pegs.

"Most peculiar," she agreed. "You say it was in a trunk?"

"Tucked into the bottom under a stack of old clothes. The moths had been in there, by the way."

"They must be old indeed if the camphor balls have gone. Was there any indication of its age?"

"None. The clothes were so tattered I could not even discern their original form. And the trunk itself showed signs of moisture damage. It had been pushed well back into a corner."

"Was the roof leaking?"

"Not that I could tell. The damage did not look fresh. What should I do with this?"

She shrugged. "Set it in the guest room. I cannot throw it out until I know what it is. It may have some value. Mr. Jenkins has some rather quaint tools on display. If we can divine a purpose for this thing, perhaps he will buy it."

Chapter Fifteen

~

Richard stepped out of the carriage, then turned to assist Millicent.

"Thank you for escorting us to the assembly," she murmured, dimpling prettily. She was making a visible effort to behave this evening.

"You are welcome, but remember that the end of deep mourning does not mean that you can throw propriety to the winds," Richard reminded her. "You will dance only the more sedate sets and will refer to your father with respect and to your mother with sympathy."

He was already having second thoughts about allowing his wards to attend. Millicent in particular had no business displaying her disreputable manners to the world. And yet he found excuses to condone this treat—it was a last fling before addressing the serious business of harvest and study; they deserved an outing after three months of mourning; it was a necessary carrot to ensure compliance to his wishes. He ignored the fact that he was looking forward to the evening on his own account. Attending balls had never been a favorite activity, especially country assemblies.

Aunt Mathilda had gone into strong hysterics over the dishonor to Gareth's memory, raging at length over his callousness and his unsuitability to act as her children's guardian. She had even accused him of promoting liaisons between Terrence and Alice and between Millicent and Darksmith.

Millicent had greeted the news that she would soon attend Miss Atherton's Academy for Young Ladies with a lack of enthusiasm that had only hardened his resolve to see her safely ensconced in that institution. And she had again aroused his suspicions. Not until after he had agreed to attend the assembly had she accepted the idea of school. Was she in touch with Darksmith?

It was possible. The man had arrived in Plymtree three days before, but was paying no attention to the locals. Instead he had established a pattern of sleeping all morning before disappearing for the rest of the day and most of the night. No one had seen him near Tallgrove, but Plymtree was only ten miles away.

Yet Millicent's agreement was not Richard's only surprise. Terrence had found him in the library shortly after luncheon. Instead of pestering him over Alice, the boy had asked detailed questions about Scott's defalcations and the present condition of the estate. He had seemed genuinely interested, but that was hard to believe. This was the same young man who had poutingly refused to discuss anything until Richard agreed to his betrothal. The changed attitude could only be a ploy to soften his antagonism.

But that thought reminded him of the apology he still owed Miss Wingrave, and he finally admitted that he looked forward to delivering it. Perhaps he would even dance with her, though his bruises throbbed at the very thought. He had refused to call in a doctor, not wanting to admit his idiocy. Nothing could be done for the ribs except wrapping anyway.

But her flashing blue eyes as she delivered that well-deserved set-down disturbed him even more than his injuries. The termagant had looked delightfully enchanting as she raked him over the coals, her auburn hair flaming in the sunlight. This quivering expectation when he thought of seeing her again was more than the lust that still assaulted him every time she drew near. He shivered.

Her disrespect for his title and position never ceased to annoy him, yet that fact irritated him even further. He had complained repeatedly about the fawning maidens and toadying gentlemen who forever tried to catch his eye, his support, or his hand in marriage. Their inability to see past his title and wealth had driven him from his mother's latest party. So why was he complaining about the one person who judged him solely on his own actions? Because she saw too far beyond his title and wealth, he admitted grimly. She exposed his flaws and held them up to his face, accompanied by impossible challenges.

He sent his wards inside while he spoke to the coachman, but lost his train of thought when he spotted Miss Wingrave similarly engaged. She was beautiful. For the first time since they had met, she was dressed in a gown that fit. Sapphire silk that matched her eyes clung as she moved, alternately hiding and revealing her legs, teasing his senses into choking desire. Though demure for London, her neckline drew attention to her generous bosom, her glowing skin set off by a single strand of pearls. Tendrils of hair escaped a careless knot, daring his fingers to touch their fire. Abandoning his coachman without a word, he crossed the yard to her side.

Penelope settled into the seat of their ancient carriage and turned a smiling face to her siblings. "It has been long since I last attended an assembly, but it is an excellent way to wind up your visit, Michael. I only wish you could get home more often."

"In time." The end of summer had been bittersweet since he started formal schooling. Aside from being separated from his family, he missed the camaraderie of the harvest.

They rode in companionable silence for some time before drawing up before the King's Arms. "Mind your manners," Penelope reminded the others as they climbed down from the carriage. Sending them ahead, she exchanged a few words with Josh, their coachman for the night.

"Good evening, Miss Wingrave."

She looked up, surprised to find Lord Carrington barely two feet away. "I suppose this means Terrence is here."

"Did you expect him to stay home?"

"The Averys have never stooped to attending public assemblies," she said with asperity, her tone condemning such arrogance. "But Alice hoped he would come."

"And so he did." Richard tried to make his voice more congenial. "He will return to Oxford next week. Dancing tonight will not hurt them."

"I suppose not."

"I owe you an apology for castigating you yesterday. And for trespassing. I meant no harm by it and spoke the truth about my motives. It was only curiosity. Ostriches are strange creatures and make fascinating watching." He offered his arm to escort her inside.

"They do at that," she agreed. He flinched when she mis-stepped in the cobbled yard and bumped his shoulder. "It would seem that Ozzie punished you quite thoroughly for doing more than look. I trust nothing is broken."

"Not that I know of, but I wish you had not added insult to injury by ripping me up."

"That was a deliberate attempt to save you further embarrassment."

"What?" Too late he noted the twinkle in her eyes.

"Admit it. By the time you escaped, your knees were shaking so badly you could hardly stand, your face was whiter than your cravat, and you were in imminent danger of swooning. If I had not stimulated your anger, you would have collapsed at my feet. But perhaps I erred. So humbling an experience might have done you some good."

He burst into laughter. "Doing it too brown, Miss Wingrave. Your own face was every bit as white, and I venture your knees were just as unsteady. Shall I claim to have saved you from mortification?"

"How ungentlemanly to call my bluff," she complained. "But you are right. I was too awash in guilt and relief to think clearly. Please pardon my unwarranted diatribe."

"Now you go too far. I acted with unbelievable stupidity and am lucky to have escaped with only a few bruises. Let us forgive ourselves and each other, and put the incident behind us."

"Very well."

"Truce?"

She smiled. "Truce."

A vase of flowers sat on a table near the entrance to the meeting room and another adorned the pianoforte inside, but that was the extent of the decorations. Old Ben tuned his violin, finally nodding his satisfaction to the other violinist and a flutist. Miss Fanshawe poised her fingers above the keyboard.

Penelope greeted friends as she crossed the room. Although she had entered with Carrington, it had appeared the barest coincidence. Everyone knew the Averys hated the Wingraves. Many were intrigued that the Averys were even attending, though none speculated about it to her.

Terrence claimed Alice's hand for the first set. Michael had already wandered off to speak to some friends, so Penelope joined her fellow spinsters.

Richard handed Millicent to an elderly solicitor for the opening set of country dances, then watched Terrence lead out a petite young lady. The way their gazes locked made her identity obvious—and stirred something that might have been envy in his breast.

Alice Wingrave looked nothing like her half sister. She was petite, with dark hair arranged simply around a heart-shaped face, her slender figure encased in a demure gown. He could see how she had trapped Terrence, for she radiated sweetness. And her behavior was impeccable. Not once during the dance did she lean too close or allow Terrence to retain her hand even a moment too long. When the figures paired her with other partners, she looked into their eyes and focused all of her attention on them. It was not the conduct of a typical fortune hunter. She was either innocent or extremely clever.

Once the dance concluded, she turned to rejoin Penelope, but Terrence murmured something close to her ear and headed for the door that led to the garden. That would not do, decided Richard, moving to cut them off.

"Are you going to introduce me?" he asked.

Terrence jumped. "I did not know that you remained strangers." His eyes condemned his guardian for judging the girl without even meeting her. "Lord Carrington, may I present Miss Alice Wingrave. Alice, my guardian."

"My lord." She curtsied prettily.

"Perhaps you can get the lady some lemonade," suggested Richard. Terrence grimaced, but complied.

"I oppose his infatuation," he stated baldly, seeing no point in skirting the issue.

"I can understand your objections. He is still very young, though that does not invalidate his feelings."

He frowned at the composed answer.

"I will be frank, sir," she continued. "I love Terry with all my heart, but I do not wish to trap him in an alliance that he may come to despise. He claims to love me in the same way, and I believe him. But Penny has suggested that he finish school before discussing the future. I doubt that his affections will undergo any change in the next months, but if you believe it possible, then by all means postpone a decision until next summer. If you are right, it will save him from making a mistake. But if you are wrong, the separation can do nought but bring us closer together."

"You are either very clever or unusually candid," he responded.

She bristled, then sighed. "I cannot blame you for being suspicious," she admitted with a shake of her head. "A marquess must spend considerable time warding off young ladies seeking his title. Send Terry away for a while. Perhaps by the time he returns, you will have learned that I care nothing for his position. I want only him."

"Does he know that those crazy birds belong to you?" he asked suddenly.

She laughed. "Yes. I have been helping them get acquainted, though please don't tell Penny. She wants to keep outsiders away for fear of trouble. But though I have never allowed Terry into the meadow, Ozzie actually allowed him to scratch his head yesterday."

He shivered, recalling his own encounter with Ozzie. Terrence returned with lemonade. When the musicians began another tune, Richard allowed the boy to lead Alice into the nearest set.

"Good evening, Miss Wingrave."

Penelope turned in astonishment. Mr. Darksmith stood at her side, his voice conveying the warmth of a long-lost friend. "Good evening, sir. I heard that you had left us."

"A necessary excursion, but my business here is not yet concluded. You are looking remarkably pretty tonight," he continued, examining her lush figure. His expression radiated blatant infatuation, but his eyes remained calculating.

She distrusted that stare. She had not forgotten his improper attentions to Millicent, and he had never before spared her a second glance. Why should he now treat her as the diamond she was not? "What exactly is your business, sir? I do not believe I have heard."

"A pesky problem of provenance pertaining to my Yorkshire

estate. A lady like yourself could never be interested in such dry stuff. Dance this set with me, for I must have the most beautiful girl in the room on my arm. All will envy me your escort."

"You flatter me, sir," she protested but allowed him to lead her onto the floor.

What game was he playing? She had no fortune that he could attach. Even her home belonged to her brother. She was not interested in setting up as his mistress—as anyone could tell him—so he had nothing to gain by pursuing her. Yet his attentions increased as the dance progressed. He praised her eyes, her hair, her lips, and every other part that could be mentioned in polite company. His hand released hers reluctantly as they moved through the figures, its pressure always greater than custom approved. His eyes remained focused on her even when he executed steps with others. It was no wonder that an impressionable girl like Millicent had fallen under his spell. At first glance he appeared to be every maiden's dream. But she detected falsehood behind his flattery. His smile rarely extended to his eyes. The tenseness never left his shoulders. His forehead often twitched as he studied her reaction to his flummery. What was his purpose? And why had he transferred his attentions from Millicent to herself?

The questions were the same, she decided as she smiled guilelessly into his penetrating eyes. By his own admission, his business was incomplete. But that business must be quite different than she had supposed. Carrington was astute. Darksmith had abandoned Millicent, so he could not have wanted marriage. Nor could he expect Carrington to buy him off. He was no longer staying at the King's Arms, yet he lingered in the area. And now he approached her. She did not believe his purpose had changed, but what could both Millicent Avery and Penelope Wingrave provide?

"Walk with me in the garden, my dear Miss Wingrave," he suggested when the final note sounded.

"I cannot, sir, for I am chaperoning my brother and sister tonight. But I thank you for a most interesting dance." She slipped away before he could say more.

But she did not get far. Mrs. Jacobson, the squire's wife, hailed her. Suppressing a sigh—the woman was always looking for new ears into which she could pour her interminable complaints—she allowed her gaze to wander over the gathering. Michael was chatting with Terrence; Alice laughed at something Elizabeth Jacobson had said, then responded with a comment that sent the other girl into uncontrolled giggles; Lord Carrington was deep in conversation with Sir Francis; and Millicent—

She suppressed a frown. Millicent had approached Darksmith and was engaged in an intense exchange of words. A moment later, the girl grabbed his arm and tugged him toward the garden door. He resisted at first, then shrugged lightly and gave in, apparently deciding to avoid a public scene.

Penelope's glance shifted to Carrington. He had noted the exchange but was on the far side of the dance floor with no hope of reaching the door before his ward escaped. His eyes darkened in frustration. Bidding a firm farewell to Mrs. Jacobson, she headed for the exit.

Millicent was murmuring into Darksmith's ear as she approached. "—Only hope is to elope."

Stifling a grimace, she set her face to an expression of relief. "There you are, Miss Avery. I have searched everywhere since Lord Carrington asked me to find you. It is all of two sets since we spoke, so you had best hurry." Her words had a ring of truth, for the girl had been in the retiring room two sets earlier, not returning until midway through the previous dance. "You will excuse us, I am sure," she addressed Darksmith.

"Of course. Ladies." He bowed with great elegance and departed.

The look in his eye boded ill. Unless her reading was out, he had been relieved to be spared Millicent's importuning and gratified that she herself was jealous enough to separate him from another woman. Odious toad! What game was he playing?

Her breathlessness returned the moment they reached Carrington's side. So the feeling could not be ascribed to surprise. She had nearly collapsed when he had approached her in the yard. Could it be his looks? A black velvet jacket set off his broad shoulders, dove-gray pantaloons emphasized a trim waist and muscular thighs, while the embroidered white waistcoat and snowy linen sparked silver highlights in his gray eyes. Candlelight glinted in his black hair. Ignoring her traitorous body, she set her face to composure.

* * *

Richard hurriedly bade Sir Francis farewell when Millicent accosted Darksmith, though he knew he had no chance of reaching the pair before they gained the garden. But when Miss Wingrave detached Millicent and hurried the girl in his direction, relief and surprise were the least of his emotions. He had watched her dancing with Darksmith, irritated at the man's blatant flirtation, and irritated at himself for being irritated. She was turning him inside out and the world along with him. But his temper had cooled when she turned her back on the blackguard. Her eyes clearly reflected distrust. He did not consider how he could read her expression across fifty feet of a dimly lit room.

"I apologize that it took so long to find Miss Avery," she said when they reached his side. "Forgive me for being sidetracked by this last set." She winked.

He nearly gasped, both at her impudence and at the way he could read her mind. She must have told Millicent that he had sent for her at least two sets ago. "That is quite all right, Miss Wingrave. I appreciate your trouble." She slipped away, and he turned his attention to his ward. "It is important that you remain at my side between sets."

"This is hardly a London ball," she snapped, obviously irritated at having her tête-à-tête interrupted.

"Manners are expected at all times, young lady," he stated coldly. "You are still in mourning. Several people have wished to express their condolences but were unable to do so because you were not where you belonged."

"You know nothing of the country if you believe they were shocked," she retorted. "We are very informal here. Many have spoken to me, including some that had previously talked with you. None expressed concern that I was not by your side."

He hardened his expression even as he kept his lips in a pleasant smile to minimize the contretemps in the eyes of the other guests. "Country or city makes no difference. A sixteen-year-old girl does not wander about a ballroom unescorted. Nor does she request a dance as you just did of Mr. Darksmith. Such forward behavior will give any gentleman a disgust of you. And do not think to confine the tale to Devon. This may only be a country assembly, but there are four men here that I have met in London. Do you think they will remain silent about your indiscretions when they return to town? What will they say when you make your bows to the polite world? I have seen girls ruined for less."

She shuddered, and he could almost hear her silent wail of despair. He could not have contrived a more effective way to end her liaison if he had wracked his brain for weeks. Darksmith's obvious reluctance to accompany her must now seem to be disdain for her importuning. Her smile could not mask the tears shimmering in her eyes.

"Do you mean that I am now ruined?"

"Not necessarily. A single *faux pas* at age sixteen will be forgiven if your behavior otherwise remains exemplary. But you will have to be careful. Your training is not good, and you cannot afford another mistake."

"I will remain by your side for the rest of the evening, my lord." She grimaced. "And I will not argue again about school. There is nothing for me here any longer." She blinked away the tears that trembled in her eyes.

"Very wise."

By the time the set ended, she had regained her composure and accepted a dance with Sir Francis. Standing alone in a corner gave him an opportunity to watch Darksmith. What was the man doing? Those fawning attentions toward Miss Wingrave had been odd enough—though he could certainly understand an attraction in that direction—but Darksmith had earlier exchanged words with Michael that had left the older man glowering. Now he was dumping the butter boat on Alice while he surreptitiously inched her toward the door. Alice seemed just as immune to flattery as Penelope had been, but she was too green to extricate herself without appearing rude.

Richard bristled. Whatever he thought of Alice, he did not want to see anyone forced outside with so suspicious a character. Penelope was too far away to help, and with her back turned to the doorway, she likely did not know the danger her sister faced. He headed for the garden himself. It was the least he could do after she had prevented Millicent from creating a scandal.

Alice was balking at leaving, her face set in that determined expression he had often seen on her sister. For the first time they appeared related. Just then the squire staggered across his path, having clearly imbibed liberally of the punch. Richard swore under his breath, for he now had no chance to reach Alice's side in time.

But a moment later he relaxed. Alice looked at Terrence, a message passing between them that made Richard's heart pause in envy. In a trice Terrence appeared at Darksmith's side, smoothly extricated Alice, and led her to Jeremy Jacobson, who escorted her into the nearest set.

Darksmith's face twisted into a scowl. Without another word, he left the assembly.

"It is the oddest thing," said Alice to Penelope after her dance with Jeremy. "Mr. Darksmith suddenly seems to believe that I am the most beautiful girl in the world. What has gotten into the man?"

"I can't imagine, not that I would disagree with the sentiment. But he cannot be sincere, for he said the same thing to me not an hour ago. I doubt that he is acquainted with either truth or honor, but neither can I think what his purpose might be. Promise me that you will be especially careful until he leaves the area. If he wishes to seduce one of us, I do not wish to risk him catching you when there is no help at hand."

"What an awful thought. And entirely possible. He tried to force me into the garden just now. Terry came to my rescue, thank God."

"I saw. He handled it quite well."

Alice frowned. "It is odd, but I could swear that Lord Carrington was also coming to help. He was headed our way, but he was too distant to reach us before Terry arrived."

"I would not call it odd," mused Penelope. "Despite our differences, he seems a man of honor." Was he merely returning a favor? Something shifted in her chest at the idea that he might care about her family.

"May Terry call tomorrow? He will soon leave for school, and I wish to see him as much as possible before he goes."

"Very well." The matter-of-fact way in which he had extricated Alice belied her impression that he was an irresponsible youth. Such a one would have created a scene that at best would have embarrassed all parties. Instead, almost no one realized that anything untoward had happened.

"May I escort Alice to the refreshment room?" asked Terrence, appearing at her side in response to another of those speaking glances.

She watched them go, musing on the tie that bound them. In her heart she knew that time would not separate those two. Perhaps Terrence was the exception to the rule that men needed several years of sowing wild oats before they were ready to settle down.

"May I have the next dance, Miss Wingrave?" asked a deep voice.

She glanced up into silver-gray eyes. "Are you sure you are up to this?" He had not yet taken the floor.

"I believe so. A little stiffness is nothing to worry about. You look remarkably fine this evening."

"Is that a compliment or a set-down for my usual attire?" She berated herself for the testy tone, but his nearness was doing odd things to her breathing. It did not help that she could recall every contour of the well-muscled body lurking beneath his elegant clothes.

"I meant it as a compliment." His eyes twinkled as they swept her from head to toe. The musicians began to play.

"Heavens! It's a waltz," she gasped, noting too late that the dancers were not arranged in sets.

"The wicked waltz. Do you know the steps?"

"I have never tried it," she admitted, feeling disappointed. This was a partner she would have enjoyed dancing with. But she had not counted on his determination.

"It is easy. Watch a moment." Only a dozen other couples were on the floor, none of them performing with grace. That fact alone would have prompted her to accept, even if her heart were not thumping along at a perfectly ridiculous rate.

His hand clasped her waist, sending a shiver across her skin—though why she shivered when his touch burned so hotly she could not explain. It took only a minute to relax into the rhythm of the dance. He was right. It was easy. She was floating.

"I must thank you for saving Millicent from folly," he said, pulling her gaze into his own.

"It was nothing. Perhaps it is different in London, but here we all look after one another's charges. It allows everyone to enjoy the evening."

"I am appreciative, nonetheless. She should know better than to ask a gentleman to dance."

"Is that what she told you?"

"I assumed it. She offered no explanation." He frowned. "Was I wrong?"

His eyes bore into hers. Even if she had wanted otherwise, she could not have evaded the truth. "She was trying to force him into the garden. I heard only a few words, urging him to elope."

His eyes closed for a moment. "I feared so. But perhaps this was for the best. I told her such forward behavior would give any gentleman a disgust of her. My words combined with his reluctance have convinced her that he agrees."

"Excellent." She laughed lightly. "You needn't worry about a repeat, then."

"Have you any idea of his purpose?" he asked, pulling her a little closer to avoid contact with Squire and Mrs. Jacobson. His eyes glittered warmly.

"None, though he is now trying to form a connection to our family. I hear you tried to help Alice."

"I was too far away to do any good."

"I appreciate the effort. I did not realize that he had accosted her until just before Terrence arrived. But I cannot imagine what he hopes to gain."

"Nor I."

"Whatever it is must be urgent. He is too anxious to hide his insincerity. Spouting the same nonsense to both Alice and I assures disbelief."

"Or else you are more knowing than his usual targets. But I hope to uncover his game soon. My secretary is checking his background."

"As he did ours?" Her eyes flashed.

"Don't rip me up here," he begged. "Enjoy your first waltz. We can fight tomorrow if you wish. But you can hardly blame me for looking up the women I was told had evil designs on my ward."

She sighed. "Lady Avery has always hated us."

"That is another situation we can discuss later. Are you sure you have never waltzed? You dance with winged feet." His fingers caressed her back, sending flames racing into every extremity.

She reminded herself that he was using seduction to gain control of Winter House. Was that Darksmith's purpose as well? But Carrington had infinitely more skill. She couldn't think. He twirled her faster, pulling her even closer into his arms. His pupils blurred, his gaze seeming to draw her very soul out for his inspection. Every nerve shivered in delight as his thigh brushed her own under the cover of her billowing skirt.

"What are you doing to me?" he murmured so softly she barely heard. "Witch . . ."

Mesmerist, she responded, but only her lips formed the words.

Chapter Sixteen

～

What the devil is wrong with me?

Richard threw the coverlet aside and climbed down from his bed, pacing the room while his mind continued its chaotic churning. Eventually he gave it up to stare out the window. Dawn streaked the sky, but its violet fingers did nothing to soothe his spirit. He forced himself to concentrate on the play of colors as the wisps of cloud brightened to rose, their edges finally flaring with brilliant gold. But it did no good. Nightmare images still tormented him, lurking behind his eyelids every time he blinked.

Penelope Wingrave.

Damn the wench! Looks like hers should be banned. What had possessed him to ask her to dance? And a waltz, of all things! She remained in his arms, her hand burning his through two layers of gloves, her bosom brushing his chest, her thigh grazing his own. His fingers curled around her waist, and he shuddered. But not with cold. Pain built in his groin. Never in his life had he felt such desire.

The exhilaration of the dance remained. His hand tingled from the shapely curve of her hip. Had he actually allowed it to drop to such an improper position? But how else could he account for their contact at so many points? Only at courtesan balls did one dance so entwined.

Again he shuddered. He must have made quite a cake of himself. It was useless to pray that no one had noticed. Only a dozen couples had participated, the others watching in envy or rebuke. His behavior gave her yet another complaint against him.

He closed his eyes, instantly regretting it. Staring at the

golden shafts of sunlight fanning from behind a cloud was safer. Startlingly lascivious dream images teased him—the generous bosom that he had actually fondled within moments of meeting her; the long legs that even her unfashionable gowns could not hide; the fiery hair that invariably set his loins to burning; the height that fit so perfectly in his arms; her soft lips opening to his . . .

Taking another turn about the room, he ran frustrated fingers through his hair. What was the matter with him? She had burrowed past all his cynicism, past all the pain Penelope Rissen had inflicted, searing her image onto his heart. One might almost suspect that he loved her.

His feet froze as shock exploded through his midsection. One hand clamped over his mouth to force down a surge of nausea.

Dear Lord! He did.

His buckling legs deposited him into a chair. How could he have fallen in love with so unsuitable a woman? She was illbred, unmannerly, independent, and had a tongue like a wasp. Again he swallowed, breaking his thoughts. *Arrogance,* screamed his conscience. *Conceited, pigheaded arrogance. You are quoting your aunt again . . .*

Her breeding might be beneath his own, but she was far from baseborn. Her grandfathers were a viscount and an earl. His were a marquess and an earl. He knew of many attachments between people who were farther apart, starting with Mark and Elaine. None provoked censure. At least half of the girls his mother championed had less exalted ancestry. And her manners were not coarse. While she lacked the training that would make her comfortable in London drawing rooms, she was intelligent and could easily learn. In fact, a quick-witted, clearheaded woman was a blessing. Hadn't he decided that weeks ago? He despised widgeons who did nothing but parrot the latest *on-dits* and prattle of fashion.

Her independence was a problem, however. Ladies did not oversee estates or raise exotic animals. And they never ran businesses. Yet he could not castigate her for doing just that. She had supported her family—literally and figuratively—for fifteen years. Without her efforts, they would have lost Winter House long ago. He must applaud her for meeting the challenge. If he were honest, that was one of the things he admired about her, for it made her unique. In his twelve years on the town, she was the only woman who had ever held his interest. And how could he castigate her set-downs when he had invited most of them. Despite his pride in judging people to the inch, he had erred badly in her case.

He snorted. He might as well humble himself totally by admitting that his celebrated perspicacity worked only in the conformable world of the *ton*. Polite society paid lip service to the rules of propriety while breaking most of them in private. But even misbehavior followed strict guidelines. After living all of his life with this dual standard, he had failed to recognize genuine honesty when he saw it.

He reeled under a wave of longing for a lifetime of such candor, deliberately recalling the fortnight he had spent at Bridgeport Abbey. Mark and Elaine shared a love that was infinitely precious. It set them apart from their surroundings, creating a world populated only by themselves. At the time he had been envious—and lonely, for he did not enjoy feeling like an outsider in company with his closest friend. Watching the way Terrence and Alice communicated without words, he had reluctantly admitted that they shared the same connection. Now he wanted it for himself.

Was it possible? Dancing with Penelope had triggered something beyond the desire she always raised. Her eyes had burned into his as if she was reading his innermost secrets. He had repudiated the idea at the time, terrified that it might be true. But perhaps that ultimate closeness grew from the very things he feared—failure, vulnerability, the mortifying admission that she could destroy him with a word. . . .

What could he do? Long fingers raked his hair, tangling in the snarls left over from hours of fitful tossing. He could avoid failure by leaving. His customary mask of cold hauteur would cover the pain until he had put her irrevocably behind him. But walking away would close the door on his one chance to find what Mark already enjoyed. Could he endure the agony of a rejection? The ghosts of his Avery ancestors urged him to stay safe, to risk nothing, to escape while he still could. But that would mean enduring loneliness for the rest of his life. He scowled. He had repudiated the Avery cowardice even before his father died. Determination had reversed his fortunes, built his reputation, and successfully controlled his family. Yet all those triumphs would be meaningless if he refused the ultimate challenge. He would stay, and he would fight for happiness.

Again he paced the room. How could he convince Penelope to start over? He could hardly blame her for lashing out at him, considering his incessant provocation. He had any number of crimes for which he must atone. On the other hand, they had enjoyed a congenial day in Exeter and had worked together at the assembly without thought.

He sighed. He could do nothing to change the past, and his credibility was nonexistent. But he must try. The first step was to talk to her and hope that she had felt the same connection.

In the meantime, he crawled back into bed, deliberately welcoming the dreams. It was the only way he could hold her in his arms.

"Are you busy?" asked Terrence from the library doorway.

Richard glanced up from the estate ledger. His ward seemed more serious than usual, in control of his emotions as he had not been in their earlier confrontations. Even yesterday's questions about Tallgrove had seemed more of a lark than legitimate interest.

"What is the problem?" he asked quietly.

"Me. Many of your criticisms were correct."

He raised his brows, but Terrence gave him no chance to comment. "Not about my love for Alice, which is stronger than ever. But I have much to learn before I marry."

"Then you will not argue about returning to Oxford."

He grinned. "Actually, I will. I ran into Michael Wingrave in town the other day. He already knows far more about estate management than I, though he is fully five years younger. Even Alice knows more, but teaching me what I need to learn will take more time than you can spare."

"What do you propose?" He could not decide if Terrence was serious or if this was a new strategy to deflect his objections—whose validity he was already questioning for himself, though he would not admit that just yet. But this explained the boy's sudden interest in the estate. Michael must have demanded a demonstration of responsibility in exchange for his support.

"To begin with, I would like a detailed explanation of Scott's shortcomings as a steward—beyond the criminal activities we discussed yesterday. And instead of returning to Oxford, I would like to spend six months studying estate management with your own steward—or someone like him if another man would serve better."

He sat back, stunned. If Terrence was running a rig, he would hardly have suggested removing himself from Alice's side for several months. The boy was more mature than he had thought, a judgment that fit well with the adroit way he had extricated Alice from Darksmith's clutches at the assembly. Had the Avery indolence bypassed him, or had his love for Alice inspired him to overcome his inherited tendencies? Perhaps Penelope was correct in claiming that the family curse was no more than profound laziness that could be surmounted. Which meant that he was doing several people a disservice by removing all incentive to see after their own affairs.

"What exactly did Wingrave say?"

Terrence repeated their conversation. "It made me furious that so young a cawker would dare criticize a lord," he admitted at last. "But on reflection, I decided he was right. I had always considered Father to be a reasonable man and expected to live my life in much the same way. But his lack of supervision allowed Scott to rob him blind. I cannot jeopardize my security by leaving my finances to chance. Yet Oxford cannot teach me nearly as much as your steward."

"I will consider it, but first we will discuss Tallgrove." He pulled out ledgers covering the past century.

"Why so far back?" asked Terrence, but his voice was curious rather than daunted.

"The Avery family has long been cursed with laziness. Seeing where that leads will be your first lesson, for you must teach your children responsibility. Your great-grandfather was proud enough of winning both a title and an estate through his own efforts that he remained cognizant of its value. When he died, Tallgrove returned a good income and embraced the most progressive techniques of his day."

He pointed out entries in the ledger to illustrate the changes the man had ordered, including the replacement of most of his outside staff. "And that is the second lesson. You will defeat laziness only if you have a compelling incentive to better your-self."

"I wish I had known him," said Terrence wistfully. "He must have been a good man."

"I believe so, though I know him mostly from the estate records. He checked them regularly, making frequent notations. Your grandfather was less attentive, and your father was worse. He inherited at an early age, but paid little attention to the land."

"Very true, but how do you know that?"

From reading his diary—but he could not mention that. Heat built in his groin as he recalled Gareth's descriptions of his li-aisons. An image of Penelope sprawled naked across the dower house bed rose so vividly before his eyes that he expected Ter-rence to see her as well. Stifling an oath, he wrenched his thoughts back to the ledger.

"A good master checks the books regularly," he said, his voice sounding stilted even to his own ears. "If he does not un-derstand an entry, he marks it so that he can question his stew-ard. A good steward insists that his master sign so that both parties can prove that the examination was done." He opened books covering the first ten years of Gareth's tenure as vis-count.

"He signed every month," noted Terrence.

"That is true, but there is no hint that he actually looked at anything. Not a single question or comment appears, nor has any entry been corrected. I don't care how good the steward was, no man can keep records for ten years without making a single mistake. Then there is the estate itself. Not one improve-ment was made, although much was discovered about better farming methods during that time. Gareth either didn't know or didn't care that his steward was ignoring new techniques. Now look at the fifteen years since Scott was hired."

Terrence rustled pages for some time, allowing his thoughts to drift to Penelope's hair. Would it feel silky to the touch, or would it burn his fingers? Probably the latter. Even thinking about it burned his fingers. And more. He realized that he was breathing too fast and forced calm on his body.

"I see," Terrence said at last. "The first year is no different, but by the second year, Father was only checking every two or three months. After that there is no hint that he looked at anything."

Except his diary. "Exactly. Now compare expenses."

Why had he thought of the diary again? his conscience demanded as another lengthy period of page rustling ensued. He was torturing himself to no avail. If he could not exercise more control, he was likely to ravish her when next they met. But the castigation proved useless. By the time Terrence spoke, he had forgotten the subject under discussion. His hands shook, recalling how she felt. Images of what he wanted to do and how he hoped she would respond suffused him with heat. He moved his chair farther under the desk to mask the painful state of his groin. But it was harder to hide the huskiness that had crept into his voice.

"I cannot tell in so cursory a glance," admitted Terrence. "But it would appear that expenses rose faster than could be explained by this endless war."

Of course. They were discussing Tallgrove. "Very good. Scott succumbed to temptation. With no supervision and no one to question his decisions, he began padding the expenses—ten pounds here, fifteen there. It would not have amounted to much in the beginning. But stealing was so easy that he set his sights on buying an estate of his own, taking larger and larger amounts. Then he doubled the rents, keeping the difference for himself. When your father died, he knew the game was up and booked passage to America. But I did not immediately take control, so temptation again won. He canceled his passage, staking everything on my staying away for the summer. And his gamble nearly paid off. He doubled his nest egg by stripping Tallgrove of much of its wealth. But he did not anticipate the war that made it impossible to escape. Nor did he expect me to discover his crimes. Perhaps he assumed that I would be the same lazy overlord as Gareth. Entrenched villains often overlook the obvious."

"You mean that a new trustee would check the books even if that was not his custom?"

"Precisely."

They spent two hours reviewing the ledgers. Richard thought he would go crazy. His mind was beyond his control, creating new fantasies from every question—Penelope braced against an oak tree, moaning into his ear; Penelope swimming naked in the lake; Penelope beckoning him into the hayloft. Increasingly lurid pictures tormented him. Often he had to scramble to cover slips of the tongue lest he disclose where his thoughts had drifted.

But Terrence finally closed the book. "I never suspected a thing. Scott has always been the bluff, hearty sort who would give you the shirt off his back if it would ease your way. How could my judgment have been so wrong?"

"It is difficult to evaluate those one has known since childhood. The important thing is to learn from your father's mistakes. Always check everything. And never allow your steward to use outdated ideas. The only way to make sure that he is aware of the latest discoveries is to learn about them yourself."

"Which returns us to my initial request," said Terrence smoothly. "May I spend the next few months studying with your steward instead of returning to Oxford? You can hardly claim I am too young. Michael will assume control of Winter House when he is seventeen. Penelope took over at that age."

His hand trembled. "She has done well by all reports. I see no reason why it could not be arranged, providing my man is willing. Afterward, if you still feel as strongly, I will not oppose your betrothal. She seems intelligent and sensible."

Joy burst across Terrence's face. "May I tell her that?"

"There can be no commitment on either side," he warned. "It is unfair to make a secret agreement that honor will demand you fulfill. You believe that your love will endure, and you may be right. But you both must have the freedom to walk away if you prove to be wrong. And you still have not dealt with your mother."

"She can move to the dower house."

"That is not enough," he warned as they put the ledgers away and headed for the stairs. "Unless you soften her antagonism, she will make Alice miserable even if she does not share the manor."

"I wish I knew why she is so adamant, for she barely knows Penelope, and has never met Alice."

"Her claims are preposterous," he agreed, drawing surprise from Terrence. "I have disproved every one." *And dug myself into a hole of mistrust in the process.* How could he atone?

There must be something that would work. And then he could kiss her again. . . .

"Then you agree that she will make a suitable wife?"

"Absolutely," he murmured, mentally threading his fingers through fiery curls and pillaging that passionate mouth.

"Alice will be thrilled."

His thoughts snapped back with a vengeance. What had he agreed to? Now he knew what Penelope had suffered the day she had to backtrack. He sighed. "She is excessively sweet, pure as the driven snow, intelligent, knowledgeable, and thinks you walk on water. But first you must deal with your mother. Her hatred goes beyond misinformation, though I have no clue as to what ails the woman." But he must learn. For Penelope's sake as well as Terrence's.

"I will talk to her." Terrence sighed. "But it is not a conversation I expect to enjoy."

"Talk to whom?" demanded Lady Avery from the nearby drawing room.

"There's no time like the present," murmured Richard.

"I suppose not." But Terrence's voice sounded as though he faced the scaffold.

"Spoken like a mature gentleman." He turned a smile on his aunt. "I have agreed that Terrence should study estate management with my steward this term instead of returning to Oxford," he announced.

She frowned. "At least that will get him away from those girls," she muttered darkly.

Terrence's hands fisted, but Richard's commanding gaze held his tongue. "At the end of that time, I will consent to his betrothal if he remains of like mind," he stated coldly.

"I should have known," sobbed Mathilda. "You are just like every other man, eager to fall into their snares. Why did Gareth not give me a voice in my children's futures?"

"How dare you?" growled Terrence. His fingers dug into the back of a chair, their white knuckles stark against its red upholstery. "If he cut you out, it was because he knew your judgment was unsound."

"Unsound? Unsound! *How sharper than a serpent's tooth is an ungrateful chil—*"

"This is beyond enough," interrupted Richard as she dissolved into tears. "Madam, I have researched the Wingrave family and can only conclude that your judgment is nonexistent and your sense is worse. I cannot imagine how you came to your unwarranted conclusions, but you do nought but tarnish your own reputation by voicing such calumny. Your characterization is wrong from first to last. Their breeding is equal to your own—"

"Terrence cannot marry that strumpet," screamed a white-faced Mathilda. "It is against all the laws of God and man!"

"What?"

"She is his sister!"

"No!" Terrence blanched.

"She is not," swore Richard, head spinning as the pieces finally fell into place. "You are wrong, Aunt Mathilda. Uncle Gareth never betrayed you, and certainly not with Alice's mother."

"You cannot hide his sins," hissed Mathilda, abandoning her weakness to stalk across the room. She yanked a well-worn paper from a drawer in her escritoire. "Look for yourself. Here is the proof that you are blind and deaf about that viper. I found it on Gareth's desk only two days before Alice's birth! Laura brags of their affair and gloats that he fathered her coming child."

Terrence moaned.

He quickly scanned the page, recognizing the writing even without seeing the signature. *I pray our child will be a boy, for Winter House should pass to your son, my love. It is as close as we can ever come to sanctioning our union. Would that we could do so in fact.—L. W.*

He had promised Penelope that he would keep the affair secret, but unless he broke that vow, too many lives would sink into misery—including Alice's.

"Gareth did have an affair with Mrs. Wingrave," he confirmed, ignoring Terrence's gagging. "With the *first* Mrs. Wingrave, Lucinda."

Terrence's horror changed to hope.

"You lie," charged Mathilda.

"Never! You are a snoop, Aunt. And stupid. Did you never note that this letter was already worn when you found it? I recognize the writing, for I have seen others in this same hand. She signed them L. W. as a way to deny her marriage, for she was born Lucinda Winterbottom."

"You knew but told no one?" she choked.

"I learned of it only last week," he said gently. "She and Gareth loved each other deeply—and very painfully, for neither enjoyed their illicit relationship. But that was long before he married you, Aunt. In fact, had she lived, I doubt he would have wed at all. He knew firsthand how agonizing infidelity could be for all parties. It is true that he fathered a son by Lucinda, but the boy was stillborn. He never once betrayed you, even after you denied him his rights. You might have found comfort and serenity together if you had not decided to make his life a misery. It was your own sharp tongue that drove him into cold disdain. And for what? Because he loved another before he wed you? You have spent a lifetime waging war against innocent people for a crime that exists only in your own head. You have destroyed your reputation and set yourself up as a laughing-stock for nothing. It will stop now!"

"Then why was he so interested in Winter House?" Her face had paled, her voice dropping to a whisper.

"His interest began long after you turned on him. I think your hatred drove him back to the past. Perhaps he wanted the reminder of Lucinda. It was her dowry and had once been part of Tallgrove."

Lady Avery was left speechless.

He had to feel sorry for her even though she had brought her suffering on herself. Her vindictiveness was a clear case of cutting off her nose to spite her face. Her antagonism toward the Wingraves had eroded her own reputation. Her repudiation of Gareth left her lonely. Her refusal to carry out her duties gave her too much time to brood, contributing to her chronic melancholy. Ignoring her children because they were also Gareth's courted their disdain. Shaking his head in sadness, he headed for the hall.

"That is the truth?" asked Terrence when they had left a sobbing Lady Avery behind.

"The truth. Your father's journal contains the details. Try not to condemn him. He suffered most of his life from guilt over an unwise love."

"Then there is nothing to bar me from marrying Alice?"

"Not morally. But Penelope also opposes this match."

He groaned. "Alice was sure she did not."

"She was wiser than I. Knowing that I would move heaven and earth to prevent your marriage—based mostly on the unsupported statements of your mother, I am ashamed to admit—she saw no reason to goad you into an elopement by ordering you away."

"So I am no better off than before."

"Not necessarily. You might try the same argument with her that you just did with me. Part of her objection is your youth and irresponsibility. Remove her fears on that score. She understands the power of love, for her father and Alice's mother were very close. And she knows about the affair between Lucinda and Gareth."

Terrence nodded. "Bringing that up would serve no purpose."

"You are learning prudence. Good luck."

He watched his ward stride upstairs to change. His encouraging words continued to reverberate in his ears. Penelope knew the power of love. Perhaps that was the answer to his own dilemma. He loved her. Could she ever return the feeling?

Hope blossomed as he headed for his room. He also had a call to make.

"Drat it all!"

Penelope shoved the pottery records aside. She had added this column six times, with six widely different results. It was useless to try again. A long, sleepless night made it impossible to concentrate.

She should have had no trouble falling asleep, for they had not returned from the assembly until well after midnight. Normally she was in bed by ten. Yet she had been unable to lie still long enough to relax. Memories made her too restless.

What had possessed her to attempt a waltz? The dance had a scandalous reputation. Even London high-sticklers reportedly looked at it askance. The vicar often decried it as an instrument of the devil, and she could see why. Dancing in the arms of an attractive man swirled devastating sensations into the pit of her stomach. Embracing him in front of the entire neighborhood made her feel like a Jezebel.

Even worse, she had thrown propriety to the winds, allowing him to draw her close enough that their bodies had touched, thus confirming his suspicion that she was a wanton. Or—horrible thought—had *she* been the one to press against him? Heat infused her face. His hand still burned into her waist and hip. Memory of her bosom brushing his coat was enough to tauten her breasts and heap fuel on the fire raging in her abdomen. The contact had awakened the ghosts of every earlier encounter. Her lips tingled. Her fingers curled into the shape of his shoulder. Scandalous indeed!

"Dear God!"

Surging to her feet, she rapidly paced the floor. What must people think of her? Never had any man affected her like this. Despite his denials, he must be a practiced rake who knew all too well how to invoke unspeakable emotions in every female he met.

Not that, she mouthed silently. She did not want to be like every other woman. Nor did she view him like every other man. Beneath his facade lay intelligence, humor, compassion, and sense. And something more that triggered a longing to seek out the safety of his arms.

What damnable stupidity! I love him.

Her pacing increased. Surely it was merely lust! She could not have fallen in love with an arrogant marquess who always believed the worst of others. He would never consider marrying a woman like her. Even her fantasies did not stretch that far.

But it was easy to understand her foolishness. He had considerable charm when he chose to exert it. She had heard of the changes he had ordered since arriving at Tallgrove. Whatever his moral failings, he was up to snuff when it came to running an estate. Rather than a wastrel like Lord Avery, he was proving to be a progressive landowner. But she could hardly ignore his moral failings. Nor could she let him guess how susceptible she was to his touch, for his own interest did not extend beyond dalliance. And despite her love, she did not want it to. All of his courtesy in recent days arose from discovering that her breeding was far from base. It was his way of apologizing for misjudging her. But he would never really approve of her, for his ideas on the proper role of women were traditional and repressive. He was accustomed to London misses, with their polished manners and witty repartee. She was unsuited to a life of idleness and gossip and could never measure up to his expectations—especially if he was confusing her character with that other Penelope's.

They would not suit, she decided, though she knew that her decision was mostly a way of coping with the fact that he would never offer. Loving him filled her with fear, leaving her more vulnerable than ever before, for he could destroy her with a word. Would he? Pain settled into her heart, but that was only to be expected. No country spinster should allow the least *tendre* for a London gentleman, even one with admirable qualities.

And the central question would not go away. Why was he investigating Winter House? He could only be continuing Lord Avery's plots despite his claims to the contrary. So she could not trust him.

She resumed her chair and frowned. Never again could she dance with him. Nor could she be alone with him lest she inadvertently betray her foolish thoughts. She had often derided her fellow spinsters for silly infatuations. Miss Partridge—who was all of forty—was currently sighing over their thirty-year-old curate, a lanky bag of bones with no chin, protruding eyes, and not a shilling to his name. But Penelope Wingrave would never open herself to ridicule by revealing that she had fallen into the same trap.

"Miss Wingrave?"

"What is it, Mary," she asked the maid, grateful to have her unproductive thoughts interrupted.

"Oh, Miss Wingrave, I'm so sorry. Indeed, I didn't mean it, and I hope you won't turn me off, cuz me poor mum needs the bit I make to keep a roof over her head—not that I could blame you if you did, cuz I failed in me duties so 'tis no more than I deserve—"

"Enough, Mary." She didn't know whether to laugh or cry over such an outpouring. Tears rolled down the girl's cheeks, unchecked because both hands clutched a thin package. "Now, suppose you tell me what happened before we consider punishments."

Mary sniffed, but a stern look silenced further wails. "A gentleman come to the door yesterday afternoon, Miss. He didn't leave no name, but he give me this package and said to see you got it."

"Then why have I not seen it?"

"I meant to bring it to you, but Master Michael said you was in the barn, and then Miz Peccles told me to fetch her some blackberries so's she could make a tart. By the time you got back, I was settin' the table and had forgot about it. Please don't turn me off, Miss."

"Calm down, Mary. I haven't the least intention of turning you off. But we have no butler, so you must handle deliveries. You have two choices for a package such as this. If the gentleman asked for a reply, you should have brought it directly to me. Did he do so?"

"No, Miss."

"In that case, you should have placed it on my desk."

"I'm that sorry." She hung her head.

"No harm was done this time," she said, taking the package from Mary's trembling fingers. "But try to do better in the future."

"I will, Miss. Thank you, Miss."

As soon as Mary left, Penelope broke the seal, drawing out several sheets of paper. Her eyes widened as she read the cover letter.

Dear Miss Wingrave,

As I mentioned at our last meeting, I discovered a detailed account of my uncle's attempts to wrest control of Winter House from your brother's hands. I would never condone such dishonor even if he had a legitimate complaint against you, but I can find no reason for his plot beyond a possible sentimental attachment to Lucinda's estate.

Be assured that I have terminated all of his stratagems. He kept meticulous records that allowed me to estimate the effect of his predations. An accounting is enclosed, along with a draft for damages. If I have missed anything, please call it to my attention.

Carrington

P.S. Set aside your fury and keep the settlement. Just as you could not accept overpayment for that broken pottery, I cannot allow Gareth to tarnish my family name.

The draft was written against the Tallgrove account in the amount of £2103 4s6d. She nearly tore it up, but Carrington's postscript stopped her fingers.

Setting the letter and draft aside she examined his figures. Fury battled horror and chagrin—sabotage at the pottery, poisoned fields, injured animals, damaged trees, the stable fire. How could Avery have been so venal? And why had she not suspected his hand in recent disasters? That was the worst insult. She, who prided herself on astute management, had never once considered vandalism. The admission was humbling.

Carrington must know as much about Winter House as she did. His figures were precise. He neither underestimated to cheat her nor overestimated to expiate his uncle's crimes. And he must have begun this reckoning long before his encounter with Ozzie. There would have been no time to do so afterward.

An honorable man. This was precisely the hedge against disaster that she had been searching for. She could set a thousand pounds aside for Alice and invest the rest in Consols. The security would pull them back from the edge—and she had Carrington to thank for it. That treacherous warmth again invaded her stomach, though his actions in no way hinted that he might return her regard. They merely deepened her feelings for the rogue. How long would it take before her infatuation faded into memory? At least she could console herself that he was worthy of her affection.

Leaning back, she stared at the bookshelves, letting her eyes caress the leather-bound volumes in the hope that they would deflect her mind from feelings that she must not entertain. She loved this room. It was one of only three that had never been remodeled, retaining the original Tudor paneling—an intricate pattern of squares and rectangles framed by heavy moldings. It had probably been a bedroom or men's retreat in earlier times, for the freestanding bookcases were a recent addition. Jake Winterbottom hung above the fireplace, staring at his third wife Jane, who smiled back from across the room. A string of seed pearls artfully threaded Jane's curls, dividing them into a pattern resembling petals. Had she deliberately mimicked one of the Tudor roses that marched in single file just under the cornice?

She shivered in an icy draft. The manor had been built just after Henry VII assumed the throne, ending the Wars of the Roses. His symbol combined the red rose of Lancaster and the white rose of York. The builder of Winter House had carved the device out of contrasting woods so that each dark flower contained a smaller light one in its center. Not even age and smoke had dimmed the white roses. Long after Henry's Tudor dynasty had given way to the Stuarts, who were themselves replaced by the Hanoverians, the united roses still smiled from the bookroom ceiling.

They were her favorite decoration—and her father's as well. He had been fond of sermon-like exhortations, his most frequent being that people should set aside their differences and work together, citing the Tudor rose as an example of benevolent harmony. Was noting the roses at this particular moment a message from on high that Carring—

Her eyes sharpened. All thought of the marquess vanished. Each five-petaled rose also had five indentations where petals met around its rim. The twelve-foot ceiling prevented anyone from reaching one. So who would ever try?

She rang for Mary and ordered her to summon Michael and Alice. Unless her mind had wandered into a fantasy realm, she may have solved a mystery—not that the answer would be worth anything.

"What happened?" demanded Michael. "Allie is out."

"Meeting Terrence, I suppose." She forbore further comment, trusting them to behave themselves. "Do you recall that odd tool you found in the attic the other day?"

"Is it valuable after all?"

"I doubt it, but I may have discovered what it is."

She would say no more until he had fetched it and found a length of cord.

"This house is old enough to have a priest's hole," she explained. "Those who did not install one when Henry VIII broke with Rome felt obliged to do so when Mary gained the throne. I suspect it might be hidden in this room. A catch mounted too high to reach by hand would reduce the risk of discovery. This pole disassembles quickly, so it could be brought into hiding to avert suspicion."

"I see," he agreed, excitement mounting as he followed her gaze. "The pegs form a circle the same diameter as the roses."

"Exactly." She looped the center of the cord around the top peg, extending the ends down either side so she could turn the wheel. "The only question is which one."

"Another question is whether the latch still works," he reminded her. "That was nearly three hundred years ago."

"True, but it will be interesting to try."

And difficult, she discovered over the next hour. She had to extend the pole until its bottom was shoulder high in order to reach the roses. It would have been simple if she had known which one to attack, but they had to try each one in turn.

"I never realized how many roses were in this room," panted Michael as he moved on to the next one.

They had started along the most promising wall—a long stretch that backed onto the butler's pantry—but had turned up nothing. Nor had their luck held on the next two walls. All that was left was the thick exterior wall, but though it was fully three feet deep, she could not imagine it housing a priest's hole.

"There has to be something," she insisted. "The fit is too perfect."

"I agree. But if such a latch existed, it must have long since rusted into uselessness. I still think the hole must be on that first wall. Here, you try for a while. My arms are dropping off."

She took over yet again, working her way along the ceiling until she was nearly back to their starting point.

"I think this one moved," she gasped suddenly.

"Let me try." Michael took over the pole, pulling solidly on the cord. "You are right." He pulled again.

"But nothing is happening." Disappointment saddened her voice. "Perhaps it is merely loose." She felt the wall underneath the rose, but it remained solidly flat.

Michael twisted the rose again, evoking a definite click. "Look, Penny. Not here, over there." He pointed around the corner where a shadow had appeared just above a bookcase.

They wrestled with the heavy bookcase for five minutes before they set aside impatience and removed its contents. After that it took only a moment to slide the cabinet away from the wall.

A four-foot-high opening had appeared between the fireplace and the corner. Molding disguised its edges. The door screeched as she pulled it open to peek inside. The space was small, perhaps three feet wide and about six long—just large enough to hold a pallet where a man could sleep during times of danger.

"Let me see," demanded Michael, bringing a candle closer.

She backed away so he could poke his head behind the bookcase.

"Marvelous! Who would have thought the old place contained a secret room?" Before she could respond, he crawled inside and gasped.

"What's wrong?" she asked sharply. "No one is in there, I hope." She shivered at a vision of moldering bones.

"Not now, but someone has been. There is a shelf in the corner." He handed her three bundles swathed in rotting fabric, then backed out, dragging a small casket.

"What in the world?" Her voice trailed off as she unwound the first cloth. A heavy silver plate with a border of leaves emerged, its surface black with tarnish. "Good heavens!" The second bundle held a matching bowl, and the third an ornate silver chalice with half a dozen gems mounted on a band just below the rim.

"My God!" breathed Michael. "Those things must be worth a fortune!"

"Probably not, but they will certainly serve as insurance against disaster. What do you have?"

A key dangled in the casket's lock. Whoever had left it in the priest's hole had trusted the location alone to guard his possessions. Michael lifted the lid and gasped.

"I don't believe it," she swore, lifting a heavy pendant redolent with rubies from the pile of jewelry that filled the box.

Michael removed a leather bag from one corner and tipped it up. Gold coins rolled across the carpet.

"Who do you think left them there?" he asked in awe.

She picked up the nearest coin and stared at it. "Charles. No number, so he must have been the first. At a guess, whoever owned the property back then hid his valuables before going to war. Many men died fighting Cromwell, and many estates changed hands when it was over."

"How much do you think this is worth?"

"A tidy sum. You can attend the university and provide a dowry for Alice. You need no longer fear the future." She relaxed with the words. Her nights of worry were over. What a day!

She had just recalled Carrington's draft when Mary shrieked. But before either of them could move, Darksmith appeared in the doorway, a cocked pistol held in a steady hand.

Chapter Seventeen

~

"What is it, Cawdry?" asked Richard.

He had been ready to leave for Winter House when his secretary sent word to meet him in the library. Such a demand was unusual enough to warrant delaying his departure.

He was still reeling from the morning's revelations, shocked at Lady Avery's charges and appalled at the childish retaliation she had pursued for so many years. Poor deluded woman. She had wasted her own life and made Gareth's a misery over a misunderstanding that could have been put right in an instant if she had only faced her husband with her suspicions. But the Avery weakness left her unable to confront trouble. Instead, she had turned on the Wingraves. Had she expected Laura to punish Gareth for revealing their liaison? If so, she had failed. Gareth had not cared that she shunned him and had not even connected her antipathy to the affair that had ended years earlier. Mathilda's futile hatred had hurt only the innocent.

He needed to atone for what his family had done. Reimbursing Penelope for Gareth's damage was not enough—

He frowned. She had not mentioned his bank draft at the assembly, though Cawdry had delivered it some hours earlier. He had been so wrapped up in other thoughts that he had not noticed. How strange.

But he had no time to ponder her odd reticence. Suppressing renewed visions of the woman he loved, he took a seat behind the desk.

Cawdry laid a sheaf of papers before him. "The report on Mr. Darksmith, my lord."

He tensed. For Cawdry to summon his employer from other business, the news must be bad indeed. "He seemed to be shunning Millicent's company last night. Or is he merely biding his time until I leave Tallgrove?"

"Neither." His voice was unusually solemn.

That familiar sense of dread crept across his back as Cawdry's frown deepened. "Is it that bad?"

"He is more of a charlatan than you feared, being the son of an Exeter innkeeper. He was born John Dougan but has publicly gone by Darksmith since leaving home twenty years ago."

"Where did he acquire the accent and manner of the upper classes?"

Cawdry sighed. "He is a gifted mimic. The Golden Stag caters to polite society, so he had ample opportunity to observe his betters. I suspect that he made the acquaintance of Lord Avery there, for his lordship frequented that inn whenever he visited Exeter. He was playing cards there the night of his death."

"I thought he died here."

Cawdry's face and voice remained wooden. "Lady Avery did not consider the circumstances of his demise to be proper for a lord."

"Surely he did not die in someone's bed!"

"No, but he had been drinking heavily and fell from his horse while returning home. His doctor had repeatedly warned him against overindulging in wine or exertion, but he evidently tried to finish the journey on foot and collapsed by the roadside. The groom sent out when the horse returned riderless found him."

"That is nothing to be ashamed of. But what does my uncle's death have to do with Darksmith?"

"They had played cards together that evening. Lord Avery was well into his cups when they started, for he had already spent six hours in the taproom with friends before meeting Darksmith. According to the serving wench, he had been maundering on about finding a lost fortune. She saw Darksmith draw him into a private parlor, where he goaded Lord Avery for details of the story. His lordship had a paper that he would not show anyone, yet no paper was found on his body. I assume Darksmith filched it."

"By following him and stripping the corpse?"

"I doubt it. A man of his proclivities would have removed Avery's purse as well."

"And what exactly are his proclivities?"

"Nothing honest, though his father believes that he works in a solicitor's office. He has run local scams under several aliases and probably has identities in other cities as well, though I have not tried to trace them. He is often out of town on business."

"We will leave that to the runners. What could Gareth have meant about finding a fortune?" he murmured, half to himself. "There is no fortune. Yet that confirms my suspicion that Darksmith is nought but an adventurer. Millicent's naïve claims would have confirmed his expectations." He bit his lip. "That's why he avoided her last night. He must have learned that her dowry is not large enough to set up a man who starts with nothing."

"Less than nothing. He is in thrall to the moneylenders to the tune of ten thousand."

"That is five times Millicent's dowry. Why then did he return?"

"I do not know," admitted Cawdry.

His blood suddenly ran cold. Darksmith had been courting favor with the Wingraves at the assembly. As Penelope had observed, he was so anxious to attach them that his insincerity showed. Were his creditors pressing him for repayment? But that made no sense. No one would expect the Wingraves to cover a ten-thousand–pound debt.

He frowned as he skimmed the report. Cawdry had been thorough, as usual. Darksmith had skirted the law for years, though he was cunning enough to avoid being caught. Mr. Dougan had accepted John's change of name without argument after the boy refused to learn the innkeeping business. His stint in the solicitor's office had lasted barely a month, though Dougan did not know that his son had been let go. Since then, Darksmith had lived by his wits. Now seven-and-thirty, he often spent an evening at the Golden Stag. But he never acknowledged a connection with the innkeeper, and few of the inn's servants knew of the relationship. Nor did its patrons. Darksmith was a cardsharp who had fleeced several customers, and a growing number of guests had been robbed. This last problem was causing custom to fall off, particularly among the aristocrats, threatening the future of the inn. Dougan did not suspect his son, for Darksmith routinely charmed his parent into believing falsehoods. But with fewer wealthy pigeons available, his own finances had taken a turn for the worse. He could run his rig only sparingly at other inns without risking detection from less credulous innkeepers. To maintain his pretense of profitable employment, he had fallen into the hands of the moneylenders.

He set the pages back on the desktop and ran his fingers through his hair. Something did not ring true. How could Gareth claim to have found a fortune when no evidence supported such a notion? And nothing explained Darksmith's recent attentions to the Wingraves.

"Summon Millicent," he ordered. Perhaps she knew something Cawdry had missed.

Millicent's face was chalk-white as she confronted her guardian across the desk.

"I won't eat you," Richard assured her. "But a problem has arisen that I need help resolving."

"What is it, my lord?"

"You have been deceived through no fault of your own. But until I understand why, there is little I can do to prevent further trouble."

"By whom?"

He handed her the report on Mortimer.

The moment she saw his name, her eyes flashed. "How dare you treat a gentleman like a common criminal?" she demanded.

"Part of the job of a guardian is to check on the backgrounds of those courting his ward," he reminded her. "Even gentlemen of known breeding often hide poverty or unsavory habits behind elegant facades. I can name a dozen lords who use public charm to conceal private abuse. Read it."

She snorted in disgust, but complied. The moment her eyes widened in horror, he walked to the window, hands clasped loosely behind his back as he gazed over the formal gardens. Her murmuring changed from irritation to pain and finally to blazing fury. "Innkeeper's son . . . debts . . . cardsharp . . . robberies . . . seduction?" The last was shouted directly at him.

"Yes, he often accepts loans from women he has seduced."

"Dear God, how could I have been so stupid?" she wailed. The pages drifted to the floor as she covered her face with her hands. "All night I agonized because my forward conduct had given him a disgust of me. How many tears have I shed over a man who was playing me for a fool? And I am! He seemed so nice! And so understanding."

"The stock in trade of a successful libertine, Millicent." Despite her shaking shoulders, he could not postpone the discussion that could only hurt her more. "This is not going to be pleasant, but I must know all the details of your liaisons, my dear. Was there anything beyond indiscretion?"

"Yes . . . no . . . I don't know," she sobbed.

He handed her a handkerchief. "This was not your fault," he repeated firmly. "But I cannot safeguard your reputation unless you tell me what threatens it. Now I know that he kissed you."

"How?" Red eyes jerked up to meet his gaze.

"I came upon you in the folly just after he left, you might recall. The look is unmistakable."

She blushed until her face matched her eyes. "Yes, he kissed me. Several times."

"Did he touch you?"

She nodded, dropping her head until he could see only her hair.

"Where?"

"My face, my arms, my shoulders—" Her voice trailed off, her hands again covering her eyes.

"Continue," he ordered gently.

"M-my b-breasts," she whispered.

"Anything else?"

Her head shook.

"So he merely loosened your gown. He did not remove it."

She nodded.

"Was eloping your idea or his?"

"Dear Lord! How did you find out about that?"

"Miss Wingrave overheard you. She will not reveal it, but never again forget that a ballroom is full of ears."

"How can I ever face her?"

"With poise. Whose idea was it, Millicent?"

"Mine."

"He never suggested it?"

"He often hinted at marriage, but he refused to elope. His sudden coldness seemed odd until you told me how forward I had been. How could I have been so gullible?" New sobs wracked her body.

"It is over, Millicent. We will put it behind us and move ahead. Count your blessings. You are luckier than many who fall prey to a determined seducer. Your virtue is intact, your indiscretions will never become public, and you have learned a valuable lesson about the danger of secret liaisons. He claimed to love you, did he not?"

"He swore so." She hiccuped.

"And you would have allowed him further liberties if he had asked for them."

Shame reddened her face as she nodded. "I loved him. He was everything I ever hoped to find in a husband. And I trusted him. How mortifying!"

"I am not angry with you," he again assured her. "If only all of life's lessons exacted so small a price. But I must know what he wanted. Did he ever inquire about your dowry?"

She frowned in thought. "No. We never spoke of money."

"Never?"

"He spoke only of me—my beauty, my charm . . ." Her voice trailed away amid vivid blushes.

"What reason did he give for being here?"

"The same tale he told you at tea that day." She bit her lip as another sob shook her body. "Sir Reginald St. Juste claims that Mortimer's estate belongs to him because the original sale was not legal. M-mortimer was looking for proof. He said that Father had found it. Since the official records were destroyed, he needed to see the ledger."

"What ledger?" His heart was pounding. Had Darksmith's purpose been to gain access to the house? But nothing was missing that he knew of.

"He asked to see the 1620 ledger. In those days, the people that owned his estate also owned ours. When his was sold, the transaction was recorded here. I tried to find the reference, but I could not read the words."

"Most records were kept in Latin back then," he said absently as his mind raced. 1620. Tallgrove would still have been in the hands of Lord Chesterton. But Chesterton had left no heir, and Cromwell had confiscated the estate. It was too far-fetched to believe that St. Juste was somehow related to that ancient family. "Why would Sir Reginald care about an estate in Yorkshire that was sold nearly two hundred years ago?"

"When you phrase it like that, it sounds ridiculous," she agreed, shuddering. "But it seemed so reasonable when Mortimer explained it. Sir Reginald is horrid. Jeremy Jacobson claims that he shoots anyone who sets foot on his estate. He cut Miss Partridge dead last month for no worse crime than wishing him a good day. Trying to steal another man's estate would be nothing for him."

"Actually, I have met the man. He is a scholar who wants only to pursue his studies. I doubt he knows anything about his own estate let alone anyone else's, for he spends his days immersed in ancient Greece."

"But why is he so surly?"

"You have run afoul of him, I see." He smiled. "Sir Reginald hates both women and children and eschews most social contacts. But that does not make him a villain. I suppose Darksmith was kissing you when he made his request."

She nodded.

"Classic seduction technique—inflame the passions until desire drives reason into hiding, at which point the victim will agree to anything." And didn't he know it. His own reason fled every time he saw Penelope. "That is another lesson you should remember. But enough of the past. Let us get the ledger and discover Darksmith's game."

Millicent paled. "It is not here," she admitted in a small voice.

"What?"

"He borrowed it, but has not yet returned it. I planned to ask him about it last night, but I had no chance."

"Did you give it to him that day you were in here?"

She nodded. "The ledger was not in the office. I had just found it when you arrived."

"But you had nothing in your hands."

"I shoved it behind that cabinet," she admitted, shrinking into her chair. "I retrieved it later and left it in the folly, expecting him to return it within a day or two, but I did not see him again until last night. Dear God, what have I done?" Her voice broke.

Richard had wandered over to glance behind the cabinet, his

mind stupidly expecting the missing ledger to still be there. It wasn't, of course, but something gleamed in the dim light. Retrieving the poker, he fished it out.

"What is that?" asked Millicent nervously.

"Some notes your father made." He recognized the handwriting. "They must have fallen out when you dropped it."

"Why would Father have been interested in so old a record?" she asked. "If Mortimer was lying about everything else, he must have lied about knowing Father, too."

"He knew him. Darksmith fleeced him at cards just before Gareth died. Gareth must have said something about the ledger." More likely, the information was on that missing paper. He had known which book to search.

"From 1620?" she scoffed.

"Gareth was researching the history of Tallgrove Manor before his death." He scanned the sheet, its disjointed phrases finally answering his questions—*margin note; hid before war; d house p hole.*

The lost fortune. Chesterton had penned a note into the margin of the 1620 ledger just before leaving for war in 1646. To guard against looting, he had hidden his valuables in the dower house priest's hole. Writing his note in an old ledger provided a further safeguard. But Chesterton must have told someone to check that volume in the event of his death, so why would Gareth believe the cache might still be there? Yet he must have thought so. It was the only explanation for his long campaign to acquire Winter House.

No wonder the Tallgrove dower house had been vandalized. Darksmith would have collected the ledger as soon as Millicent returned to the house. He had left the King's Arms in the morning and must have spent the next three days looking for someone who could read Latin. Needing no further access to Tallgrove, he had no use for Millicent, so he moved to Plymtree. That night he vandalized the current dower house. Not until he failed to find a priest's hole did he steal the Tallgrove files and learn that the original dower house was now Winter House. So he set about cultivating the Wingraves.

But they had not fallen for his seductive patter. Penelope was too knowing, and Alice's heart was bestowed elsewhere. What would be his next move? Terror gripped his soul at the possibilities. A desperate, unscrupulous villain might try anything.

"What is wrong?" asked Millicent nervously.

"I understand his game," he said. "And he is more dangerous than I supposed. You have been very helpful. Thank you."

"Is there anything I can do?"

"Nothing more. Stay here and do not approach him again. I will see that he does not bother you. By the time you stage your come-out, this will seem no more than a bad dream."

"I do not want a come-out. After watching my parents constantly snipe at each other, I refuse to marry without love. But I will never love again. Or trust again. It is too painful." She slipped away before he could respond.

He shook his head. Her words echoed his own vow of ten years earlier. He prayed that she could put Darksmith's betrayal into perspective before it ruined her life. It had taken him far too long to achieve a balance between prudence and credulity.

But more important matters drove her from his mind. At last he understood the feeling of doom that had plagued him ever since receiving Aunt Mathilda's summons. It had grown so powerful that he could hardly breathe, and could only warn that Penelope's life was in danger.

Chapter Eighteen

$\backsim$

Darksmith's hand remained steady. "You have saved me considerable trouble," he gloated. "Thank you."

"What have you done to Mary?" Penelope's calm voice belied her pounding heart. She had already suffered too many shocks this day.

"She'll live." He gestured with his pistol. "Move away from the treasure."

"How did you learn of this?" she asked, stepping gingerly behind the desk as Michael backed toward the window. "We knew nothing of it until ten minutes ago."

"Lord Avery." He ignored her gasp. "His ancestor must have been crazy to build a new dower house when he still had this one." He was inching toward the chest.

"So you were the one who wrecked the dower house," snorted Michael. "What a sterling example of gentlemanly behavior. But then you are only a *faux* gentleman."

Darksmith's hand twitched.

"I always suspected that you were a slippery character," mused Penelope, relieved when the pistol turned from Michael to herself. If he twitched again, she did not want Michael in the line of fire. "You never seemed the sort to care for schoolgirls, and I could not accept the theory that you were after her dowry. Everyone knows the Averys have no fortune. But you were looking for information, weren't you?"

Michael had also noted Darksmith's shifting attention. He sprang. She screamed, but instead of firing, Darksmith slammed the butt of the pistol into the side of Michael's head, felling him with one blow. Blood welled from a cut, the red stream vivid against his white face.

Fear closed her throat. She should not have baited him. He was more dangerous than she had thought.

"Foolish boy!" he snapped, drawing a large bag from under his cloak. "Put everything inside." The pistol jerked menacingly.

Furious but impotent, she dared not refuse. Michael's future would now slip through her fingers. Carrington's draft would guard against default, but it would not substantially change their situation. So they were destitute. Again. She slowly transferred jewelry and coins, trying desperately to think of a way to disarm him, but no plan emerged.

"Now go get the rest," he demanded when she had placed the last of the plate inside.

"What rest? This is everything."

"You lie! Avery swore there was a vast treasure hidden in there."

"How would he know? No one else even suspected the priest's hole existed."

"His ledgers tell of it. Some toff hid a fortune before he left for war. But he left no son, so it is free for the taking. Gold beyond imagining. A king's ransom in jewelry. Plate enough to grace the largest table."

She backed away from the bag. "Unless the ledger included an inventory, the details could only have come from Avery's imagination. Who can believe the drunken mumblings of a dreamer? There it is, Mr. Darksmith. Gold. Jewelry. Plate. If you doubt my word, look for yourself. The door is still open." She gestured toward the bookcase that still partially blocked the entrance.

He plunged forward, but immediately halted. "You think to trick me, but I will not fall into so obvious a trap," he sneered. "You go first."

She hesitated until he jerked his pistol. There was nothing to do but comply. Yet if she allowed him to lock her in, what was to prevent him from killing Michael?

He followed her slow footsteps, remaining eight feet behind her. She had reached the bookcase when Alice screamed.

"Michael!"

Penelope whirled to see Terrence in the doorway and Alice surging forward. Before she could shout a warning, Darksmith pivoted, his pistol glinting in the sunlight that streamed through the window.

"No!"

Quick as lightning, Terrence grabbed Alice around the waist and threw her behind the desk. "Stay down!"

Penelope took advantage of Darksmith's wavering attention to seize the poker. But it grazed the fireplace surround, drawing his eyes. Terrence charged, trying to tackle him low. But Darksmith was faster. The pistol fired even as she swung.

"Terry!" choked Alice.

The poker slammed into Darksmith's upraised arm, its hook slicing his flesh, but he ignored the wound. Before she could strike again, he grabbed her and twisted the weapon free.

"Enough!" he growled, pressing a knife point into her throat. His arm held her in a steel band despite the injury that dripped blood onto her gown.

"Leave him," he barked at Alice, who was bandaging Terrence's arm with his cravat.

"Do as he says," moaned Terrence before slumping into unconsciousness.

"Into the priest's hole," commanded Darksmith. His voice was strained and Penelope could almost read his mind. He had no idea how many servants might be in the house. The shot would draw anyone within hearing. Unfortunately Mrs. Peccles had gone into the village.

"Do it, Allie," she gasped as the knife prodded deeper. Something warm trickled down her throat.

Alice nodded, crossing to the secret door. With a final anguished glance at Terrence, she ducked inside.

"Now it's your turn, Miss Wingrave," he mocked, forcing her forward. Only at the last second did he remove the knife and fling her against Alice. Before she could turn, the door banged shut. The bookcase screeched as he shoved it against the wall. Not a flicker of light penetrated their prison. She ran her hands over the opening, but there was no sign of a release. Was it high on the wall like the one in the library?

"What have I done?" moaned Alice.

"This is not your fault."

"We should have run for help."

"Instead of screaming? There was no time to think." A door slammed in the distance, increasing her anxiety. Had he grabbed his bag and left? Or had he killed Michael and Terrence first? But that was preposterous. The pursuit would be far more intense if he faced a charge of murder. He would be lucky to escape the country as it was—unless he had already made travel arrangements with a smuggler or fisherman. They were only five miles from the coast.

"I hope Michael and Terrence are all right," sobbed Alice.

"Terrence will be fine," she stated firmly, refusing to consider any alternatives. "As for Michael, we can only hope for the best. You know head wounds always bleed freely."

"W-what is g-going on?"

Penelope drew her sister close. The girl had long been afraid of the dark and was shaking from that as much as from reaction. "It's a long story," she began, but a smothered curse cut off her words.

"Are you all right?" demanded Terrence, grunting as he tried to move the bookcase.

"Thank God," sobbed Alice. "We're fine, but what about you?"

"Don't worry, love. I was faking. He barely grazed my arm. How does the door open?"

"Find the pole," Penelope answered. "Michael dropped it behind the chair nearest the window."

"What the devil?" a new voice exploded into the library.

"Lord Carrington!" exclaimed Penelope. "Thank God you are here. Go after Darksmith. He shot Terrence and stole a bag of jewelry."

"In a moment. Are you all right?"

"Yes, but—" She brought her chaotic thoughts under control and resumed in a calmer tone. "Terrence can't manage the pole with only one arm. The latch is on the outside wall, the seventh or eighth Tudor rose from this corner."

"Right." A murmuring ensued that did not fully penetrate the door. Finally the latch clicked open. "Find Darksmith," she begged. "Michael's future is in that bag." Richard's eyes met hers with a promise she could hardly believe.

"Come, Terrence," he ordered. "He must have seen me coming, for he fled on foot, leaving his horse out front."

"But your arm," protested Alice.

"It's fine," Terrence assured her, already striding from the room.

"Help me," Penelope begged, pulling Alice's attention away from the men. "We must turn Michael over so I can examine his head." The bleeding had slowed, but a disconcerting amount of it had soaked into the carpet.

"What happened?"

"Like Terrence, he tried to attack Darksmith but was too far away." She checked his breathing and sighed in relief. Both heartbeat and respiration were steady. Together they lifted him onto the couch. Penelope fetched a basin of water before explaining all that had happened since the moment she opened Carrington's package.

"Who would have believed it?" said Alice with a sigh. "Terry will be appalled to discover his father's plot."

"Are you sure he does not already know it?"

"Positive." She stared. "So that is why you dislike him. Why did you not say?"

"I do not dislike him," she protested. "I merely thought him unusually young to consider marriage, which made me wonder about his reasons. But without proof, I could make no charges, for it was possible that his attraction was genuine. At least with the treasure exposed, he can have no ulterior motives for seeking your hand."

"You will approve, then?"

"If he is of like mind when he returns next summer."

"He is not going back to Oxford," said Alice. "He will study estate management at Carrington Castle instead."

She smiled, tying off the bandage around Michael's head. Perhaps Terrence was more responsible than she had thought. His quick action to keep Alice safe had already convinced her that he was not faking infatuation.

A roar of outrage erupted in the distance.

"Ozzie! Dear God, they must be near the enclosure." She raced to the doorway. "Stay here! Keep an eye on Michael and find Mary." With that, she was gone.

"What happened?" demanded Richard as he and Terrence galloped around the house.

"I've no idea. Alice and I walked into the middle of it." He described the scene in the bookroom.

"He had a knife to her throat?" His icy fury kindled speculation in Terrence's eyes.

Richard's blood boiled. He had noticed blood on Penelope's throat and gown when she emerged from the priest's hole, but had not stopped to consider where it had come from. The bookroom resembled a slaughtering pen.

"Most of the blood on Miss Wingrave came from Darksmith,"

said Terrence, pulling his mind out of a red haze. "She laid his arm open with the poker."

"Good for her." But he winced at what she could have suffered. "What was Darksmith after, anyway?"

"A treasure." He explained Gareth's plots.

"I had no idea," confessed Terrence shakily. "It's a wonder Alice will even look at me after what my parents have done to her family."

"She may not know."

"Then I will tell her. She deserves to learn it all."

"Again you surprise me— Hush!"

The boy raised his brows.

"There he is," he whispered. Darksmith whisked around a corner. "That lane leads to the woods. If you circle around, we can trap him. These hedgerows are too high to jump on foot."

"Right." Terrence dug his heels into Darksmith's sluggish mount and cantered across a pasture.

Richard walked Jet forward, wondering whether Darksmith's pistol was reloaded.

Darksmith glanced over his shoulder as Richard entered the lane, uttered a lurid curse, and started running. But he had managed only a few steps when Terrence blocked the exit.

"Hold it," ordered Richard.

Darksmith drew his knife though he could barely grip it. Penelope had badly damaged his arm. In order to fight, he would have to drop the bag and shift the knife to his left hand.

Terrence inched his horse between the hedgerows.

"It is over," announced Richard coldly. "Drop the knife and the bag."

"Stay back or I'll stab your horse," threatened Darksmith, slicing the air with his dagger.

"Give it up, old man," advised Terrence disgustedly. "You can't possibly kill both of us."

Darksmith twisted nervously from one to the other as they moved inexorably closer.

"It's over," said Richard softly.

"No!" Darksmith flung himself over the gate and into the ostrich compound.

"Come back, you fool!" screamed Terrence. "They will kill you."

Richard lunged for the gate as Ozzie let out the loudest roar he had yet heard.

"Don't be stupid!" Terrence grabbed his arm before he could follow.

They watched helplessly as Darksmith veered toward the barn, choking out incoherent sounds as he identified the approaching beast. He must have known it was hopeless. Ozzie's strides each covered twenty feet, racing the length of the meadow in seconds. A clawed foot lashed out, catching Darksmith on his shoulder and glancing into his head. He dropped like a rock.

"Easy, Ozzie," called Terrence.

Ozzie lifted Darksmith's left arm with his beak, then cocked his head in puzzlement before letting it fall.

"Relax, fellow," urged Richard, fighting to make his voice as soothing as possible.

Cleo joined her mate, her head skimming the grass as she examined this new toy. Darksmith groaned, and Ozzie rested one foot on his chest.

"At least he's not dead," murmured Terrence.

"Don't move or Ozzie will tear you apart," Richard advised as Darksmith's eyes flickered open, widening at the sight of Cleo's head a foot from his own. She prodded his ribs.

He whimpered.

"Shut up, you fool," said Terrence coldly. "Ostriches are territorial when they are nesting."

"Nesting?" whispered Richard.

Terrence nodded toward a sand-covered hillock where two enormous eggs glistened in the afternoon sunlight.

He gasped when the boy slipped through the gate. "Now who's being idiotic?"

"Ozzie knows me," he replied. "Stay there," he added as Richard followed.

"I met Ozzie yesterday, though I would not count on his remembering that fact fondly," he said. "But I suspect there is safety in numbers. And you can hardly handle the birds and rescue Darksmith at the same time. If we let Ozzie kill him, it will cause trouble for the Wingraves."

The bag lay halfway across the field. Fluff clawed at it until an ornate ring fell out, which she promptly ate.

"No!" Darksmith had seen and jerked in protest. Both Ozzie and Cleo struck him.

"Don't move and don't talk," warned Richard again. "One more sound, and we will leave you here."

"What kind of intruder did you catch, Ozzie?" asked Terrence softly, sidling closer to the birds. "If you want to live, Darksmith, you had best let go of that knife," he continued in the same tone as Mortimer's hand tightened. "If you do the slightest damage to any of the birds, Ozzie will tear you limb from limb. So far he is merely playing with you, but he is capable of disemboweling a horse with one kick. That knife has no chance of killing even one bird, let alone the twelve that now surround you."

Darksmith's eyes swiveled. The last vestige of color drained from his face, but his hand relaxed, allowing the knife to fall free. One of the youngsters tugged on his hair, but he swallowed his curse, finally accepting the danger of his position.

"Leave the knife alone, Ozzie," advised Richard softly. "If you eat it, you will shred your guts."

Ozzie cocked his head at the unfamiliar voice and gurgled. At least it wasn't that challenging roar, but he let Terrence resume his soft murmuring. Several of the juveniles lost interest and wandered away to peck at the haystack. Fluff abandoned the sack to nibble the buttons on Darksmith's coat. Two came off and disappeared down the bird's throat.

A gasp sounded from the gate. Thank God!

"How do we get out of this fix, Penelope?" he asked, keeping his voice soothing. Neither of them noticed his form of address, but Terrence's brows rose. "Sorry to let him bother Ozzie. I had no idea he was so stupid."

"I never thought to find you in here again," she said as she crossed to his side.

"Terrence claims to know Ozzie, but I thought it might take two of us to distract him. Much as I detest this piece of scum, I would not like to see him damaged any further."

She met his eyes, and his heart pounded. "Can you drag him to the gate alone?"

"Certainly." Though he knew why she asked. His bruised ribs felt worse today, especially after his recent burst of activity.

"Good. Terrence can't lift so much weight at the moment. He and I will distract the ostriches while you make your escape."

"How?"

A thump sounded from the corner of the field, whipping Ozzie's head around.

"That's right, fellow," murmured Penelope. "I brought you a treat. He adores pears," she added for Richard's benefit. "We collected a basket of windfalls this morning. Thank heaven Josh hadn't brought them down yet. Terrence, show us your skill with the ladies. If you can bring Cleopatra there, I'll entice Ozzie. The others will follow."

Terrence laughed. "Come on, Cleo, old girl." He draped an arm around her neck and rubbed her breast. Penelope did the same with Ozzie. The parade of ostriches nearly made Richard laugh. Necks craned toward the pears, but none dared pass Ozzie's dignified pace.

"If you make a single wrong move, I'll turn Ozzie loose on you," he threatened as Darksmith flexed his fingers. He recovered the pistol, dropping it and the knife into the bag. "Can you walk?"

"Of course." But it was nought but bravado. As Darksmith tried to sit up, he swooned. Shrugging, Richard grasped the fellow's shoulders, and dragged him to the gate. Four men clustered on the other side.

"Take him to the house and lock him up," he ordered. "Then send for the magistrate and the doctor." They loaded Darksmith into a farm wagon as he turned back to Penelope. "All clear."

She nodded, giving Ozzie a final pat before leading Terrence to the gate. "Well done," she congratulated the boy.

"Very well done," Richard echoed. "You are a good man to have around in an emergency." He untangled Jet's reins from where he had jammed them into the hedgerow and fastened the bag behind his saddle.

"You got the treasure," she said softly.

"Most of it. Fluff ate a ring." He lifted her up, then mounted behind her.

"It shouldn't hurt her," said Terrence, pulling his own horse alongside.

"Ostriches are always eating bits of gravel," Penelope explained, more to distract her mind from his encircling arms than because he needed the information. "They particularly like anything shiny."

"Like the buttons Fluff pulled off Darksmith's waistcoat. Or the ones Ozzie stole from me." Richard chuckled. She could feel it rippling through his body, sending shivers into her own.

"We shan't see them again," she said. "I'll not kill Fluff, even for a piece of jewelry." She turned to Terrence, who was staring at her with blatant speculation. Did he suspect her old-maid's foolishness? "Why don't you ride ahead and see after Darksmith," she suggested. "Alice will need help."

He flashed the warmest smile she had ever seen before pressing his mount to a gallop.

"Does that mean you've decided to favor his suit?" asked Richard, tightening his hold and drawing Jet to a walk. Now that the crisis was past, his bruises made riding any faster difficult.

"I am thinking of it. He has a cool head in a crisis."

"That he does." His voice turned serious. "He wants to study estate management instead of returning to school. I told him it was an acceptable alternative. If they are of the same mind in six months, I will give them my blessing."

"So Alice said. Did he know about his father's plots?"

"Not until I told him just now."

"What of Lady Avery's antagonism?"

"Based on a misunderstanding." He explained. "I had to break my vow to keep your mother's affair secret."

"I cannot blame you for that," she assured him. "I would have done the same."

"Thank you." He hugged her but loosened his hold when she stiffened.

Penelope stared into the distance until she was sure her voice would not betray her. "I feel sorry for Lady Avery. She has had a wretched life."

"She doesn't deserve your pity," he protested. "If she had confronted Gareth, her suspicions could have been laid to rest years ago."

"But not everyone is strong enough to face their fears." She hesitated. "My lord, I must thank you for the packet you sent. I would have mentioned it earlier, but I only received it this morning."

"The accounting was accurate?"

"To the penny. I cannot believe you know so much about my affairs. And I must extend my apologies for suspecting you of continuing your uncle's scheme."

"I can hardly blame you for that. I've suspected you of enough plots of your own. May we set aside past differences and start again?"

She nodded.

"Thank you. Do you feel up to telling me how this confrontation with Darksmith started."

"Of course, but I have already been through it once and would prefer to wait until everyone is present before doing it again. Both Terrence and the magistrate will wish to hear the details."

"Understandable." She had stiffened again, so he pushed Jet faster, arriving at the house five minutes later. Was she in shock? Did she still mistrust his motives? Or did she find his touch distasteful? Cold seeped down his spine.

Alice was waiting for them in the hallway.

Penelope paled. "Mic—"

"Michael is fine," Alice interrupted. "And so is Mary. I had already summoned the doctor before they brought Mr. Darksmith back."

"Where is he?"

"Upstairs. Terry is watching him."

Richard nodded approval. "I want to speak with him."

"So do I. And I must see after Michael." Penelope seemed torn over what to do first.

"Michael is sleeping in the bookroom," said Alice. "And I honestly mean sleeping," she hastened to add. "He woke up and spoke with me an hour ago."

"Then we will not disturb him until the doctor arrives," decided Richard. He offered his arm to Penelope and followed Alice upstairs.

"If you don't lie still, I'll tie you down," swore Terrence as they approached the guest room. "Or would you prefer to play with Ozzie some more?"

Darksmith muttered a string of curses that abruptly ceased when Richard pushed the door open. "You! I should have followed my instincts. I knew this job was turning sour the moment I met you."

"No one can escape justice forever, John Dougan," he replied, watching the color fade from the man's pale cheeks.

"You know everything, then."

"I doubt it, but I know enough to send you to Botany Bay for several lifetimes. What I don't know is why you waited so long to claim the treasure. Lord Avery died three months ago."

"Why should I satisfy your curiosity?"

"Perhaps to avoid a charge of assaulting a lord. Transportation might be preferable to hanging."

"I did nothing to you," he protested.

"You have forgotten that Gareth's death elevated Terrence to the viscountcy," said Penelope, nodding toward the arm that still wore a bloodstained cravat.

Richard loomed over the bed. "Why did you wait so long, Dougan?"

Darksmith crumbled. "Avery spent an hour mumbling about a 1620 hoard, but he refused to discuss the details. Even that damned paper he guarded so close didn't help. His writing was terrible, and the words meaningless."

"If he guarded the paper so well, how did you get it?" asked Terrence.

"Lifted it from his corpse."

All but Richard jumped. "Later," he murmured when he saw the objections rise to Terrence's lips.

"It wasn't until the duns started hounding me that I managed to connect his mutterings with his scratchings and work out the truth. If only I'd done it earlier, the treasure would be mine. Or if Chesterton hadn't written his damned note in Latin, or somebody hadn't discarded a perfectly good dower house."

"And that's that," Richard said, leading the others to the bookroom.

When the magistrate finally arrived, Penelope described Darksmith's attack. She let Carrington explain his capture. She was too tired to think, and much too tired to control her countenance. She knew she had slipped several times on the way back to the house, unable to maintain the aloof facade that would hide her infatuation. But his arms had been so comfortable, so warm, so exciting . . . She trembled. Had he noticed?

She lost track of the conversation. Memory overwhelmed her senses, recalling his hard body, his taste, his smell. . . . She needed sleep. Too many shocks had piled atop one another, all made worse by her fitful night. But before she could retire, she must thank Carrington for his help. Without him, the treasure would be gone. She frowned. Where had that bag ended up?

"Are you all right?" Richard's question snapped her attention back to the bookroom. It was empty of all but the two of them.

She jumped to her feet in panic. "Where—?"

"You fell asleep," he interrupted, nodding toward the window that was lighted only by the glow of a fading sunset. She must have been asleep for hours. "Terry and Alice are upstairs with Michael, and Darksmith is in jail. Are you all right?" He touched the mark on her throat. "He cut you."

His nearness left her breathless, and his fingers turned her knees to jelly, but she could not let him sense her weakness. "I am fine. It was only a nick to keep Alice in line." Black spots danced before her eyes.

He heard the strain in her voice and saw her pale cheeks blanch further. He pulled her close before she could collapse, though he tried to keep his touch comforting lest she think he was again assaulting her. So far she had been grateful enough for his help to ignore his earlier misdeeds.

"There is nothing you need do at the moment," he assured her, stroking her back. "Just relax. You are still in shock, my dear. Despite your nap, you can hardly remain untouched by the kind of day you have had. Hush," he added as she burst into tears. "Michael will recover. Terrence is fine. Mary has nought but a bump on her head. There is nothing Darksmith can do to any of you now." His hand brushed the hair back from her face as he half carried her to the couch where Michael had lain, and sat down with her in his lap. "It is over, and everyone survived."

"I was n-never so s-scared in my l-life," she admitted shakily, sliding her arms around his waist as she burrowed further into his embrace.

"When he threatened you, my love?"

But she was sobbing harder and did not hear him. "D-don't you ever g-go near Ozzie again!"

His heart stopped. After all she had been through, what had terrified her was seeing him with the ostriches. A wave of tenderness engulfed him. "If you introduce me properly, we won't have that problem in the future," he suggested, pulling her head free. Her eyes widened at the implications, her lips parting with a soft gasp.

He couldn't help himself. He kissed her and drowned in the taste and feel and smell of her. But his euphoria bore little resemblance to his earlier lust. Gone was anger, cynicism, and all trace of guilt. His newly unlocked heart overflowed with warmth and happiness. His need for her ran deeper than desire, but before he could bring himself under control—for the last thing he wanted was to confirm her suspicion that he was a libertine—her mouth opened and her fingers slipped under his coat to knead his back. Lightning licked along his nerves, inciting moans that echoed her own.

Penelope was stunned. Heat swirled, building unbelievable fires in places she had never thought of. She arched into his embrace. *Wanton!* screamed her conscience, but she no longer cared. She needed his arms, his caresses, his insatiable kisses to soothe the terrors of this day. And more. But she abandoned thought, threading a hand into his hair and reveling in its silky texture. His lips trailed kisses over her face; his teeth nipped at her ear, sending new sensations shivering through her body. His tongue slid along her throat to take the sting from the knife wound. She moaned. Again.

"Marry me," he gasped, teasing her breast with wicked fingers.

Her eyes focused. "Are you serious?"

"Absolutely."

"But society would never accept me." Her voice cracked, revealing her vulnerability. Dear Lord! She was exposing her foolishness. Sliding off his lap, she paced to the fireplace and back as her head shook in a vain attempt to clear her mind.

Richard froze. The independent, confident Penelope afraid? *I can hurt her so easily.* Stunned by the realization, he groped for the words that would carry off his impetuous proposal. "Of course society will accept you. You belong there as surely as I do."

"Belonging and acceptance are very different, my lord. As I have been shown countless times. You could never want a wife whose behavior called censure upon your head."

"My arrogant blathering comes home to roost, I see," he murmured. Laying his hands on her shoulders, he turned her until he could look into her eyes. "Short of parading Ozzie and company into White's, there is nothing you could do to embarrass me. A marchioness can commit any number of *faux pas* with impunity."

She giggled. "Ozzie at White's! What a delectable image! I never would have expected it of you."

"You wound me." His exaggerated pout elicited new giggles. "I would love to see Brummell sans buttons, sans quizzing glass, and sporting a purple eye. The man has become too arrogant by half." He sobered. "You need not fear society, Penelope. Most likely, you will come to scorn them for the empty-headed creatures they are.

And that is fine with me. All I ask is that you not try to emulate them, for I have never met a society lady that I could tolerate for long. They are insipid creatures without substance. It is you I want to share my life with, my dear. I love everything about you, especially those traits that I have been criticizing since my arrival. Forgive me, love. I was terrified by how much I cared."

"Are you sure you really know me and are not assuming virtues I do not possess because I resemble a girl you once loved?"

He cursed himself for ever mentioning Penelope Rissen. Pulling her closer, he planted a soothing kiss on her trembling lips. "I was guilty of that when first we met, assigning you all of her traits—lying, scheming, greed, vengeance. I no longer believe you harbor any of them. In fact, all you have in common is the most glorious hair I've ever seen, eyes that outshine the darkest sapphires, and a bosom that has robbed me of much-needed sleep."

She scowled, but he nipped her earlobe before exploring her mouth.

"Seriously," he said at last, his voice huskier than before, "you are nothing alike otherwise, and I am glad. I love you, and only you."

She quirked her brows. "You do understand that I have a continuing duty to Alice and Michael."

"Duties I understand very well. I suffer an abundance of them myself. Perhaps you can help me decide which ones are necessary and which ones prevent my esteemed family from standing on their own feet."

"Gladly." She smiled. "I love you, my lord. Irrevocably. So I suppose I have no choice but to wed you."

"Richard," he ordered.

"Richard."

"It had better be soon," he murmured, fondling that well-loved bosom. "I can't keep my hands off you."

"I've noticed. How about next month? I think I can make arrangements for Winter House by then."

"Good." He grinned in sudden mischief, the lopsided smile sending tingles clear to her toes. "I have a growing urge to play fairy godmother, my love. Your priest's hole makes an adequate pot at the end of the rainbow that will set Michael up quite nicely—we examined the treasure while you slept. Perhaps you would care to claim Lord Chesterton as that long-lost relative. But

I also recall something about three wishes." He kissed her. "Ask and you shall receive."

Her eyes widened in surprise, her entire body melting as his silvery gaze pulled her in. "Are you serious?"

"Never more so. I love you, Penny. I want nothing more than to fill your life with joy from this day forth. Let me make you happy."

"You will, for my first wish is you. Never have I been more content than when I am in your arms." They tightened around her. "As for the other two, what more could I want?"

"I'm sure you'll think of something." He pulled her into another heady embrace that would never have ended if someone had not knocked on the door. Terrence and Alice entered.

"Wish us happy," ordered Richard, refusing to release her.

"Wonderful!" enthused Terrence, turning to Alice. "That means that you will be—"

"—living at Carrington Castle," she completed, blushing.

Richard stared into Penelope's eyes, reading the same conclusion that blazed in his own. "Christmas, I think. They will not—"

"—change their minds," she completed. "I'd best train someone from Tallgrove to take over the ostriches."

"Excellent. We'll delay our wedding trip until January."

"And it will be to—"

He grinned. "Rome. Athens. Perhaps Egypt."

Penelope's arms slid around his neck before she recalled their audience.

Alice grinned. "May we go tell Michael?"

She nodded. The door had hardly shut before Richard pulled her back into his arms.

"Some fantasies really do come true," she murmured as his lips covered hers, driving rational thought away.